Dark Enchantment
Janine Ashbless

BL

This book is a work of fiction.
In real life, make sure you practise safe, sane and
consensual sex.

Published by Black Lace 2009

4 6 8 10 9 7 5 3

Copyright © Janine Ashbless 2009

Janine Ashbless has asserted her right under the Copyright, Designs
and Patents Act 1988 to be identified as the author of this work

*All characters in this publication are fictitious and any resemblance
to real persons, living or dead, is purely coincidental.*

First published in Great Britain in 2009 by
Black Lace
Virgin Books
Random House, 20 Vauxhall Bridge Road
London SW1V 2SA

www.black-lace-books.com
www.virginbooks.com
www.rbooks.co.uk

Addresses for companies within The Random House Group Limited can be found at:
www.randomhouse.co.uk/offices.htm

The Random House Group Limited Reg. No. 954009

Distributed in the USA by Macmillan, 175 Fifth Avenue, New York, NY 10010, USA

A CIP catalogue record for this book
is available from the British Library

ISBN 9780352345134

The Random House Group Limited supports The Forest Stewardship Council [FSC], the
leading international forest certification organisation. All our titles that are printed on
Greenpeace approved FSC certified paper carry the FSC logo.
Our paper procurement policy can be found at www.rbooks.co.uk/environment

MIX
Paper from
responsible sources
FSC
www.fsc.org   FSC® C0130

Typeset by Palimpsest Book Production Limited, Grangemouth, Stirlingshire

Printed and bound in Great Britain by
CPI Antony Rowe, Chippenham, Wiltshire

For Annie
who asked for a story

Contents

Dishonour

My name is Raihn and I am third concubine to Lord General Mershen. I was born in Halghat of the White Cliffs, in the east of the Eternal Empire, the sixth child of a prosperous perfume merchant. When I was eighteen my parents offered me as a gift to the Glorious General upon the occasion of him passing through the city, in the last throes of the civil war. My lord was most graciously pleased to accept me. This is a story about Lord Mershen. I want you to hear it.

When news was brought that armed riders were approaching swiftly up the mountain road and that they did not bear the Imerho family banner, Surya ordered the servants to leave the house. Most obeyed, heading into the cedar forest; those that were left – and the slaves who had no right to flee – she told to hide in the cellars and the grain tubs in the kitchen. Above all they were not to attempt any kind of armed resistance: the House of Dark Needles had never been built to be defensible, and there were no soldiers among the men General Imerho had left with his only daughter. This was the oldest and the least accessible of the family's holdings, their last refuge. It would not, she knew, remain so for long under any attack.

Having made the one decision left up to her – flee or surrender – Surya paced the polished wooden floors, sick with fear, clutching her bow. It had a short span but was deeply recurved when strung, and it was the only thing that gave her comfort. A quiver of bronze-tipped arrows hung at her hip.

If a soldier must surrender, her father had said long ago, *then he should show that the choice was his. There is no respect for the helpless.*

Like all men of his class Imerho was full of military advice and Surya had grown up in awe of him. She would have liked to have had the poise of her mother, who'd accompanied her warlord husband to the very edge of the battlefield where she would live or die as he did, but Surya was too young and too untried for such stoic courage. She knelt briefly before the family shrine and thrust incense sticks into the basins of sand, but the gilded statues of the gods grinned at her with more than normal vacuousness it seemed, and mocked her trembling prayers: *Let it be good news. Let it be peace. Let it be mercy.*

It was to be none of those things. She knew that when she heard hooves on the hard earth outside, heard a man yelling commands to keep the rear covered, and the order: 'With me! Quickly!'

She ran to the window and looked down upon a dozen horses and men milling about before the house – men with the long hair of soldiers, and the uniform of the Imperial Army but the cloaks of a noble's household. The hot breath of the horses mingled with the mountain mist, and dew hung in the plumes of the helmets. A burgundy pennant bearing a white egret ensign swayed in a soldier's grasp. She knew that livery, and for a moment her heart crashed against her breastbone. She could see no faces because of their bronze helmets, but heads were tilted watchfully towards the tall façade of the house.

Burgundy cloaks, the white egret. It was Lord Mershen's colours. She tasted the brief elusive sweetness of hope, remembering mornings in the Imperial Palace at Antoth even as she retreated from the window and the searching gaze of the men. Then doors slammed open below, echoes bouncing down the wooden corridors of the ancient building, and boots drummed on the boards. They hadn't removed their shoes. Such flagrant disrespect for the house would have told, if nothing else did, of their intentions.

But, a part of her protested, *he was ... He smiled ...*

Recollections of winter mornings half an Empire away tangled her fingers as she bent and strung her bow. Mornings had been reserved on the Palace Field for the young women of the Imperial Court to practise the arts considered proper to their age and gender and class: horsemanship and archery. Not that they were ever expected to use those skills in battle, but for the Irolian people the raising of warriors was a matter of pride. *Lions are not born of ewes*, as her father had said. So Surya had, along with the dozens of other unmarried noblewomen resident in the palace, clattered out dutifully on horseback each morning to ride at full gallop up and down the lists, turning their small horses with a twitch of the reins, shooting at targets both before and behind them from the saddle. It was a minor form of entertainment for the noblemen of the court too, assessing the marriageable women for skill and grace and looks.

Lord Mershen had been a regular spectator. He'd always had some sort of reason to be there, she noticed: a meeting with other members of the Imperial Council, a game of tiles, a healthful stroll across the palace grounds. Always some excuse to be there, watching. At first she hadn't even differentiated him from the other noblemen until, leaning on the balustrade one morning, he'd caught her eye and told her, 'I should have you in my archery corps.' His eyes had crinkled warmly when he smiled. She'd blushed. After that she'd been aware of him every time; it had rattled her somewhat, and made her practise with more determination.

Protocol, of course, meant that she couldn't talk to him

without her father's permission but only smile and look coyly pleased. She'd hoped that Mershen himself would make the proper enquiries to her father, but these hopes were dashed along with so many others as political strife had split the Imperial Council. She made do with gossip: that he was unmarried, and regarded as a competent soldier but stubbornly apolitical. An honourable man, they said in public – which meant that he lacked ambition and behind the scenes he had few allies.

Then the civil war had washed over them all, sweeping so many noble houses away, and alliances and favours and ambition had been tested to breaking point. And honour, it turned out, still had hard value. Now he was here, and of all men, all the Emperor's loyal men, that it should be him – Surya didn't know what to think. Perhaps he would help her. Perhaps.

But deep down she knew that if he were truly an honourable man he would not permit himself that.

Surya had a half-formed intention of waiting for them in her father's audience hall, where she felt some dignified and defiant attitude might be struck. But her nerve failed her when she set foot in the corridor; it was patently too long and exposed for her to retreat all the way down, so in a flurry of panic she slipped into the family sitting room opposite the shrine and pulled the door shut. This was the room where her mother liked to lie on a day couch and watch the ever-changing clouds as they broke and formed and flowed upon the mountains. A screen door in the far wall gave access onto the balcony and Surya wondered if it was possible to slip out that way, to drop into the garden and scale the wall in her embroidered robes and flee into the forest.

It wasn't. The door slammed open and a man's voice shouted, 'Here! Sir!'

Surya whirled, nocked and drew in one motion, determined that she would go down proudly, as her father would wish it. But her best intentions vanished as a man in full armour pushed into the room and she backed up several steps, only halting when her thighs connected hard with a rosewood cabinet.

'Lady Surya.'

The bleached tunic was stained with mud – and with a reddish filth that was not mud – but there was gilding on his breastplate and helm. He was followed by a squad of soldiers even more dirtied than he, brandishing long-bladed spears. Their bronze kilts rattled with every step as they fanned out.

'Lord Mershen!' she gasped.

The one in the ornate helmet held up his hand and turned his head briefly. 'Hold.' His voice was as she remembered it, but hoarse from bellowing on the battlefield. As his men halted he pulled his helmet off to give her a long, even stare. There was no warmth in his face on this occasion. He looked grey and sweaty and two grim furrows were etched down to the corners of his mouth. 'Put the bow down, Surya, and we will talk.'

Nodding, she lowered her bow and slacked the tension. It was a relief to be told what to do, even by him.

'Wait for me outside,' Mershen ordered his men. Surya, feeling light-headed, watched as the soldiers withdrew. Walking back to the door, he kicked it shut then dumped his helmet on a cupboard top.

'The war's over then,' she said, wondering how she could sound the words when there was no breath in her lungs.

He nodded.

'My father?'

'He's dead.' There was neither regret nor triumph in his voice.

No need to ask about her mother then, she knew: Lady Imerho would have opened her wrists when her husband's standard fell. 'My brothers?'

'All died on the field. None were captured.'

'Oh.' She knew she should be proud of them but she felt only dizzy. It wasn't real. None of this could be real. 'All of –'

'You are the last of Imerho's line.' He was a tall man and the armour looked like it belonged on him: far more so than the courtly robes she'd last seen him in, almost a year ago.

'May his star look down upon us,' she whispered.

Very pointedly, he did not echo her words. 'Lady Surya . . .'

For a moment the room seemed to swim. 'I am a poor hostess,' she said, her dry voice cracking a little. 'Would you care for a drink?'

Softly, he shook his head. 'No.'

'My father's estates produce the finest plum brandy in the Eternal Empire.'

'That's not what I came here for.'

'You've been sent to kill me?' she said faintly. The other possibility flared like a firework in the night. 'Or am I to be taken to the Emperor?'

Mershen's mouth twisted. 'The Radiant Emperor considers that only the expurgation of Imerho's bloodline will fit the crime of his treachery. No descendants, Surya. None may pray for him.'

She covered her mouth. She had no cause to expect anything less, but the fear was like a black tide rising in her.

'I'm sorry, Surya.' His voice dropped, became gentle. He sheathed his blade and pulled his cloak over his head, discarding it.

'He made you do this?'

Mershen blinked, like a wince. 'I volunteered.' And when he saw the betrayal in her eyes he added: 'I will make it swift and honourable. There are others who would not, Surya. You must be brave, as your brothers were.'

'My brothers . . .'

'All died with unbroken hearts. No one can question your family's courage.' *Just their loyalty*, he left unsaid. 'Now you must live up to that.'

He doesn't want me to start screaming and weeping, she thought, recognising the command in his words. That would sicken him. 'I'm not ready,' she whispered.

'No one is. But you are of warrior blood, Surya. You can do this.' His eyes held hers, implacable but not cruel. He was the object of all her fears, and yet perversely the only source of comfort.

She stared. 'Yes,' she said at last.

'Is that gold thread in your robe?' he asked, and she nodded. 'Undo it. Better you bare your neck.' Quietly his hand went to rest on the pommel of his blade. He sounded calm; if any man was capable of being a reassuring executioner then it was he. But there was something in his eyes that betrayed him.

Dry-mouthed, Surya laid aside her bow and fumbled with the fastening at her throat, perversely ashamed that her fingers were so clumsy. Every loop of braid was agonising. She pictured the way he'd smiled at her from the palace balcony, the smile she'd held secretly to her heart. She did not really know this man, she reminded herself. She only knew that he'd watched her warmly, long ago. At that memory her heart cracked. 'I have a request,' she blurted, not looking at his face. 'Before I die.'

'Yes?' Mershen folded his arms, a little wary.

Under her fingertips the pulse in her throat was hammering. 'Honour my wish, please, my lord.'

'What is it?'

'Do you remember the women's archery practice at the Imperial Palace?'

Ever so slightly he let his guard down. 'Of course.'

'You'd watch us.'

The hard line of his mouth softened. 'Upon occasion.'

She bit her lip. 'You'd smile at me when we passed.'

'Yes.' He was almost smiling now, sadly. 'It was one of the better parts of my day.'

'You were ... fond ... of me?' Her voice nearly cracked.

He nodded, his dark eyes filled with regret.

Surya took a deep breath. 'I don't want to die a maiden.'

Those eyes widened. 'What?'

'You smiled at me. Do you know what you did to me? That became my reason for going each day. I wanted that smile. I wanted the way you looked at me ...'

A line appeared between his brows.

'... I thought about you all the time. What it would be like if you did more than smile. What your hands would be like on me. What you were under those robes.' She should have been scarlet with shame saying these things to a man, but the blood had fled from her face when he entered the room. 'When the war started I prayed for your safety, just as I prayed for my brothers' lives. More so. I hoped there would be peace. I wished in time you might ...' With a supreme effort she dragged her gaze up to meet his, finding it astonished and full of pain.

'You're shaming yourself,' he said thickly.

'I don't want to die, Glorious General, not without knowing what it is like: the feel of a man's skin on mine.' She took a faltering step forwards. 'What it would be like to have you on me, and in me, as I have dreamt. Please. Before you –'

He closed on her, his hand gripping her arm. 'This is wrong,' he rasped.

'And what *you're* going to do isn't?'

He flinched. 'Have it your way.' Seizing her by the shoulders he whirled her sideways and slammed her against a pillar, nearly knocking the wind out of her. His hands were rough and determined; he tore straight through the fastenings of her robe and wrenched the cloth open, ripping the thinner material beneath to bare her breasts. Surya shut her eyes, shrinking back into herself; he was too big, too strong, too fierce. He smelled of sweat and horses. Under his armour he was all hard muscle and his thighs were crushing hers. His hands grabbed her soft little breasts like he wanted to squeeze the life from them.

I asked him for this, she told herself. I will bear it. I will endure it. It's what I wanted.

He was panting hard through clenched teeth. This wasn't even lust: it was anger. Anger at her for rejecting his honour, anger at an emperor who would insist on such a task – and most of all anger at himself. Involuntarily she cried out as his fingers bit painfully into her flesh. Without warning he went still, one hand on her shoulder, one squashing her left breast, her nipple pinched between his fingers. With his head bowed over hers, he made a noise almost like a sob. Then, 'Surya.'

She bit the inside of her lip to staunch the tears that were burning at the back of her eyes.

'Do you really want this?' he groaned.

She whimpered. Then he lifted her face to his and kissed her. His lips were dry and a little chapped, and there was no anger in them at all, just deep pain and a fervent, haunted desire. She shook beneath them, opening to him, dissolving as his kisses soaked into her. He tasted of wine and blood and exhaustion, but he was warm on her cold skin and she pressed against him, trembling. A tear she had not held back slipped down over her cheek and he caught it on his thumb before brushing his lips across the planes of her face, as if he were tasting her skin.

'Have you prayed to Tesub?' he breathed, his mouth hot at her ear and throat.

'Hhh?' She was incapable of speech at that moment.

'Ask her to accept your maiden sacrifice.' He was pulling at the strapping of his breastplate. His words burned.

'Ah.' Of course; it was the ceremony for the wedding night: to offer one's maidenhead to the goddess as a pure sacrifice. A woman who did not – oh gods, he was kissing her throat now and her whole body was shaking with the heat of those kisses – risked dying impure and being rejected by the gods. Oh. The tears were back again, brimming in her eyes. 'I don't know the words.'

He pulled back momentarily to look her in the face. 'Nor do I.' He shrugged his breastplate off and laid it to the floor, deliberately making as little noise as he could. 'Think. You must have heard women talk.'

'Yes.' *Think?* She couldn't think. His big strong hands were on his belt now, uncinching the kilt of straps that protected his thighs. There was blood all across his scraped knuckles. There was a green stain on the front of his tunic from the breastplate. She touched the fabric, feeling for his heartbeat beneath the padded linen. He grabbed her hand and pushed it down to his crotch. Beneath his tunic and calfskin breeches something surged hungrily to greet her.

'Divine Tesub,' he groaned, prompting her.

'Divine Tesub . . .' Her mind was capable only of focusing on one thing: that this was *him*, this was his cock. This was what she had dreamed of and blushed over in secret and shaped in the hot still air of her bedchamber. He was making her touch it. He was moulding her fingers round its thickness. He was breathing hard as she measured its length with her clumsy hands. 'Divine Lady, I am a virgin,' she breathed. 'Give me courage this night.'

'Good.' Whether he was referring to her prayer or her actions, she couldn't tell. His voice was low and urgent.

'Let me give my husband pleasure – Oh!'

'What?'

'You're not my husband ...'

'It will do,' he promised.

'Oh. Let me give him pleasure that he may teach pleasure to me.' Her words were coming out in a stumbled blur, her focus torn between them and the live thing in her hands, muscular as a snake. 'Accept the blood I shed, Divine Lady ...'

He was peeling away the belt that held her quiver of arrows.

'Accept my ... my sacrifice, Divine Lady ...'

He was loosening the drawstring on his breeches.

'Divine Tesub ...'

'Is that it done?'

Surya gaped and nodded. There was more: something about bearing the wound given to her, something about fertility, but she couldn't remember the words because the soldier's weapon had sprung out unsheathed into her grasp and she could not get over the heat of him, the girth of him, the solidity.

Mershen touched her lips. 'Done well, Surya.' Then he pulled up the skirt of her robe and slipped his hand between her thighs. Flesh parted before his fingers just as her lips parted under his. She was wet; it came as much of a surprise to her as to him. She shook, grinding her spine against the pillar. No one had ever touched her there; no fingers but her own had done *that*. His fingers were rough-textured but careful in their movements, slipping up her shallow furrow.

'Yes?'

She nodded, wide-eyed.

'Good.' He was smiling, but it was not the warm conspiratorial smile she remembered; it was something wilder and harder edged and loaded with foreknowledge and regret. His fingers slipped in and out of her, painting her the bright hot colours of desire. She felt like she was changing shape under his touch, being moulded into new contours. Her own hands slackened, bereft of direction. She couldn't even see him properly; her eyes kept fluttering closed of their own accord. 'Good,' he murmured again, then slid from her and grasped her under the curve of her rump, lifting and holding her close to him as he carried her over to the couch nearby. The couch, Surya thought dimly, where her mother used to lie and watch the clouds caress the mountaintops.

She could feel his erection pinned between them and pressing into her as he took those few steps. He laid her down upon the padded brocade, readjusted her skirts and the hem of his tunic, then bent over her, guiding his cock with his hand. Surya got her first proper look at that swarthy, turgid length, angled towards her from his open breeches, the skin so tight it was glossy.

'You know what to do.' It was barely a question.

'Yes,' she whispered, parting her thighs. Blood from her: blood from him. It was the way of their people.

He butted up against her sex, slipping a little in her juices till he found the angle. Then Mershen moved his hand from his cock to her mouth, covering her firmly as he pushed home. She arched her back involuntarily, trying to withdraw, but he pinned her tight and surged in, and she couldn't cry out or even breathe so she bit him, hard. Then he was still again, and there was air and his blood in her mouth, and they were both panting and sweat was running down his temples.

'That's it,' he grunted through bared teeth. 'I'm in. I'm in. It's done. You took it.' She saw the bloody crescents left by her teeth on his palm as he withdrew his hand. He licked his thumb then delved down between them to touch her at the point of their juncture. And then all the pain went away – though he was still hard as teak within her, though he was rocking in deeper now, push by push, stretching her wider – because he was sliding his slick thumb over her clit, teasing the pain from her flesh and transmuting it to pleasure.

She forgot the pain and the fear. She forgot everything but what it was to feel him moving on her, to feel his mouth on her skin as he bent to her breasts or nuzzled her throat, to feel the unyielding hardness of his thighs pressing hers apart. She tasted the salt of his sweat and slid her hands up under his tunic to grasp him about the ribs and back. Her fingernails dug into the declivity of his spine. His muscles worked under her hands like those of a galloping horse. His gaze brushed hers, boring into her yet unseeing. His hair swept her face and clung to her lips and tongue, sharp with the taste of smoke. Only dimly at first did she recognise his desperation: that he had fought in battle, butchering men of his own blood, then ridden two days from the field to do something his soul recoiled from. He was exhausted and frantic and needy, heartsick and burning with lust. His thrusts grew fiercer. He groaned curses under his breath. He was taking her and taking from her. Ravishing her. Burying himself in her. Drowning in her.

She opened within, layer after layer, to receive him. She'd never felt so huge, as in the end she encompassed the man, the mountain they lay upon, the world and the burning sun itself.

He called upon the gods as he came, despairing.

Afterwards he lay quietly upon her, their hearts racing together. Then he eased himself up on his elbow and stroked the hair back from her wet brow. 'I didn't hurt you ...'

'No,' she lied.

His lips tightened. 'Surya ...'

He didn't look like a man who'd just taken his pleasure;

he looked stricken. She wondered to see it. At this moment – just for this moment, while the sunlight still streamed through her veins – she was free of fear. She touched his face with her fingertips, memorising those dark eyes and that warm mouth for her journey. She could not bring herself to smile, but there was no tension in her as she closed her own eyes and turned her head away, baring her throat. 'Be quick.'

He heaved himself from her, his hands reluctant to let her go. She felt the wetness between her thighs, the pulse in her belly. She heard his feet on the floor, the clink of his swordbelt, the long intake of his breath. He would be skilful, she knew, with the blade. It would be swift. She touched her breast with her fingertips, where his hand had last lingered. He was not unkind. He was simply a man of honour, doing his duty as best he could when it left him no choice.

But there are limits to every man's honour.

For far too long he held his action, while Surya clung to the fading sunlight glow in her breast, willing it not to die. Then she heard him step forwards. He took her wrist. He pulled her upright and she sat, head swimming, trying to focus, feeling the burning in her rent sex.

'Get dressed,' he told her.

As she obeyed ineffectually, tugging her skirt down and fumbling the torn edges of her robe across her breasts, he followed his own command and donned his armour and cloak. He didn't look at her. Automatically, she smoothed her hair.

'What ... ?' she whispered.

He put his finger over his lips, casting her a sharp impersonal glance. Then he went to the door. As he opened it his body blocked the gap, and she was not in the line of sight of anyone in the corridor.

'Captain Felic,' he said, the hoarseness of his voice more

marked than ever, 'I want you to see to the body.' He ushered another man into the room, then shut the door behind him. Surya saw a soldier whose long hair was greying and she shrank a little into her seat, conscious of her torn clothes. He looked her in the face and raised his brows.

'Sir?'

Mershen put his hand on the captain's shoulder and spoke to him in a voice so low that Surya could make out none of the words. The instructions took some time. Felic chewed the inside of his cheek and blinked hard, but showed no other sign of emotion. Then Mershen turned to look at her one last time. 'Wait till nightfall,' he said thoughtfully.

'Sir.'

The Glorious General left without another word to her, without a smile, without explanation. The soldiers' boots drummed on the corridor boards, and when they were gone Felic went and sat himself in a chair, stretching his legs out. His expression was mostly one of resignation.

'What was his command?' Surya asked.

'We wait. Until nightfall.'

My name is Raihn and I am third concubine to Lord Mershen. I was born Surya, daughter of General Imerho, may his star look down upon us, and when I was eighteen I was slain and reborn. I was brought secretly to Lord Mershen's private house on his ancestral estate, where I now live. It was four months until I saw him again. He is risking everything by keeping me alive and we have to be careful.

I live with Mershen's other concubines. There are only three of us. They've treated me kindly, to my surprise; they know nothing of my true history and nothing he or I do must arouse suspicion. He does his best to keep up with us all. It's a good thing he has a most spacious bed.

I am happy, though I miss using my bow. It is a noble-woman's hobby not normal among other classes.

I tell you all this now, my child, while you are still within me. It must never be spoken aloud. Mershen says that when you are born he will adopt you. But the Radiant Emperor must never know that the bloodline of Imerho lives on.

Pique Dame

At last my governess and the other girls go. Pauline lingers for a while, anxiously, but I don't encourage her. It's a relief to be on my own.

My words are sweetly plaintive, falling like raindrops through the air.

I remove my house gown, preparing for bed. I've told the maid to leave the French windows open, because the night is fresh now that the rainstorm has passed. I light my candle, turn back my sheet and brush my hair out. But I'm restless. I climb upon the bed then spring off again. My agitation grows. I should be looking forward to my marriage to Prince Yeletsky, but I cannot. Ever since that chance meeting in the Summer Gardens, my heart has been thrown into turmoil. That lowly soldier who looked at me with such burning eyes – what spell has he cast on me? Why am I trembling at the mere thought of him? Why can't I think about anyone else – even my betrothed? There is a flush on my girlish cheeks now that has never been there before; it's like fire has taken the place of blood in my veins; it's like my mind is no longer my own. His handsome face haunts me. I touch my breasts, feeling the stirrings of strange new yearnings in them. I run my hand across the flat of my belly, aware that it is another's touch I really need, but not truly certain what it is I would want him to do.

There is a noise at the shutters.

Hand on my heart, I retreat in fear. Someone has climbed to my balcony from the garden below. I see his figure framed against the night sky as the doors are thrown open and I cry out in recognition. It is the soldier – Herman.

Into the room he strides, pain and desire in his wounded eyes. He loves me, he declares. But he cannot have me; I am too far above him on the social scale. He is only a lowly officer in the Tsar's army, and I am the granddaughter of a countess. If only I would take pity on him! But no – he must never think that he might be able to attain my love, so he has come to bid me farewell. This night he will kill himself, so that the agony of lifelong separation might be avoided.

I beg him to reconsider.

There's a noise at the door – a knock, my grandmother's voice. She's heard noises from my room and wonders why I am still up. Herman dives back behind the louvered shutter as she enters, and I try to look nonchalant. The Countess chides me and orders me back to bed, and as I pretend to acquiesce she departs.

In half-a-dozen strides Herman is across the room, kneeling at my bedside, seizing my hands in supplication. I tell him he must go. If he goes it will be to his death, he declares. If only he could know that I love him as he loves me, that the same fire burns in both of us. If I would kiss him – if I would only yield my lips to his – if I would only answer his passion with mine, then he would live in everlasting joy.

He's on the bed now, his arms around me. I protest, but feebly. He is strong and insistent, his eyes and his voice holding me captive as much as his hands. I arch beneath his taut body, my breasts heaving against his chest. He has one hand in my hair now, and I can't tell if he's holding me up or bearing me down. Though I try to wriggle free, every movement I make somehow opens me further to his caresses and works me further into his embrace. He wants me. He cannot bear to let *me go. He must have my love now. And as he bears me to the mattress and moves upon me I yield helplessly before his passion and my own, sliding my arm about his neck and sinking back as he takes full possession of me. His lips hover over mine.*

The curtain falls on Act 1.

That moment almost hurt. The transition was wrenching: all at once I was no longer virginal Russian noblewoman Lisa, but back in my own somewhat older body. My hair wasn't golden but a light brown – it just looked blond under the stage lights – and it wasn't the dashing obsessive Herman whose weight was upon me but Elliot Wells, the lead tenor.

We held our places, trying to control our breathing, because it's not totally unknown for a stage curtain to go bouncing up again so it's best practice to freeze in place for a while. He was heavy on my thighs and the heat of his body was making me tingle. Not that I was objecting. The stormy passion of the scene, the soaring vocals of our duet, the fearsome intensity of his eyes – I'd hardly been acting as I portrayed Lisa's arousal. I wondered again at the perversity of the director's decision not to let us kiss before the curtain fell. Over and over during months of rehearsal, this same music, played on a tinny piano, had brought us to this climactic point without ever permitting any resolution.

It's easy to get lost in a passionate role. There's a reason why actors and singers aren't so good at monogamy.

Stagehands hurried on all around us, grabbing the props. Beyond the heavy curtain applause was still raining.

'OK?' said Elliot, still not moving, still not taking his eyes from mine. Between the tight rows of his braids his scalp gleamed with sweat: this was hard work.

I nodded, panting. The aftermath of our duet burned inside me.

'You were amazing,' he murmured. From a professional like him to an amateur like me, on our opening night, that's a high compliment. I felt myself blush beneath my stage make-up.

'Elliot! Tanya!' Our stage manager Leo had scurried on. He had to keep his voice down but his enthusiasm was unmistakable. 'Did you hear that? They love it!'

Reluctantly, it seemed, Elliot heaved himself to his feet and held out his hand to help me up, while I straightened my dress, trying to cover the fact I was feeling flustered. 'Tanya's got real ability,' he murmured. 'You should try out for a professional company, you know.'

I was damp between my legs I realised, trying not to squirm.

Leo squeezed my shoulder. 'Don't say that! I need her here!' His head whipped round. 'Careful with that!' he hissed at two hands who were wheeling in a draped pillar for the ballroom scene and almost tipping it.

Distracted for a moment, I lost track of Elliot. When I looked around he was heading into the wings. *Pique Dame* is a particularly hard opera for the principal tenor because Herman is on stage and singing in every scene. My own part was somewhat briefer, as Lisa would commit suicide when she realised that Herman's true devotion was to gambling and that he was using her to acquire her grandmother's card-playing secret. That role was quite enough of a challenge for me. But at least we were singing the French version rather than the Russian; memorising our words had been that much easier.

Leaving Leo to chivvy the backstage crew, I slipped through the wings and down the stairs to the female dressing room to glug bottled water and get changed into my ball dress. The second act would be upon us before we had time to cool down.

Dizzy with excitement and adrenaline, I was still thinking about Elliot Wells, wondering if his lingering touch was entirely method acting. We'd only met six months ago and had only been rehearsing hard together for three. I'd found him, well, *reserved* – perfectly polite and very professional, but slow to thaw, as if an operatic arrogance went with that artsy little beard. Maybe that was my own fault for holding him so much in awe. He was in the chorus of the English National Opera and I, like the rest of the cast here, was only a keen amateur. Don't get me wrong; he wasn't slumming it down here with the Danley Opera Company, he was advancing his own career. Professional singers vie for lead amateur parts because they want the roles on their CV. But I was lucky to get the chance to sing with someone so good and we both knew it.

And I was lucky in another way entirely: that he was so handsome. Most tenors in my experience were short, fat and balding. I don't know why that should be, but I've always found baritones to be much better looking, even though they don't often play the romantic leads. A tall charismatic tenor is a happy surprise. A tall *black* tenor is as rare as hens' teeth. Opera, that most middle class of art forms, is not exactly full of singers from ethnic minority groups.

Working with Elliot was not doing anything for my peace of mind.

I hurried through the changing room, nearly tripping over the ballgowns that were being flung on in a last-minute panic. One end of the room was screened off for the Countess and myself, the contralto and soprano principals: that small privacy and our own chairs were all the privilege we were afforded.

'You looked good out there, dear,' said Mary, the chief wardrobe manager, over an armful of taffeta. I'd gathered she'd been backstage on every production this company had done since it was started. 'Very nice.'

'Thanks!'

'I never realised what hot stuff this Tchaikovsky was, you know.'

I grinned and lifted the curtain to our little chamber. The mirror lights had been switched off and the space was in shadow. Just for a moment I thought I saw a slight, dark figure sitting in my chair, head in hands. Then the light from the room behind me shifted in as I changed my stance and I saw that the room was empty.

Odd, I thought. But I didn't have time to worry about it. I had to get into my costume for the masked ball, and meet my betrothed.

The opening night was a thorough success and I couldn't have been more pleased; this was my first principal role with an opera company this big, and though it was an amateur company it was a top-of-the-range one, with costumes and sets as good as any you'd see in a professional show. It was only the participants who didn't get paid for what they did.

After the final curtain fell some of the cast went to the pub to celebrate while others went home and the backstage crew scrummed down into a technical discussion. I hung around chatting for a while, but ended up getting changed back into civvies alone, humming to myself my riverbank aria. I was just putting my earrings on when Elliot lifted the curtain and looked in on me.

'Hey.'

'Hi there.'

We stood smiling at each other, not entirely sure of ourselves. Elliot's silence before he next spoke was just that little bit too extended. All of a sudden the room felt too warm.

'I was wondering if you would like to go out for a drink,

Tanya.' His invitation was measured and polite, but it could not be construed as casual. His eyes said everything.

'A drink?'

'There's the bar at the Hilton.'

'I'd love to.' I ran my hand over the back of a chair. 'But I can't.'

He raised an eyebrow. 'Hm?'

'I'm . . .' I bit my lip. 'I'm married.'

'Ah. Fair enough.' He smiled ruefully. 'So am I,' he admitted.

'I'd have liked to though,' I blurted out as he turned away. 'You know.'

He held me with his gaze one beat longer. 'Yes. I know.'

A moment of aching frustration passed between us, unspoken. Then he stepped in towards me and I thought that he wasn't taking no for an answer. He took my hands in his and I thought how big and warm his were compared to mine. And I thought I was sure I was capable of denying myself – but not if he pushed it, not if he took control, not if he touched me. Please, I thought, just kiss me and it won't be my fault.

Stooping, Elliot brushed his lips to my cheek. 'I think it's probably a good job we're not on tour together, don't you?'

'Yes,' I whispered.

'Goodnight, Tanya.' He left me breathless and shaking – and alone.

I sat down heavily, feeling the air go out of me like from a punctured tyre. I should phone home, I told myself, my fingers fluttering over my face. I should speak to Tim and his voice would remind me who it was that I loved, who it was I could come home to every night and find always pleased to see me, pleased to slide into bed beside me, pleased for my success and my passion and my pleasure in an art he understood not at all. Tim would have bought a bunch of flowers to congratulate me on my opening night, and would have a bottle of my favourite wine open. We would make love because I'd be too wired and hyper to sleep, and it would be quite wonderful and satisfying.

None of which made one whit of difference to how I was feeling now. My panties were soaking. My insides churned, craving Elliot's touch, the smell of his skin and his cologne, the sound of his voice. His beautiful, perfect voice. For a few moments I relived in my head our lovers' scene on stage, hearing again our two voices intertwining passionately, seeing his body moving down on mine. It was too much to bear. With a groan I shook my head and reached for my car keys, but my fumbling fingers knocked them across the dressing table and into the wastepaper basket. As I scrabbled among the crumpled make-up-smeared wipes, I realised that I was in no condition to drive. Frustration was making me clumsy and unfocused, and the itch between my thighs was too cruel to be ignored.

With a quick glance out through the curtain I ascertained that there was nobody else in the changing room. Well, I told myself wryly, this wouldn't take long. I stood with one hand on the glass of the mirror, hitched my skirt with the other hand, and delved into my panties. If I need to come quickly, that's the way to do it: on tiptoes, my legs straining, my thighs braced. A peek of white cotton and a flash of mouse-brown hair under the folds of my skirt were the only visible naughtiness, but my fingers confirmed that I was slippery, that my clit was engorged and stiff. I fingered myself with quick vibrating movements. In the mirror I could see the tension in my jaw, the deep hunger in my eyes, the strain of my breasts against my tight blouse.

What if he comes back? I asked myself, strumming hard. What if he comes back through that curtain to ask me again?

Would I be able to stop in time or would he catch me working off my frantic desire for him? Would he stand and watch, delighted, or would he pull up the back of my skirt and wrench down my knickers and stuff me hard from behind with his eager cock, just as I deserved?

Reflected behind me, in the shadow behind the costume rack, two eyes glinted. A dark figure stirred.

I froze, more confused than shocked. Movement behind me ceased. When I looked over my shoulder I was as sure as I could be: there was no one else in this cubbyhole of a room. The shadows were simply not deep enough to conceal a human being. It had been a trick of the light.

Nonetheless, there was a strong feeling of eyes upon me.

My heart racing, I turned back to the mirror. 'Watch if you want,' I whispered, thrusting out my lower lip. This time I fingered myself all the way to orgasm, my legs trembling with the strain, my boobs out-thrust and shaking, a blush storming my cheeks. And in the reflected room a shadow watched with avid eyes.

Pique Dame ran for a week, every night. It was hard work – physically, vocally and emotionally. I'd taken leave from my day job, but even so this pushed me to my limits. Elliot was as polite as ever and didn't try his luck on any following evening, but it wouldn't be entirely accurate to say that he backed off; on stage every night he seduced and ravished me with predatory zeal, ripping the seams of my costume on one occasion. His body imprinted itself on mine as if he were branding my flesh. Lisa's virginal reluctance became flimsier and more transparent. Our singing reached new heights of emotion; we seemed ready to tear each other apart in our passion, and my character's anguish as I discovered him false became raw with pain.

For a short time that opera consumed my life. I have never been happier.

At home I tried to rest my voice as much as possible, not daring to chatter but miming to Tim when I needed to communicate. I also ambushed him daily in his home office, dragging him from the computer to fuck me on the bed, the sofa, the living-room carpet and – memorably – over the lip of the bath. I was high with tension. I was on heat. Tim was bemused but willing enough to indulge me, and did not question my horniness. I could hardly tell him it was because I was gasping for the show's star performer.

Back at the theatre, our mutual desire was articulated in silence as much as in song. The ravenous look in his eyes as he stalked me across the stage during the ballroom scene made me quake. The private and knowing smiles we exchanged when I watched over his shoulder in the mirror while he had his make-up dusted on made my heart leap painfully. It was as if we shared a secret language.

It didn't go entirely unnoticed, the tension between Elliot and I. The producer was heard to mutter darkly that if that seduction scene got any steamier the paint on the flats would start to run. But this was theatre, and opera at that; nobody disapproved. Emotion was what it was all about. Everyone capable of fancying men had a crush on Elliot anyway, and all the female chorus were completely aflutter in his presence.

On the Thursday afternoon I approached the wardrobe mistress casually. 'Is this theatre haunted, Mary, do you know?'

She cast me an amused glance. 'The opera been getting to you, darling?' *Pique Dame* is after all a tale of supernatural vengeance, and the make-up of the Countess' Ghost was particularly grisly. The final scene, where Herman went mad and killed himself, still made the hair stand up on my neck even after several performances.

I smiled. 'I mean it. Does it have a ghost?'

'A Grey Lady, you mean? Or some Victorian gentleman in a top hat?' She waved a hand at the building around us, which certainly looked like the proper setting for a traditional theatre ghost. It was Victorian red brick and cavernous, and full of tiny backstage corridors that rose and dropped and branched. I stood my ground though, determined.

'A skinny black guy in grey overalls.'

She stopped smirking. 'You've seen William?' She raised her voice. 'Ted! Come here!' When Ted ambled over she added: 'Tanya's seen William!'

'Oh, that's good. I thought he might have gone.' Ted was one of those elderly gentlemen that you find in amateur theatre; they take tickets and sell programmes and wedge themselves firmly into every management committee available.

'William?' I said faintly.

'He hasn't been seen in a couple of years. I thought he might have faded, you know. Ghosts do.'

'You know his name?' I don't know why, but having a name to put to the shadowy face made me feel uneasy, as if he were suddenly more real.

'Well,' laughed Mary, 'he's not an old ghost. Nineteen fifties, I think.'

Ted nodded. 'He came here on that ship, the whatsit . . .'

'The *Windrush*?' I guessed.

'That's the one. From the West Indies.' He looked pleased with himself. 'Worked here eight years, first as a carpenter and then as stage crew. Never a day off, they say. Hard working, and kept all his money carefully. He was saving up to bring his wife and children here too, you see.'

'So what happened?'

'Oh, nothing terribly dramatic. He just passed away quietly one night, behind the scenes. Aneurysm or something, I should think. The sad thing was that his family was on a boat headed to England at that very moment. He never got to see them again.'

'That's awful,' I said.

'But if his ghost shows, that's supposed to be a very good sign for a performance; he's taking an interest. It's not at all common. You've seen him, have you, my dear? Whereabouts?'

How was I supposed to tell them that I'd glimpsed him every night since we opened, in the wings or corridors or dressing rooms? That I could feel him watching me whenever I went on or off stage? That when I was alone he came to hungrily watch me undress? 'The green room,' I muttered feebly.

And I lay awake that night thinking what it would be like to be separated from my spouse for eight years, working for the day that we would be reunited, a day that would never come. Not to mention being stuck in a foreign country, treated as some sort of oddity at the very very best. Poor William. Had he found distraction among the flighty and curious actresses who passed in succession through the theatre, or had they been only a source of temptation and torment? Had he really stuck it out for eight long years? I didn't think I could go that long without my husband without going crackers; celibacy was not in my repertoire. Wasn't it the case that even with my man in my bed every night I was panting foolishly after another one? Why couldn't I just be content?

In the dark I snaked my arms around Tim's sleeping form and kissed the nape of his neck, as if trying to apologise.

The ghost's attentions might have been a good omen, but things were not going smoothly. As the last night of our run loomed the atmosphere grew not just more strained but distinctly odd, and though we should have been settled into our routine by now all sorts of little problems were sparking off without warning. The lighting rigs were playing up and different corners of the stage would be plunged into shadow or lit in peculiar colours, despite the lighting operator swearing that there was nothing wrong with the electrics during the technical run-throughs. The dressing rooms were always either too hot or too cold. Leo and the conductor had a huge row over, as far as I could tell, an entirely imaginary series of slights, and the orchestra threatened for an hour to walk off the production – musicians being the only performers who get paid for their efforts, and so having no loyalty to the show. Prince Yeletsky, who was a seasoned trooper of the amateur circuit, suffered unaccountable attacks of nerves and barely made it onto the stage one time. The Countess complained that the make-up was making her eyes itchy and bloodshot, and certainly her facial appearance even as a living woman was haggard. A family in the audience complained bitterly that they had brought their children along to an opera because it was *culture*, and they hadn't expected the final scene to be so *nasty*. They got their money refunded.

But the singing was magnificent. Despite all the peripheral problems, I'd never been in a production sung with more passion. The fact that everyone seemed tense and out of sorts translated into dramatic energy the moment we were in front of an audience.

On the last night I stationed myself in the wings as the overture played. We had a full house yet again. The reviews had been glowing, even in the national papers. I wasn't due onstage for some time, but I didn't want to miss a thing, and that moment in the first scene where Herman stood beneath the tempest, arms outspread and his wet shirt clinging to his chest, and swore he would triumph over fate – oh, that was a moment I particularly looked forward to.

'Our last time,' said Elliot, and I nearly shot out of my skin. I hadn't noticed him moving up behind me. I struggled to compose myself.

'Well, it's been incredible. I've ... I've learned so much.'

'I meant what I said before, Tanya.' He had to stand quite close to me so as not to shout over the music, and his chest brushed my arm. 'About you trying out for a professional company. There are auditions coming up for the ENO chorus; with training you've got a real chance.'

'Ah.' I didn't know how to respond to that. I shook my head. 'That's kind but ... I don't think so. I'm not ready to face that level of competition. You know, the unending bitchiness and the sleeping with musical directors ...'

He chuckled.

'And,' I added more seriously, 'the travelling away from home and the daft hours. I'd have to give up too much. It's just not me, I'm afraid. I love singing opera, but it's not my whole life.'

He nodded. 'I hope you don't regret the opportunity later then.'

Was he still talking about my career? 'Regret's not the worst thing to live with,' I said sadly.

'That's true.' He glanced towards the curtain. 'Is your husband out there tonight?'

'Yes.' I smiled. 'Despite the fact he's absolutely tone-deaf and thinks opera is plain silly.'

Elliot's forehead wrinkled. 'Perhaps we should tone it down for tonight then. We don't want him getting upset.'

'Oh, Tim won't worry. He's not the jealous type.'

'Well.' He brushed my bare arm with the back of his fingers, very gently. 'I'm certainly jealous of him.'

I parted my lips, but I had no answer to that. His gaze lingered on me as if he were searching my soul. I felt my heart begin to race.

'I'd better get into place,' he murmured as the safety curtain started to lift and reveal the tabs. Then he withdrew into the shadows.

That final performance was like a fever dream. Whatever was going wrong with the lighting, it changed the settings by degrees until the stage was eerily lit like an impressionist film, all inky shadows and blue highlights. I could see Leo's grimace of fury from his position in the wings stage-left, but there was nothing he could do about it, it appeared. The players flung themselves into their roles, seemingly determined not to be outdone by the melodramatic staging. And when I made my first entrance, promenading at the Countess' side through the Summer Gardens, I understood why. A blue light in the rig overhead seemed to be shining into our eyes when we turned to look upstage, plunging the audience beyond into darkness. It created a most peculiar feeling of disassociation from the reality of the theatre, as if we were trapped in our own little world and the stage was a bubble of light floating in blackness. We emoted fiercely in an effort to communicate.

But the sound was wonderful. Every note, perfectly true, soared thrillingly in the auditorium. After the first scene I came dizzily off stage, feeling almost drunk with the power of our voices. Janice, who played the Countess, gripped my arm hard, and I was shocked to see tears running down her cheeks.

'Are you all right?' I asked.

'It's just this make-up in my eyes,' she said, turning her face away. But her speaking voice sounded like it was trembling.

Then the second scene began: the seduction scene. As soon as I stepped into character I felt the outside world recede and the fervid reality of the opera take its place. I became Lisa, at least in part. I wasn't remembering rehearsals and stage directions; it flowed through me as if I were living it for real, as if there could be a world in which people sang their every thought out loud. I listened to my female friends' pitiful attempts to cheer me up with genuine impatience; I bid them farewell with heartfelt relief. I flung myself around the room in an agony of virginal frustration.

Then Herman appeared at my balcony window. My heart crashed in my chest.

We sang that night like I've never sung in a duet before or since, every word meant for real, our mutual desire raw and naked. Herman's voice seemed to batter upon me, one moment caressing and the next filled with violence. We circled each other, we reached to touch each other, we drew away. He caught me from behind and pulled me against him and I felt his physical arousal in no uncertain terms even as his hands mauled my hips and bit into my shoulders, stalking the lines of my flanks. I'd have bruises tomorrow, I realised dimly. His fingers smeared my lipstick. I could smell his heat and his cologne. His muscles felt like rock under his military uniform.

When the Countess interrupted us, so briefly, I found I was actually unsteady on my feet. I sank onto the edge of the bed. As soon as she had gone Herman took advantage of that, moving in upon the forbidden territory. His body language was unmistakable by now: if what he wanted wasn't going to be offered up freely it would be taken by force. Only a maiden would be innocent enough to think his pleading and his need were all about love, not power and avarice. Only a virgin could be naive enough not to realise where this would inevitably end. Only a girl like Lisa would not think twice about where her own desire was taking her, or the consequences of her new-found appetite. I ran my hands over his chest; I should have been fending him off but I was kneading his flesh. I writhed in his arms, rubbing my body against his. He had my thighs parted, my gown hitched up to reveal the line of my bare leg, his own bulk pressing in on my sex and turning its softness to juicy pulp. Even as the notes poured from my throat a part of me was aware of the stony hardness of his erection, trapped by his breeches but pressing into me greedily.

My consciousness was fractured into kaleidoscope colours. The performance. The emotion. The words. The cock. The aching need between my legs. We hit the last few exultant phrases with our voices intertwined like our limbs, and he surged upon me and held the last note.

The curtain did not fall. The lights did not go out.

Breathless, I stared into his eyes. Elliot's eyes; not Herman's. I saw the slightest widening as he acknowledged something was wrong. The music swept on to its conclusion.

Oh hell, I thought, we were going to be left frozen on stage, in silence.

But the orchestra was better than I could have given them credit for. As the main drape hung obstinately unmoving, high over the stage, the musicians picked up the music almost seamlessly from an earlier phrase and swept on into another round. As far as the audience was concerned it was only Herman and Lisa who had frozen in place.

Elliot raised his eyebrows as if to say, *The show must go on.* Then he kissed me. I tasted the pine-pitch tang of the lozenges he'd been eating. It was the first time our lips had met on or off stage, and six months of dreaming and denial grounded themselves like lightning with that one kiss, the colours dancing behind my eyes. For that moment the world seemed to collapse in around us, but it was all too brief. He kissed deep and sweet but he didn't linger, making it look good for the audience. As his lips left they tore away from me a groan of pleasure that only he heard. His eyes held mine for another second, searchingly. He must have discerned the bravado to match his own. I could feel his chest heaving as his lips descended to my throat, his gasps gusting hot on my skin; he was fighting to recover his breath after the duet, and my breasts heaved too as I laboured for air. I rolled my head back, letting my hair fall across the bedspread. Part of me was praying for the curtain to drop. Part of me was praying that it wouldn't.

Elliot groaned, his erection grinding into me through our clothes. He must have been as frantic as I was. From my upside-down position, I glimpsed in the wing Leo slumped over the stage controls and at his shoulder a slim figure with an expression full of years of loneliness and need, watching us on stage – watching as if finally something had brought him to the point of release.

Elliot bit my breasts with tremulous urgency, through the material of my gown. I dragged my fingertips across his hair. The music swirled around us, lifting us on its furious tide. They weren't going to stop, I realised. The curtain wasn't going to fall. We were going to have to carry on acting our parts. I felt a kind of holy terror – not of Elliot, but of what we were doing. The ritual we were enacting. The forces focused upon us, along with all those eyes. I've been nervous before going on stage, but never like this, and never had it been combined with such a hot desire.

Then Elliot hitched himself upon one elbow and reached between us to his breeches. Stage costumes might look elaborate with buttons and laces, but in reality they are all Velcro and press studs, designed to pull off as simply and quickly as possible. It was easy for him to open his trousers and free himself. It was easy, under the disguise of those stark shadows and the rumpled folds of my gown, for him to pull aside the sodden gusset of my knickers and angle his beautiful stiff cock into my waiting wetness. They must have thought out there that we were wonderful actors: my spasm of shock, his lurch as he embedded himself into me, the look of poised awe and intent upon our faces before he began to thrust.

And it might seem odd but that moment as his cock split me open felt like my gift to Lisa, to the sweet foolish girl sacrificed so cruelly for her love. It was the moment that made it worthwhile. But don't think I'm trying to excuse myself by saying I'd let the character take possession of me. Her desire and mine had a single object, but my lust – a primitive desperate need to be opened and rived asunder by this man – was my own. To be fucked by Elliot Wells, to feel his hips roll on me and his wonderful cock deep and hard inside me, was everything I had dreamed of in my most private fantasies. That we were doing it before witnesses only forced me to accept my culpability and thrilled me to the core.

See how much I want him. See how he pleasures me. See how my need for his cock overwhelms my sense of decency. Watch as he fucks me senseless, you voyeurs. Have you ever seen anything so elemental?

After that I did not worry about the audience; singers and actors are after all exhibitionists at heart. I even forgot to worry about Tim, who must have been watching as his wife fucked with another man, wrapping her bare thighs around his hips, sinking her fingers into the cloth at his back. Without an inch of obscene skin showing, we still demonstrated in the most graphic manner two people frenziedly screwing each other. Man on woman, sweat flying, mouths open with ecstasy, hands tugging at one another and the bedding, my ankles hammering his calves. His thrusts were deep and forceful, like some thundering drumbeat underlying the music. Were they aroused, the watchers? Did men stiffen and women spread in their scarlet velvet seats, hot with *culture*? They must have suspected, surely. Some of them must have realised. They might even have been able to hear my cries over the music's final crescendo and Elliot's deep groan as he followed me into orgasm and spurted his come deep within me.

Then the curtain fell.

And in the wings the shadow smiled, before fading away.

And Their Flying Machines

Unable to sleep, Charlotte went up to the Flight Deck.

She'd tried to sleep. She'd tried to distract herself by playing patience, and by talking to her friend Louisa about the upcoming season, and by attending tea dances and tennis parties and the Hambletons' charity ball 'in support of our heroes', but nothing had worked. For three days she'd had the sick feeling of anticipation in her stomach, and now it was so bad she couldn't even doze off for more than half an hour at a time. She'd awake sweating and frightened, sure that she'd missed the alarm klaxon that every nerve was tuned to. The klaxon that would summon the pilots to their ornithopters.

It was thirty floors up the interior of the Peak to the Flight Deck. She could have taken the lift, but it was the middle of the night and she felt it too cruel to waken the attendant. Besides, the exercise was a distraction, the struggle a blessing. She watched her flying boots take the stairs, one riser at a time. She made herself go slowly. She remembered the first time she'd ventured up here, when she'd been wearing a white summer dress down to her ankles and little white calfskin boots with scalloped heels. She wouldn't, she reminded herself, have been able to climb thirty storeys back then, not in that dress and those boots.

Then, she'd taken the clanking wrought-iron lift and emerged blinking from the gaslit dimness of the interior tunnels into the wide cavern that was the Flight Deck. Past the ranks of ornithopters and the clusters of busy engineers the flight apron gaped onto empty sky; only the tips of the surrounding hills were visible, lit by the evening light. A single ornithopter flickered into view as it swept westwards in its patrol circle.

She paused inside the doorway, taking it all in. The pilots in their blue leather overalls, checking their machines over or striding away to well-earned R&R. The engineers, far more numerous, in brown, intent upon the machines. The sense of tension, the scurrying, the babble of conversation and orders and the clang of metal. The sweet familiar smell of machine oil.

The ornithopters themselves were less familiar. They were military standard models, bigger than her own Skylark Celestial and weighted down by their twin blunt-muzzled aether cannons. Charlotte bit her lip. An ornithopter at rest was hardly a beautiful thing; nothing like the shimmering darting dragonfly that it became in flight. But these machines looked positively brutal. They were grey where the paint had been burnt off and pocked with projectile holes.

She turned to the first man to pass randomly within range. 'Could you possibly tell me where I might find Chief Engineer McGregor?'

He looked surprised, and his eyes swept her up and down, but he pointed to a knot of men who were working beneath one of the flying machines. 'He's the one in the waistcoat, miss.'

Thanking him, she followed his pointing finger. The men were trying to hoist an engine into the ornithopter's empty carcass. Neither engine nor vehicle body looked particularly new. Most of the men wore brown boiler suits. The only man obviously wearing a waistcoat was squatted on his haunches, peering up into the machine's belly and instructing the engineers as bolts were tightened in order.

'Excuse me? Mr McGregor?' she asked when there seemed to be a momentary, triumphant lull. The men, who hadn't even noticed her until now, went quiet, staring over their shoulders.

'Chief McGregor,' he said, not looking round but reaching up to wipe a bleed nipple with a rag.

'I'm Charlotte Laindon-Royse. I wrote to you.'

He manoeuvred out from under the machine and stood, wiping his hands on the rag. Suddenly he was quite tall, and broad-shouldered to go with it. His hair was swept back and ran to greying curls behind his ears. His eyes were cool. 'The Honourable Charlotte Laindon-Royse,' he said, speaking with a noticeable brogue, and Charlotte remembered her headed notepaper with an inner wince. 'I remember. But I don't remember writing back.'

A few of the young men sniggered audibly.

'I only need a few minutes.' She could feel her pale cheeks flushing.

'Minutes? They're in short supply around here.' He glanced around the Flight Deck. 'Along with everything else.'

'Well,' she said, 'I came to offer to help you with that.'

For a moment he studied her face. 'Five minutes,' he pronounced, throwing his rag to the nearest man. 'Get this engine secured, lads.' He extended his hand to the right. 'My office, miss.'

His office was a room of leaded glass at the end of the hangar. Inside it was hung with wooden blinds. There was a desk, a narrow cot bed, the innards of at least two ornithopters and a huge quantity of mess; the place seemed to be used as a dump for everything that had no place in the pristinely ordered Flight Deck. He had to lift a battery pack off a chair to offer her somewhere to sit. He remained standing, and folded his arms.

'Well, Miss Laindon-Royse?'

He was what her father would praise as a 'salt-of-the-earth workman'; one of that breed of educated practical men that had created Victoria City – technological wonder of the age – from a spire of raw rock, and helped build the Empire. He made Charlotte feel like a child. She took her courage in both hands.

'I want to volunteer as a pilot.'

Credit to the man, he neither laughed nor choked, though his eyebrows went up. 'Oh,' he said, glancing towards the hangar then frowning.

She hurried on: 'I can fly. I have my own ornithopter; a Celestial. And I won the Ladies' Race and a silver medal at the airshow last year.'

'I see.' His knotted brows didn't part. 'Very ... nice.'

She flushed anew. 'I think that's worth something, don't you?'

'You think it qualifies you as a fighter pilot?'

'Of course not.' She wished she hadn't sat down; she felt at too much of a disadvantage. 'But you're desperate for pilots. It's in all the newspapers. I could be trained up. I want to do my bit – before it's too late.'

'Well, I'm sure that there's plenty of useful war work that you could volunteer for –'

'What? Knitting socks and boiling soup? A lot of use that'll be if the enemy take Victoria! It's vital to keep up the air defences, everyone knows that. You need pilots.'

'I need *fighter* pilots.'

'And all those men in the Volunteer Air Corps, they were fighter pilots before they joined up, were they?'

He exhaled, clearly restraining himself from snapping at her. She left him no space.

'They want to defend their country. That's enough for them and it's enough for me. I don't want to just sit here helplessly waiting to see what happens.'

'And do you know what the casualty rate is among pilots?'

'That's why you need more of us, isn't it?'

His jaw tightened. 'And you want to end your days in a smashed and burning ornithopter on some God-forsaken hillside, do you? Because that's what happens to most of my men. I can count on one hand the number of pilots who've been with me since the start of the war, Miss Laindon-Royse. The chances of your getting through unscathed are ridiculously low – this is not a job for a lady.'

'What are my chances if the enemy break the line and reach the Peak?' She thrust her chin out. 'How unscathed do you think we ladies will remain then?'

The Chief Engineer ground the heel of his hand into his forehead, leaving an oily streak, and changed tack. 'Well why haven't you approached the Volunteer Air Corps if you're so keen? Lord Atherstone might have a place for you.'

Charlotte bit her lip. His grey eyes bored into her. 'Lord Atherstone is my fiancé,' she admitted.

Out of nowhere the ghost of a smile touched his face, like sun on a winter mountainside. 'I can see him having problems with that, then.'

She averted her face slightly.

'What does your father think of this?'

'I'm twenty-one.'

He hid the flicker of surprise not quite well enough. 'Well, good for you, but I'm not asking you to marry me.'

'I'm legally an adult. I can take this decision myself.'

'And what would Lord Laindon say if his daughter was brought back charred and limbless? Or not brought back at all?'

'I want to do my part,' she repeated quietly but fervently. 'I can fly. I'm wasted doing anything else.'

He shook his head. Then, to her utter amazement, said, 'All right, lass. Show me what you can do.'

She stared, her heart starting to thump as it caught up with the tidings. 'I'll have to go fetch my –'

'You do, do you? If the raid klaxons go off you think you'll have time to pop home and get your toy?' His mouth pulled sideways. 'You'll suit up and take one of my scouts. Now.'

Turning away, he searched down a coat rack laden with grimy flying suits and selected one. 'Probably the smallest,' he said, throwing it at her. 'Get it on.'

Charlotte blinked, holding the heavy padded leather out from her clean dress. 'Excuse me ...'

'Shy, are you? Not the most useful trait in a fighter pilot.'

She was going red. 'You could –'

'Yes, you're right. I could convert my office to a ladies' changing room for the duration.' He pulled a fob watch from his waistcoat pocket. 'One minute or you're wasting my time.'

She bared her teeth, flung the flying suit over the desk and went to work on her dress fastenings. Luckily it was a summer outfit, with the minimum of buttons. It came off quickly. Chief McGregor watched coolly as she loosened her waistband and dropped her underskirt to the floor, revealing long white drawers and stockings.

Faintly, from outside, came a joyous whoop: someone had noticed and such light relief was truly welcome. Charlotte clenched her teeth and ignored them. She had no time to change her tightly laced boots so she shrugged the leather suit on over the lot: footwear, bloomers and lacy chemise. It was so big that it didn't even snag on her heels. And it smelled strongly and malely of sweat; the musk made her head swim.

Conflicting emotions – humiliation and pride, outrage and fear and hope – washed through her from all directions, creating chaotic eddies.

Tightening the straps in a desperate attempt to make the baggy garment wearable, she glared at the Chief Engineer, her cheeks crimson but her lip mutinous.

He lifted one sardonic brow. 'Well, you might have a weight advantage,' he allowed.

'Helmet?' she demanded, pinning up her hair.

He threw her one from a pile. 'This way then.'

He led her out to the smallest ornithopter in the row. They had an audience now of grinning men, but he barked at them and they retreated to their duties. 'In you get,' he instructed. 'Take her out; show me some moves. I want to see a one-eighty drop roll. Don't go beyond the harbour perimeter.'

Charlotte found this the easiest part of the whole process. Once she was buckled into the seat, she felt her confidence surge back. She knew how to fly. Nothing else in her life might be under her control, but this machine was. Nevertheless she was cautious at first, and a minute later glad she'd been so because with its armour this ornithopter was heavier than her own, with a higher stall-speed and pedals that were awkwardly stiff. Once she was used to them she was able to put the machine through its paces. Keeping in sight of the Flight Deck she spun and tumbled under the summer sky, looped the patrol ornithopter and finally scudded back onto the apron. She knew she'd acquitted herself well. She walked back towards Chief McGregor and his group with her cheeks glowing with excitement rather than offended pride, her blood singing in her veins. Even having to hitch up the flying suit did not dent her sense of vindication.

The Chief Engineer waited with his arms crossed over his

broad chest. He nodded as she stood in front of him. The other men were smiling, not unkindly this time.

'I can fly,' she said, looking him in the eye.

'You can fly,' he agreed. 'But when an enemy 'thopter comes at you out of the sun and there's shrapnel ripping through the bodywork, will you scream and freeze or can you *fight*?'

And he slapped her hard across the face.

If she hadn't been so charged with exhilaration she might have shrunk back and burst into tears. But she was burning with pride. She staggered, stared, and then launched herself at him, striking him in the face with her first blow. After that he caught her arms and pinned her out of reach.

She spat at him.

'That's the reaction I want,' he said, his eyes no longer cold. 'You'll fly scout until you're trained on the guns. Cartwright, take her to the Osprey and show her how to strip down the ammunition belts.'

That was a few months ago. Tonight she wore her own flying suit of cream leather cut snugly for a female figure. Tonight she entered the Flight Deck without trepidation. She wasn't even the only aviatrix in the Royal Ornithopter Brigade any more, two others having followed in her footsteps since she had set the trend – though Alicia Holdstock was getting all kinds of pressure from her family to give up such low-class company and fly scout for the more genteel Volunteer Air Corps.

Charlotte had no problems with the company she kept. The crews, mindful of her status, were more restrained towards her than they might be to one of their own class, though they did not modify their general behaviour at all. She turned a deaf ear to the crudest of their conversation, but she liked their humour and their camaraderie. She liked their professionalism.

Of course it was impossible that she share their whole lives. While they bunked in barracks near the Flight Deck, ready at a moment's notice, she was isolated at home. She did her best to be ready for action, and wore her flying kit at all times. She didn't shy away from unpopular or dangerous missions, and the Chief showed her neither favouritism nor hostility.

When she stepped out onto the Flight Deck, she found it silent except for the faint roar of the boilers. The lights were dimmed, the shutters down over the apron. She walked slowly down the ranks of machines, pausing to touch their metal flanks as if they were sleeping horses.

Nobody else was about. They would, she supposed, be asleep at this hour, or if like her they could not they would be entertaining themselves in a public house somewhere, though with restraint. Unlike the V.A.C. who deemed it proper to fuel their pilots on champagne, here the Chief did not permit drinking on the Flight Deck – in fact he wouldn't let anyone fly whose breath betrayed the smell of alcohol. The pilots grumbled but obeyed.

He was awake tonight though. Her heart bumped a little to see him. He sat at a workbench, lit by a spotlamp, absorbed in his special project – a bulky complex chunk of machinery that people said was supposed to be an entirely new design of phlogiston engine. Most of the time it hid under a tarpaulin as the Flight Deck was too busy for speculative engineering.

'Chief,' greeted Charlotte as she got close.

He glanced up at her briefly. He was busy smoothing a perforated brass disc bigger than his spread hand with a file the size of a toothpick. 'You should be asleep at this hour, Laindon.'

'I can't.'

He grunted under his breath, his attention on the machine part.

She folded her arms and paced in front of the bench. 'I just can't sleep. I keep worrying – what if I miss the call out? What if I can't get here in time?'

He sat back then, chewing his lip as he regarded her. 'You're not going to fly at your best if you've not rested.'

She wondered if he'd seen himself in a mirror recently; there were black shadows under his eyes and lines were beginning to etch themselves deeply into his face. 'I just wish it would start,' she complained. 'It's the waiting that's the worst.'

'No.' His voice was low. 'The longer the attack takes, the more likely we are to have our allies in place to help us.'

'But I can't wait! I want to fly! I feel sick when I eat, and I can't sleep, and all the time I'm listening out, and I think if it takes any longer I'm going to go crazy. I mean – this is it. Everything hangs on this! Can't you send me out on reconnaissance, Chief?'

'At night? We need to conserve fuel, Laindon. You know that. The sentry systems will warn us in time.'

She spun on her boot heel, breathing hard. 'I've been through the drills so many times. It's not helping. I'm going blank on things I should know. I find I can't remember what day it is, or what I'm supposed to be doing –'

'Laindon!' He held up his hand, arresting her mid-flight. His eyes held her. 'It's all right. Come into my office. I've got something there that'll help.'

What was that? she wondered as she followed him. A bottle of whisky? It didn't seem likely. The story among the crew was that when he'd been younger he'd had trouble with the bottle, but nowadays he was a hymn-singing teetotal Nonconformist.

But she trusted him. Everyone in the Ornithopter Brigade trusted the Chief, even if he was a swine to work for. As for Charlotte, she would do anything he told her, willingly. He'd let her fly.

Inside the office, Charlotte watched as he adjusted the blinds so that the slats shut out the world. There was a jerky tension to his movements. Whisky, she thought. It has to be. Only when he shot the brass bolt on the door did she feel the first stab of doubt.

'Chief?'

Then he turned towards her and she saw the intent in his eyes, but she couldn't believe it, couldn't react even when he took her shoulders and shoved her up against a wrought-iron pillar and pressed his mouth down on hers in a fierce kiss that ate her breath. Even when he released her bruised lips she had nothing in her lungs to scream with. He grasped the hair at the back of her head without any gentleness and she let out a squeak.

His hard, handsome face was fierce with desire. His eyes burned. He kissed her open mouth again, triumphantly, relishing the softness of her lips and the slipperiness of her tongue. His thighs trapped hers.

'Yes,' he whispered as he pulled her head back and kissed her throat. He hadn't shaved recently and his stubble rasped on her neck. She could feel the threat of teeth in his kisses.

'No!' she gasped.

'Why not, lass?' he growled. 'Am I not good enough for you?' The hand that wasn't pinning her head moved to the front of her flying suit and worked dextrously at the hooks and eyes holding it closed. She pushed feebly at his hand with her own, but she was weak with shock. He revealed the silk chemise beneath the leather and his hand moved on her breastbone and her left breast, chafing the nipple into reaction. 'Now don't tell me a girl of your spirit hasn't tried some things out with her fiancé already. I'll bet Lord Atherstone has had a handful of these pretty wee things.'

Her breast seemed tiny in his broad hand, but when he thumbed her nipple it filled with electricity.

'Please!'

'Please?' He laughed. 'Of course, lass.'

'Please don't ...'

'Oh now. Don't go disappointing me, your ladyship.' His pelvis pressed against hers and she found it difficult to believe how heavy he was, how hard. His hand worked her breast, more teasing but equally as implacable. 'You're no coward.'

She tried to reply but he kissed her words away like he would eat her protests. Then he drew back. His breath was hot on her lips, his grey eyes boring into her brown ones. She didn't understand why her body was responding to none of her commands, why it was awash with heat and as limp as boiled laundry.

'Have you ever touched a man's prick?'

She whimpered.

He abandoned her breasts to fumble at the fly of his trousers, popping the buttons. His lips curved tauntingly. 'Have you touched Lord Atherstone's prick?'

She couldn't answer. The world made no sense to her any more and the room was spinning away into darkness. The only thing in her world was his hard body and his hard eyes and the hand that was taking hers and guiding it to his crotch as he released his proud erection.

'Was it like this, then?' He folded her fingers around an incredibly hot thick length of flesh and she shook from head to foot.

Comparing Lord Atherstone's slim dart to this thing was like comparing a Skylark Celestial to a gunship.

'Ah.' For a moment the fire in his eyes dimmed, as he visibly enjoyed the sensation of her fingers on him. 'Lass.' He smiled. 'You should take a closer look.'

Stepping away, he pushed her to her knees in front of him. She came eye to eye with his flushed and turgid cock.

Charlotte now discovered that men of the lower orders did not shave their body hair. His balls nested, bulging, in dark curls. And his member – well, she had only a prior knowledge of Freddy Atherstone's to draw upon, but if this was a typical working man's cock then it was as honed and strengthened by labour as the rest of his body. A spill of clear moisture slicked the swollen glans that thrust from his foreskin.

'Like it?' His voice was misleadingly tender. 'Not too indelicate for you?'

Then he pressed her to his crotch, rubbing her face in his scent, on the stiff pole of his arousal. He wasn't particularly cruel about it, just very thorough – as if he were marking her. When he'd rubbed every inch of the contours of her face with his prick he stroked back her tumbled fringe with his fingers. 'Put it in your mouth.'

Charlotte obeyed him. He was the Chief and she was a pilot. He was in control.

She'd done this before. She'd done it with Freddy. When they'd been playing tennis together or dancing, and he was limping with arousal, he liked to shoot his seed into her throat. Freddy tasted yeasty and sour. Chief McGregor, she found, as she wrapped her lips around the plum of his cock-head, tasted of smoke and machine oil and salt. He spoke, but she couldn't hear what he was saying because of the blood roaring in her ears. He pushed himself deep into her mouth, down to her throat, until he found the point at which she choked, and then he pulled out again. She laved his slit with her tongue, no longer thinking or trying to think.

He groaned. Then with one hand and then the other on her head to guide her, he made use of her mouth while he undid his shirt buttons, shucked off his upper garments and pulled his long-sleeved vest over his head. Only then, with some reluctance, did he draw her to her feet.

Bare-chested, he wasn't quite as hairy above as below, but still intimidating, sculpted by his work to inexorable muscle. He kissed her lips, then pushed her back to the pillar again.

'I can taste my prick on your mouth,' he whispered. 'And I'm going to make you taste your quim on mine.'

Both hands went to the fastenings down the front of her flying suit. He revealed her swiftly from breast to crotch, the silk of her undergarments springing out between the edges of cream leather. And as he worked, because he was for the moment no longer holding her, Charlotte finally found her strength. As he wrenched the suit off her shoulders and pushed it down to her hips she began to fight back.

It was a strange fight in some ways; she didn't cry out for help or scream abuse at him. She fought in silence except for gasps and whimpers. She struck at his hands and his chest, but when he picked her up and carried her over to the narrow cot bed, although she twisted wildly in his arms, she didn't hit at his eyes or his throat or anywhere that might have caused real damage. He threw her down on the bed and grabbed her leg in order to unbuckle the bootstrap. She kicked at his chest and thighs but not his head. She felt a white flame in her own breast, a roaring need for violence, for struggle, for resistance, but not for victory. He smacked her flailing limbs away and pinned her and forced her legs apart. He had to fight for every inch of the silk-clad body he stripped of its protective leather. She thrashed like a wild thing in his grip, but she didn't grab at any of the machine parts in easy reach to strike him with. She made him sweat and flush and grunt, made him roll her and bear her down and grip her until she cried out in pain. By the time he finally pulled down her long drawers and forced her thighs apart there was a look of fury on his face to match her own. She planted her foot on his chest and nearly managed to pull from his grasp; he responded by heaving her towards him by the ankles until her whole abdomen was clear of the bed, she was upside down with only her shoulders and head on the blanket and her legs in their incongruous thick woollen socks scissoring either side of his head. He took her hips in a bear hug. Then he stooped and thrust his mouth into her fleece.

Charlotte went still. It wasn't possible to fight with his mouth wet on her sex and his teeth pressed into her flesh. She crossed her heels behind his back and cried in defeat as warm waves of sensation rolled over down her spine and the blood filled her head. Lord Frederick Atherstone had never in all his days tried to do this to her. She'd never imagined that anything could feel so good as that mouth on the pearl of her clitoris, the soft sucking and the long strokes of his tongue and the prickle of his stubble in the wet folds of her sex.

She surrendered. He ate her. And at the last moment, as she was starting to heave and buck in a new and inner struggle, he laid her down on the bed and before she could register the loss of his mouth he was pushing his big cock smooth and hard into her, covering her with his body and thrusting stroke after stroke, until the lightning ignited and suddenly she was coming on his cock, coming hard, as she had never intended to do. And as she parted her lips to cry out, he kissed her and she tasted her own sweet-sour tang, just as he had promised.

She was still dazed and burning when he rolled onto his side and pulled her with him, rolling under her on a bed so narrow there was only room for one. He was still hard. He hadn't come. He sat her astride him, impaling her anew on his length, and he put one hand on her breastbone to push her up into a sitting position. She wanted to curse him then, and tears burned in her eyes. He couldn't be ravishing her if she was on top, could he? She looked down on his broad chest, glazed with sweat. She tried to get off him but he grabbed her hips and rammed her down on his cock, deep enough that she saw stars.

'Bastard!' she hissed, sinking her nails into his skin.

He bared his teeth. 'Still not good enough for you?'

He licked his thumb and pushed it between them, where his body joined with hers. He need not have bothered with the extra lubrication; the junction was steaming hot and as slippery as an oil bath. She groaned and twisted on his thumb as he found her pearl and began to rub it. She forgot she was being forced. His hips moved beneath her. His cock stirred her within. She arched her back and pressed against him and opened to that brazen length. He reached beneath her damp chemise to stroke her breasts as he made her come for a second time.

Only when she was wrung out did the Chief Engineer take his own reward. He was not delicate about it. He rolled her off him and manhandled her into position on the bed, on hands and knees, with an urgency in his movements that – despite all his forcefulness – had been lacking before. He knelt up behind her to plough the narrow furrow of her sex. She pressed her hot face to the blanket and let him have his way, his hands tight on her hips, his thighs pummelling hers, his scrotum slapping her puffy lips. His thick cock pistoned in and out and she thought of the movements of mighty steam engines, the slickness of oiled steel, the burning phlogiston fire. His movements quickened and she thought, He's going to come now. And despite everything somehow she welcomed the thought.

'Bloody hell, yes,' he said.

Then he pulled out and took himself in hand and with a grunt sprayed dollops of spunk on her splayed cheeks, one on the small of her back, one that slopped on the crack of her arse and dribbled down to her anus. Heaving for breath, he put his hand on her bottom and massaged his jism into the pucker of that hole. Charlotte, incredulous, felt the iris soften and yield. With a push he popped the first joint of his oil-stained thumb into her most intimate orifice, and she felt her legs give way. It wasn't an orgasm. Could an orgasm begin at the back entrance and flare up the spine like that? It flashed through her limbs like lightning and she collapsed upon the bed, tissues pulsing, head spinning.

He followed her down, covering her body with his. He wasn't heavy any more. He ran his hand down her side and pressed his lips to the curve of her shoulder.

They were still lying there panting when the klaxon began to blare.

Two months later the war was over. The homeland had held on for long enough. Their colonial allies had came through.

The official victory celebration was held in the Royal Hippodrome, though it spilled out into all the streets and taverns of Victoria City. In the gilt and plush interior the various military and auxiliary companies were paraded and presented before His Imperial Majesty so that all they had done might be publicly acknowledged. Each combatant received the newly struck Cross of Victory. Several members of the Volunteer Air Corps were awarded the Imperial Star – though none of those honours went to the Ornithopter Brigade, who had after all been *paid* to risk their lives daily.

Charlotte joined her brigade for the fly-past and display, then the presentation of the medals. The engineers in a fit of solidarity wore their brown overalls instead of their Sunday suits for the presentation; the pilots wore their flying kit.

After the rest of the ceremony, which they watched from their reserved box, surrounded by gilded plaster cherubs that the men found risible, there was food laid on and dancing. The brigade broke up as people went to find their families or pillage the buffet tables. Charlotte reluctantly left her companions and presented herself and her medal to her father and mother, who were so proud that for once they almost refrained from scolding her. She loaded a plate and circulated among her peers and drank an incautious amount of champagne until Lord Atherstone took advantage of a lull in the conversation.

'Charlotte, darling, would you care to dance?' The orchestra was just warming to a polka.

'Of course, Freddy.' She put down her glass and offered him her hand.

He hesitated. 'You'll want to go and change, of course.'

The smile faded from Charlotte's lips as she looked down at her brand-new flying suit. She was rather proud of it. 'Will I?'

'Well, it would look rather ridiculous, wouldn't it?' He swept his sandy fringe off his brow.

'Ridiculous?' She took a step away from him.

They had the attention of their little circle now.

'I mean, for dancing, darling. You'd look rather foolish waltzing like that.'

'Would I?'

He was getting flustered. 'Well, it isn't really *you*.'

'No.' Her mouth tightened. 'On the contrary, I think it *is* me.'

Turning on her heel, she stalked away. He didn't try to stop her, and she was pleased. Only when she passed a mirror in the corridor outside did she pause, and then it was momentarily, to look at herself. She touched her face. She had a scar now where a piece of flying glass had laid her left cheek open to the bone. She was rather proud of it when she wore her flying suit; it was reminiscent of the duelling scars that men of her grandfather's generation wore. But when she changed back into a dress it became all of a sudden a horrible blemish. And there were other scars: a pink weal across her collarbone; a burn mark down her right forearm from when she'd brought her ornithopter successfully home even when in flames. They did not look good in the low-cut short-sleeved dancing dresses fashionable at the moment.

Charlotte felt suddenly queasy. She couldn't look at herself any longer.

She set off through the crowds. She patrolled the veranda over the lakeside and the ballroom, the public dining area on the terrace and the champagne fountain. Everywhere people were singing and stuffing their bellies and getting as drunk as possible. An unusual mixing of the social classes was visible, and other behaviour that would have been unthinkable at any normal time was sparking off in darkened corners, as alcohol and relief went to people's heads and they gave way to celebratory practices that ranged from the risqué to the positively debauched. Charlotte blinked in surprise and hurried on. She saw several groups of her old flying comrades, but avoided them all. Only when she checked inside the Aviators' Chapel did she admit to herself that she was looking for Chief McGregor, but he wasn't there.

I need to speak to him, she told herself. This is my last chance. I need to . . . say goodbye.

He'd been with the ornithopter ground crew at the awards and the parade of course. She hadn't seen him since the ceremony finished and they all split up.

In all these last weeks he'd said nothing to her about what had passed between them in his office. His demeanour had been exactly as before. Not a word or a glance had betrayed that any such incident might have taken place. And on her side she'd never told anyone.

She found him when she returned to the private box that had been allocated to them among the cherubs on the third tier of the hippodrome. On the main floor below, the party was in full swing, but when she opened the door she found him sitting on the floor with his back to the balcony, invisible from below, facing the disordered ranks of chairs. His knees were bent up, his arms propped on them, and a large brown bottle swung from one hand.

'Chief?' Charlotte glanced around quickly. There was no one else in sight.

'Laindon.' He looked melancholy, she thought. He was down to shirtsleeves and his braces had been slipped from his shoulders to pool on either side of him.

'You're on your own?'

'Oh, I've had years of practice drinking on my own. Don't you worry.' Then he noticed the expression on her face and softened, adding, 'It's ginger beer. I've been really pushing the boat out.'

'Are you all right?'

'Bloody ecstatic. Can't you tell? Three-quarters of the pilots who came through my Deck are dead – but at least it's over.' He waved the bottle in her direction. 'Care for some?'

She came forwards to take the bottle from him, then sat on

one of the chairs to drink. It fizzed on her tongue and burned in her throat; it was ginger beer just as he'd said.

'Believe me now?' he said with a small smile.

'Thanks, Chief.'

'There's no reason to call me that now.'

Charlotte felt a pang. 'I'd rather.' Then, because she felt foolish perched higher up than him, she sat down at his side, her back to the balcony wall. He took another sip from the bottle.

'I suppose things will have to go back to the way they used to be now,' she said.

'No. Things never go back after a war. Things move on. Your people are going to find that out sooner or later.'

'My people?'

He shook his head. 'Sorry.' There was an uncomfortable silence for a moment.

'What are you going to do now it's over?' she ventured.

'Me? I'll be leaving. There's always work for an engineer anywhere he chooses to go. And I want to travel. I want to go overseas. I want to fly again.'

'You do fly?'

'Course I do.' He looked exasperated. 'I'm just too bloody big for a war ornithopter and my reactions aren't up to dogfighting any more. That's a job for young lads … and,' he added with a nod in her direction, 'young ladies.'

She smiled. This was the Chief she knew, at his most mellow. But she couldn't reconcile this man with the one who'd pinned her down in his office and made bestial use of her body. She felt the blood rise in her cheeks. She looked at her hands, at the fingers knotted together. 'Before the Battle of the Peak,' she said falteringly, before she ran out of the air that was rapidly leaving her lungs. 'You know, that night –'

'I gave you what you needed.' He wasn't looking at her. He

was staring straight ahead, through the ranks of chairs, or perhaps at something a hundred miles away. His voice was quiet and emotionless. 'You were overwound, like a watch spring. You were in such a state with the waiting that you were going to seize up at the controls, or not going to be able to get into the ornithopter at all. You needed something to snap you out of it. You needed something to fight against. You needed something to take your mind from the battle. I gave you what you needed.'

Charlotte's throat worked as all the answers and the questions and the accusations fluttered round inside her. 'What I needed?' she croaked at last.

'You flew. And you lived.'

'Nothing to do with what you needed then?'

His eyes darkened. He spoke more softly. 'I've needed you since the day you set foot on my Deck, full of fire and pride.' But he still didn't look at her.

'You hated me that much, for being – what I am? And for you being what you are?'

'No. I don't hate you.'

And Charlotte, wrestling with words that did not seem to connect to his demeanour and with a present that seemed not to connect to the past, could not understand what he was saying. Why didn't he look at her? Why was he so quiet? 'You were so ... rough,' she managed to hack out, her own voice so torn up that it hardly sounded like it belonged to her.

'Oh, I can be rougher than that. Rough as you like, when you need to do battle. Or gentle as you want.' He turned to look her in the eye at last, his own eyes full of storm and sorrow and yearning without hope. 'Whatever you want, Charlotte.'

And it came to Charlotte that his burden was to be on the far side of a gulf so vast that no matter how loud he shouted at her, it only reached her as a whisper.

'Oh.' She started to tremble. There was only one thing that spanned that abyss. 'Gentle, I think,' she breathed.

There was a yard of carpet and an infinite void between them; they reached across together and he took her in his arms and pulled her into his lap to kiss her. His mouth was gentle this time, just as he'd promised, but no less hungry. His arms were no less strong. His touch burned through the leather of her suit and set her body aflame. He tasted of ginger and endurance and disbelieving joy. He pulled her astride his thighs and she kicked over the bottle so that ginger beer fizzed across the scarlet carpet.

'You are ... a little white hawk ... I release ... from my hands ... in the dawn,' he murmured, kissing her throat. 'And you come back ... back to me ... You smell of the clean sky ... and the clouds.'

She was shocked that he owned such words and tears brimmed in her eyes even as she whimpered with desire and writhed upon his lap. 'I always come home to you,' she whispered. 'I want to come back.'

Then he took hold of the front of her flying suit and unhooked it all the way from neck to crotch. He kissed her through the pearly-grey silk she wore there – much daintier than her wartime flying chemise – and his hot mouth left cold patches on the thin material. He pulled her right up over him, so that her breasts were in his face and she was leaning on him, her bottom cradled in his arms. She could almost see over the balcony but she shut her eyes and lowered her face over his head, smelling the spicy pomade in his hair, stirring the untidy curls at the back of his neck with her fingers, feeling his lips and his teeth on her as he pushed her chemise up over her breasts and nuzzled upon the bare flesh. He teased her nipples with his tongue, his suckling an exquisite pleasure. She pressed her pubic mound against the hard wall of his torso and groaned unrestrainedly. She was burning. The sheath of leather about her body was an unbearable frustration.

Just as she was beginning to think she might come if only he would bite her nipple properly, he let her slide down into his lap again. They kissed, breathless, open-eyed; not in wonder or hunger this time but knowing, and almost afraid of what was going to happen. She sought the thick bulge of his cock through the wool of his trousers and felt it heave against the pressure of her hand.

'You're sure?' he whispered, so softly the cherubs could not have heard him.

She nodded, not trusting herself to speak. Their lips met in melting union. She broke away first, so that she could look down and watch her hands open the buttons of his fly. His erection beat like a heart under its caul of fine cotton. He helped her draw it out into the light and she grasped it in both hands, stroking the velvet skin that slid so enticingly over such hardness.

He slipped one hand carefully down the front of her flying suit, cupping her pubic area, fingertips sliding into wetness. It was a tight fit.

I will stroke him till he spends, she thought. He will come in my hands just as I come on his.

But she had no chance. He was much, much better than her – either that or more versed in self-control. His hand squeezed and his fingers stirred and she lost concentration, forgot to stroke, swayed on his thighs and sagged against him. He had to hold her upright with his other hand as within brief minutes he rubbed her slipperiness into squirming, gasping, flushing crisis and tipped her into a defeat she regretted not one whit.

'Does that make up for what I did before?' he asked, brushing his lips across her scarred cheek as she opened her eyes and tried to focus again.

'It's a start,' she allowed, regaining her grip on his cock.

He looked at her intently, his smile fading, a vertical line between his brows.

'Bugger this,' he muttered. Then he pushed her gently from his lap and tucked his decidedly unco-operative prick into his clothes again, his fingers fumbling on the buttons.

'What's wrong?'

'Nothing.'

'Where are you going?' Charlotte cried as he stood up.

'To bed.' He stooped and picked her up, cradling her easily in his arms. 'And you're coming with me. Don't waste your breath arguing.'

'Yes, Chief,' she said.

'James. Or Jim.'

'Chief.'

He laughed. He carried her right through the long corridors of the Royal Hippodrome down to where the ornithopters were parked on the plaza. They passed people Charlotte knew, and she twined her arms about his neck and looked at their shocked faces doe-eyed, pleased that Freddy would know about this long before morning, that there would be no need for awkward negotiations.

As they approached the ornithopter bays they walked straight past a bunch of engineers and pilots who were drinking together. They gaped at the sight of their Chief with Charlotte in his arms, then began to cheer and stamp their approval. Even the Hon. Alicia Holdstock, who was draped over the laps of three engineers, flashed a grin and waved.

Charlotte took a look at the Chief's face then. It was set with determination but there was a glitter of a proud smile in his eyes. He caught her glance and right in the doorway to the bays he paused, ignoring the whooping of his men, and kissed her.

Charlotte knew then that he was right. The war was over. Nothing could go back to being the same.

Ruby Seeds

'Champagne cocktail?'

He materialises at my elbow, a glass in either hand, as I'd hoped. He's been watching me on and off for an hour, but my going out on the balcony has spurred him into action. There's an autumnal bite to the night air so we're almost alone. I give him a sideways smile.

'You don't look like a wine waiter.' Then I take the glass, which has been overfilled. The cocktail is a pale red. My fingertips brush his.

'No?' His grin is insouciant. 'What do I look like then?'

I put my back to the balcony railing. The drop to the hotel terrace garden below is two storeys and the cold rail rests right across my bare shoulder blades, an inch above the back of my glittery dress. I give him an appraising once-over, rewarding him for his cheek. In truth he doesn't look like a waiter because he's too old, and too dishevelled compared to the slick youths who've been doing the serving. His tie hangs open at his throat. His face is bony with a broken nose and green eyes and incongruously dark lashes. He has intriguing hands: long and craggy, the knuckles prominent. 'You look like you might be fun,' I tell him.

'Patrick.' He tilts his glass towards me.

'Saffy.' The champagne flutes kiss and then we watch each other as we sip. The taste takes me by surprise: something that pink should be sweet but despite the fruity aroma the cocktail is sharp. Memory comes in a rush: *Yellow rind breaking in his hands reveals a treasure of packed translucent arils like gems, not the insipid pink of fruit from modern supermarkets but a deep, luscious, almost purple red, juice running from the crushed tissues.*

With a sharp intake of breath I refocus on my surroundings: the hotel balcony, the party, Patrick. 'How do I look to you?' I wonder.

There's a hint of teeth in his smile; he recognises he's being challenged. 'Bored with the party.'

I'll grant him that, though he doesn't score high. 'I've been to a lot of parties.'

'At first I thought you were one of the athletes.' That gives his gaze an excuse to drop from my face and go exploring. 'A swimmer maybe, with a strong beautiful shape like that. But –' he rescues himself from simple lechery by suddenly focusing on my hair and face with uttermost seriousness: on the black dreadlocks, pale skin, gold piercing in the side of my nose '– that's not a swimmer's hair. You're track and field perhaps. On the other hand, you're drinking. None of the athletes drink, not the night before the first heats. So maybe you're like me, attached to a corporate sponsor. But – forgive me – you don't look like a corporate drone either. Too much of an independent spirit, I'd say. So you're a mystery.'

I giggle, pleased by his ingenuity – and by the raw, tight lines of his body under the eveningwear. 'And a mystery is intriguing?'

'I find it irresistible.' His green eyes tread a dangerous line, leavening their appetite with a hint of twinkling self-awareness. My own body squirms with impatience but I force myself not to seize him.

'I won't ruin it for you then.' I brush the rim of my glass down my neck. 'Some things you'll have to work at finding out.'

'I'll enjoy that.' He's standing very close now. The electricity between us is delicious and I can't hide a shiver as he brushes the back of my wrist with his fingers. 'Are you cold?' he murmurs, tracing a line of goosebumps up my arm.

'A little.'

'Shall we go back inside?'

'No.'

His gratification is undisguised. He knows I am his for the taking. 'Well,' he suggests, 'my jacket, then.'

Slipping it off, he furls it gently about my bare shoulders. I ease away from the rail to make it easier for him and am enveloped in his warmth and the perfume of his skin and whatever male scent it is he wears. My sex responds to the pheromone shock by blossoming into wet petals. He runs his fingers down the lapels of the jacket, those big knuckles just brushing the jut of my breasts, his grip saying *I could pull you to me*, his eyes promising a rough landing. I'm still holding my glass. When he looks down it's there between us, tilted towards him, the carnelian contents threatening to spill.

Then Patrick lifts an eyebrow, the merest brush of his fingertip outlining the ring on my third finger.

'We're separated,' I whisper. Most men don't care, even when they do notice.

'Ah.'

'Nearly a year now.' I don't know why I have to say that and I'm annoyed with myself as the words slip out.

'Shall I?' He moves to take the glass from my hand, but I'm quivering with tension and in the exchange I manage to spill a little down the side and onto his fingers. I laugh and lift the flute and his hand in both of mine, so that I can lick the dribble first from the cool hard glass and then, my eyes never leaving his, from his fingers. I lap those knuckles and suck one long finger into my mouth, teasing the sensitive skin with my tongue even as I hold it captive. 'Oh God,' he says softly, with reverence.

I take the glass and throw it over my shoulder. It hits a bush somewhere in the garden below. He touches my mouth with his other hand too, as if wondering how much I can fit between my full lips.

'There's got to be a quiet room somewhere ...'

'No.' I pull my lips from his fingertips. 'Out here.' I watch the look of surprise and doubt and delight flash in his eyes, and I lay my hand on his shirt front. Under the cool cotton his stomach is warm and flat. I slip a button and ease my fingers in through the gap, finding firm flesh. That's too much for him; he finally steps in to close the gap between us, his thighs brushing up against mine, his hands taking my hips. His lips scout gently across my upturned face, checking for hostility and finding not even token resistance

'We're a bit visible,' he murmurs.

'Then we'll have to be careful.' He has a lovely hard bulge of anticipation in his trousers already, I'm pleased to find. 'I promise not to scream if you don't.'

I lick his bottom lip, then catch it in my teeth and give it a teasing nip, just as my hand goes to work on his cloth-covered erection. As our tongues meet he gives a thick little groan. Then he surprises me by taking the initiative and sliding his hand up between my thighs. He doesn't have to lift the hem of the dress far to find the velvet mound of my pussy under the flimsiest of silken triangles. It's shaven smooth, a fact he discovers as his fingers stroke me softly through the cloth. His tongue stirs my mouth in assured counterpoint to the movement of his hand.

I can't help the noise that escapes as he finds the edge of the silk at the crease between thigh and pubic mound, but my moan is kept private by his lips. It's a secret between us – like the secret movement of his finger slipping beneath the fabric to caress my bare flesh, soft and slow. Like the secret rush of heat to my sex. Like the hidden cleft of my sex lips that he inevitably finds. Suddenly I'm not soft velvet under his hand any more, I am hot liquid melt and his fingers are delving the shallows of my furrow, back and forth.

Our tongues still dancing together, we shift our stances very slightly. I ease my legs open to make room for his hand. He leans in to me harder, arching me over the rail. To any observer it ought to look like we're simply locked in a deep kiss. From the balcony windows the partygoers will only be sure of the hand he has locked on my hip, not the one plundering my panties. They'll see the arm I have draped around his neck, not the way I'm stroking the thick bulge in his trousers, squeezing his tumescence greedily. They might guess, but however avidly anyone is spying upon us they cannot be sure.

What if he loses patience? Will he blow our cover? Will he pull the front of my dress down to expose my breasts, hoist my skirt and fuck me properly in full view of them all? The thought makes me wetter still. His fingertip skids in slippery circles upon my clit, stealing my senses.

He's *perfect.*

Then it all falls apart.

'Saffy!'

I jerk away from him to see Demi standing with legs braced and one hand on her hip, her face sour. His fingers slip from me. 'Shit,' I say, hopelessly.

'What the –' Patrick turns to take in the sight of her voluptuous curves, the blond-streaked hair that belies the toast colour of her skin. She glares at him. He rubs his wet fingers together, dazed. His erection is like a fist pushing against his trouser front.

'What do you think you're doing with her?'

'Um.' He's fazed by her vehemence. 'Excuse me?'

'Saffy's with me!'

'Jeez,' I mutter, pulling down the hem of my dress. 'Patrick, meet Demi. Demi, this is a nice guy I was just having a bit of fun with.'

'Slut.' She takes me by the arm and all but hauls me out of his.

He's looking from my face to hers, trying to work out how he should react.

'I should put a shock collar on you, you little slapper.'

'You'd enjoy that, wouldn't you, you bitch?' I snarl.

'Watch your mouth!'

Patrick brightens. 'Hey, if you two are together we could always go for a threesome.'

Demi draws herself up, lip thrust out furiously. 'You stupid man,' she sneers. 'You vile little man.' Snatching his jacket off my shoulders she throws it onto the railing, and it hangs there a moment before slipping off over the edge of the balcony and disappearing into the darkness below. Patrick, half-paralysed, watches with his mouth open as it falls from sight. 'You'll stay away from us if you know what's good for you,' Demi announces.

'My wallet,' he says plaintively, going to look over the edge. 'My phone.'

'Come on,' she orders, pulling me away.

I obey, whining below my breath. Being with her brings out the worst in me, turning me instantly into a sulky brat again.

'Hey!'

'I just can't trust you around men, can I?' she complains.

'Hey! That was my jacket!' Patrick has recovered enough to get angry.

As Demi turns back to face him I take the opportunity to

step aside and, as they start to argue, I slip quietly away. I'm seething with arousal and frustration and resentment, but I have enough of a cool head to get the hell out of there. It's going to end badly, I know. I weave through the sardine-packed partygoers – they're all a bit drunk by now but not a single hand squeezes me in passing: this crowd is just too well-behaved – and make a line straight for the elevator, catching it as the doors close.

Its floor and walls are carpeted in wine-coloured fabric and for a moment my inner vision flashes: *Juice running down his fingers as he strips the rind away, scattering ruby seeds as he peels them from the yellow inner pith.*

Then I'm back in the present. It's nine floors to the hotel lobby. The big lift already has two occupants: a man and a woman pressed together in the far corner. I can only see her back as I slouch against the wall; he has his hands on her hips and he's looking over her shoulder at me. He's silver-haired, and his pupils are dilated. I know it would be polite to glance away but I stare truculently. It looks like they're just having a bit of a cuddle, but from the faint movement of muscles in her arm I realise she's groping him. She's got his cock out, I surmise, shielded between their two bodies, and she's playing with his length. His feet are splayed. I think he's too far gone to resist. His gaze drops from my face to my breasts, his face masklike, his breath coming shallow.

It's just what I'd wanted from Patrick. Everyone's getting some but me.

I lick my lips, tasting the remnants of my lipstick. Nine cool floors of tinkling Vivaldi and her stroking him off, and him looking at me in my tight brief sheath of scarlet sequins. I lift my right hand to my breast and cup the swell of flesh for him. I can feel my nipple, as hard as a button. His eyes widen. I stroke that button, knowing that I'm pressing all his even as all my nerve endings ache. His breathing is louder, faster, harsher.

Then we reach the lobby – and I'm the only one to leave the elevator. My panties are so wet I actually feel the night air as a cool touch between my thighs, reminding me of what I have been denied. I ache with all the formless bitter passions of an adolescence I've long abandoned.

It's so unfair! I roar inwardly. That bitch Demi wants to control my whole life!

I stomp off down the midnight streets, my heels clicking on the stone slabs like snaps of a whip. I want to get lost, or at least I don't want Demi catching up with me, so I take several turns down minor roads and alleys, clattering under the cement cliff faces, deliberately heading away from the upmarket area the hotel is in. What I really want is to find a strip joint and watch some pole-dancer shimmy her big ass in front of rapt faces, losing myself in other people's lust, forgetting for whole moments at a time the gnawing emptiness within me.

I need ...

Self-pity swamps all my senses, including my common sense. I'm crossing an open-air car park towards what looks like a promising glitter of multicoloured neon when I'm suddenly recalled out of my inner world by a throaty growl.

It's a motorbike. A big black-and-chrome monster that looks like it would break your leg if you lost your balance and let it tip. It's moving slowly down the far side of a double rank of cars, paralleling my route, a little further back. Pacing me. The rider isn't wearing a helmet, though he does have shades on, and sunglasses after dark is never a good sign. His long hair is held back by a bandanna, he's got a black leather jacket on, open, and a black shirt beneath that; that's all I can make out at that distance, in this light, with the cars ticking between us.

My heart goes *ker-chunk* down into the pit of my stomach. And instantly a hundred thousand years of terror are right there in my bloodstream: I'm a deer in a wood; I'm a hare on the high wolds; I'm a girl in a meadow. I'm *prey*.

He turns his head slightly, watching me, neon glinting on his shades.

There's no one in sight, though there are plenty of cars here. I leave my lane and duck away between two 4 × 4s, hearing the bike engine rev behind me as soon as I change direction. I don't run; I haven't got the strength to, just yet. My heart's hammering. I zigzag down the aisles of cars, heading for a different corner of the car park. Every time I look around the bike is there, moving smoothly, tracking me. This isn't my imagination.

The whole car park is a roughly levelled rectangle, the roads on each side sloping more markedly. I hope the set of concrete bollards with looped chains will thwart him and I clatter down the steps beyond to street level. The bike engine roars as he spots what I've done and changes direction, heading for the exit. As soon as I'm on tarmac I break into a trot, hurrying past the beetling face of a Chinese supermarket. My heels aren't made for this and sound agonisingly loud to me.

The road dips towards an underpass and the desultory traffic on the city freeway overhead drowns the buzz of his engine. It's unlit down there; dark enough to mask me for a moment. I stumble swiftly into the shadow of the tunnel, keeping close to the tiled wall. Somewhere there's a double *thunk* as wheels pass over a manhole. Just as I reach the far side of the underpass I hear the distant drone of an engine deepen to a growl behind me, and I realise that I'm perfectly silhouetted against the lit street beyond. I corner left, hustling along but not running: I can't run in these heels. This road, tucked into the shadowed curve of the flyover, is full of tiny shops with steel shutters drawn down over the windows and doors; most look like the shutters never get raised. It goes on and on in a great shallow curve, and I know there's no chance of me outrunning the bike in plain view. There's no chance of me outrunning him at all and he must know that; I think he's deliberately holding back. There's a gap between a Halal butcher's and a hairdresser's called Cutting Crew and I break across the width of the road, not daring to look back. If I look, or if I really run, I'll panic.

The side road turns out to be no more than an alley, without streetlights. Steel skips and overfilled bins line either side, alternating with doors that look like they're armoured to hold back police raids. There are more streetlights at the far end though, and I stumble onwards, panting. It stinks of damp and garbage down here. My painted toes splash though a cold puddle. The ground is uneven, the tarmac rotted and cracked. The bike engine flares, sounding like it's directly behind me, then it sinks and dies to nothing.

I stop and turn. He's there at the entrance to the alley, setting his bike onto its kickstand. My mouth has gone dry. I retreat a few steps, my legs wobbling. His face is shadowed but I can tell from the tilt of his head he's smiling to himself. I whirl and see for the first time that between me and the lights, the width of the street is blocked by a chain-link fence.

For a moment I despair.

It's the sound of his feet that breaks me from my trance: big biker boots crunching on the grit, heavy and unhurried. With a whimper I plunge to the fence, splaying my hands across the cold metal net. With the faint hope of finding a gap I hurry from one wall to the other, but the mesh is unvandalised, meeting galvanised poles at either end. Just my luck. There's nothing else for it: I kick off my strappy shoes and try to get a purchase on the fence. I've never climbed chain-link in my life, though it looks easy in the movies. It hurts like hell on my toes as I heave myself up one arm's length.

It's too late. He reaches up and snags me off the fence, catching me briefly before he slaps me face first into a brick wall, not hard enough to really hurt but hard enough to knock the breath out of me. In the same movement he's up behind me, pinning me to the damp bricks, his hands heavy and groping, his crotch pressed like iron against the cushion of my backside.

'What are you scared of?' he growls in my ear. His voice is deep, even for a guy of his size, and thick with excitement. 'Nothing to be scared of. I'm not going to hurt you, am I?'

I gasp, shaking.

'You're dressed like a hooker,' he continues, finding the hem of my skirt and pulling the stretchy fabric up to bare my cheeks to his cold, heavy hands. 'A hooker shouldn't be scared, should she?'

'I was just at a party,' I squeak.

'Oh.' He kneads my bum and my hips. He smells of leather and violence. 'Nice party? Meet anyone interesting?' With that last word he slips his fingers right between my cheeks, into my most intimate cleft. I'm hot and sweaty and wet from running, from fear, from the smell and the touch of him. And I squirm like crazy, but there's no escape from his fingers.

'No.'

'Don't believe you, honey. How long since you had a man in here?' His callused fingers are spreading my pussy lips. There's nothing I can do to stop him. 'Fucked anyone tonight?'

'Not for nine months,' I sob.

'Liar.' He sounds amused. 'You dress to pull.'

'Plenty of games on the porch,' I insist. 'No one's been in.'

He chuckles. 'If that was true, your muscles would have tightened right up. Let's have a look, shall we?' He pushes one – no, two – fingers deep inside me, then grunts with surprise and appreciation, even as I moan with discomfort. 'Well, what do you know,' he murmurs, working his fingers deeper in, through my welling juices, 'nice and tight after all. Just right for my cock.' A shove of his leather-clad crotch into the soft muscle of my bum lets me know he is painfully hard. His voice is almost a caress now. 'I might hurt you just a little bit. But it'll be worth it.'

He steps back, planting a hand between my shoulder blades to keep me pinned in place, while he skins down my knickers. They were never any barrier to him, so brief and flimsy are they, but I think he likes the look of them stretched across my spread thighs. My chest and belly are so flattened against the wall that my butt is inevitably forced out, the full swell jutting towards him as if I'm presenting it.

'Oh yes,' he says. I hear the clink and tug of a belt being uncinched, the pop of studs, the tiny roar of a fly zip, the catch of his breath as he handles himself.

'Let me suck your cock!' I plead.

'What?'

'Please.' I sound desperate. My cheek where it's pressed to the brick feels numb. 'Let me suck your cock.'

He hesitates. 'Well. If you're offering, hon.'

He releases me momentarily and I turn. In the dim light I catch only a partial look at his unshaven face; most of him – hair, bandanna, glasses, leathers – is darkness. He hooks one finger in the front of my dress and I can't even tell if he's smiling as he pulls down sharply until my breasts pop up over the material. My nipples spring free and he catches them both, one in each hand, pinching them between thumb and forefinger and twisting until I gasp, but I can't pull away from him because that would hurt more so I fall against him. Then he pushes me down on my knees. In this alley there could be anything on the floor: broken glass, needles, indescribable filth. He doesn't care. I end up kneeling in a puddle, grit under my bare shins, tits out and my skirt still rucked up to my hips, my panties down around my thighs. I put my shaking hands on his leather-clad legs and feel the unyielding muscle beneath, and I lick my lips because I need to be moist for him.

'That's a good girl.'

He's already out, imperiously erect, and the sight nearly stops my heart. The distant lamps lend his length a pale sheen. The smell of leather rides his body heat. Then he guides me to him and there's no preamble, just the charged solidity and the bulk moving over my tongue, stretching my mouth, colliding with the soft back of my throat, and the groan of his pleasure. For a moment I think he's going to use my mouth as a cunt and just fuck me, but after that first impetuous thrust he relaxes, his hands slackening on my head. I can feel his thighs quivering. I draw back, taking breath, drowning in the leather-and-sweat masculine smell of him and the sharp salty taste as my tongue is given room to move over his thickness. His scrotum is clenched high, almost spherical under my fingers.

The pomegranate, round and pallid and packed solid with seed, breaks under his strong hands. Juice as dark as wine runs out over my belly as he plucks the ruddy jewels from their nest, filling my navel, trickling over my skin and running round my waist to drip on the sheets. It will stain me. He tries to clean it up, licking the spills from my flesh, lapping the pool that has formed in my navel, kissing up the seeds that have fallen, but it's impossibly messy. One cannot eat a pomegranate with decorum. I am juiced and sticky, my belly heaving with suppressed tremors. He laughs and licks me deliberately to make me squirm, knowing me ticklish.

I suck him eagerly, hoping that once satisfied, even for a moment, he will be gentler. 'Oh, that's right,' he murmurs, looking down on me, pulling back my hair so his view is unimpeded. 'Your mouth makes such a fine cunt, hon. Perfect for my big hard cock.'

He's wearing a ring just behind the head of his dick. No, not a ring, a little bronze snake, coiled snugly about his girth, its flattened head capping the eye of his glans. I let my tongue play with both serpents, wondering how the ornamental one stays on when he is flaccid. Maybe he never is. Maybe he's been hard since he set out tonight, on the hunt. Then I work out that the snake pierces his flesh and I shudder with fear and a strange, sick excitement. I take him to the back of my throat and moan, longing for the tidal rush.

He feels my eagerness and tilts my head so he can look at me. I can make out nothing beyond the shine on those glasses. 'Good,' he whispers. 'Very very good.' Then he plucks my lips from his swollen glans. 'It's not going to save you though.'

Pulling me to me feet, he scoops me up bodily without ceremony or any obvious effort and dumps my arse on the sloping plastic lid of one of the garbage skips, making an almighty clang. My bare skin would recoil from the grubby stickiness but I've no leisure to worry about such things, as he rips off my panties – literally rips them, snapping the elastic. The skip holds me at the right height for penetration and, forcing me back on my elbows and splaying my knees, that's exactly what he intends to do.

'Now,' he says simply, his face over mine as he guides his big cock with its bronze ornamentation to my pussy.

Gripping my hips he pulls me down sharply onto him, piercing me to the core. I feel the metal spiral as it slips in. I feel him spread my sex with his thickness, and it's so unfair that I'm not ready for this, that I'm not used to it any more. I try not to squeal but it tears from me. He's sweating, he's shaking – he wants this so much. My arse skids around on the plastic bin lid and he has to hold me in place as he thrusts. It all makes a noise, the lid and my heels banging on the skip, my gasps and his groans. Lights come on, scattered across the black brick faces. A window opens noisily overhead.

No one calls out. The watchers do it in silence.

All my resistance has deserted me and I fall back upon the plastic incline. My exposed breasts are banging wildly up and down as he thrusts into me and I can hardly draw breath; there is no part of my body that he doesn't seem to have invaded. He reaches forward one hand with hardly a hitch in his rhythm and shoves his calloused fingers into my mouth. I can taste my sex on him. There's a ring on his third finger and it bites into my lip.

He rolls a single ruby aril out of the sticky crowd, using only a fingertip: up the length of my torso, over my ribs, between my breasts to my collarbone and my throat. There is such longing in his expression, such absorption; my supine and passive body is everything to him. As he tips the fleshy seed over the angle of my jaw he lifts his eyes to mine, pleadingly. He has never given up, though I've offered him no hope. He rolls it around my lips and then tenderly slips it between them. For a moment we both hold our breath. Then I let the tip of my tongue protrude, the pip balanced upon it. For a heartbeat we are motionless. Then I close my lips, and bite down upon the seed. It is sour and sweet at the same time, as fragrant as perfume, and tears swim in my eyes as I swallow. It's the first food I've eaten since he brought me here.

In his midnight eyes light blossoms. Very gently he plucks another pomegranate seed from the platter of my belly and feeds it to me. Then he places the third between his own lips and leans over me. His mouth brushes against mine. I take the pip from him, and as its juice wets my lips he kisses me. He tastes of wild sour fruit and ruby-red desire. I twine my fingers in his dark hair as I open to him, to his mouth and his passion.

And in the back alley of a midnight city the man in black leathers brings both of us full circle and almost collapses over me, his shudders bone deep as he comes and comes. He goes down on his elbows and his long hair brushes my bare skin. I lie quiescent but for my panting as I recover from the pounding he's given me, and my sex feels awash with him. He pushes himself up onto splayed arms to stare at me with blank plastic eyes. His lips curve. With an unsteady hand I remove his shades so that I can see his eyes at last, and all at once I can read his expression: the satisfaction, the relief, the rueful acknowledgement of what I do to him. Sweat speckles his brow and upper lip.

'I'm sorry, Seffany,' he says in that husky voice that sends shivers down my spine, 'I couldn't wait.'

He always was too impatient, I tell myself. If he'd been just that bit more restrained when it came to the pomegranate seeds he could have had me for four months, or six, or all year round, but three seeds had been all he'd been able to hold himself back for. I laugh as I cup his face, feeling the dark stubble harsh on my hand. How can you blame someone who wants you *that much*?

'The snake was … a nice touch,' I giggle.

'Ah.' He runs his tongue over his upper lip. 'For you. I hoped …'

'I like it.'

A great deal more gently than he's been so far, he scoops me up into a sitting position and I twine my arms about my husband's neck and we kiss, and laugh between kisses because it feels so good. He kisses like a parched man drinking great draughts of water, holding me tight against him. When he's temporarily slaked he nuzzles my throat and ear and hair and whispers, 'Are you all right?'

I wrap my hands in his long coarse hair. 'I went half-mad missing you.'

He nods, understanding. 'Time to go home.' Slipping his cock from me and readjusting his clothes, he picks me up and I wrap my legs about his waist. He holds me as lightly as if I were a child and carries me carefully back down the alley. I have eyes only for him: for that dark stern face and those broad shoulders, for that hard mouth that can be so exquisitely tender. I'm perversely scared he'll lose me before he gets me safely back.

'A good year for you, Seffany?'

'I live for the winter. You know that.'

'How's the family?'

'Same as ever.'

'How's your mother?'

'Still hates you.' Freed from my enthralment to her and from the black swamp of emotions that it entails, I can sympathise with Demi; she has good reason to resent what the family has done to her over the years. When she finds out that I'm missing she will be angry enough to tear the leaves off the trees, and she will rage and weep and withdraw from the world, but there'll be nothing she can do about it for now. Me and my husband have all of three months together, guaranteed, before she pulls legal strings and forces us apart once more.

Hades shakes his head, smiling that at-least-I-try smile. Then we reach the bike and he sets me on my feet.

'Nice bike.'

'Thought you'd like it.' He swings astride it and indicates the seat behind him. It's a bloody big machine; my legs don't come near to touching the ground. The saddle is soft though, and comfortable against my pantyless flesh. I can feel our combined wetness oozing from me to grease the leather.

'Nice,' I repeat, holding the bar behind me. My skirt has ridden right up my thighs. He slides a hand up my leg, tucking the limb close against his, all but baring me.

'Let's see how far we get before I have to fuck you again.' He pulls me tight up against him, wedging himself into the angle of my thighs so that I can feel his solidity through the leathers, stirring my bruised flesh and awakening my appetite anew. I wriggle against him, reaching round to squeeze the bulge of his crotch. My need pleases him and I hear the intake of breath between his teeth. He kicks the engine into life and I feel the throb of the engine through my spine. 'I wouldn't want you to go cold on me,' he says.

There's no chance of me going cold, I think as he pushes the bike forwards off its stand. Though the world freeze over, I'll never lose this heat. The bike growls like a lion as we ride. As the street lamps flash past overhead and the kerbstones peel back and the road drops away beneath our wheels, I look briefly up, catching a last glimpse of the city skyline as we plunge steeply down the road to the Underworld, and he takes me home.

Cold Hands: Warm Heart

'So, what are we doing here?' I asked when we'd finished dining on the cold mutton and potted meats from the hamper, washed our distinctly bachelor repast down with a passable Chablis and finally settled back with brandy – from crystal glasses, carefully packed – and cigars that were produced from a humidor which looked both oriental and antique: Morgan might have no talent for picnic dinners but he could be relied upon to provide excellent smokes. I glanced around at the shrouded furniture that cluttered the parlour where we were sitting. 'If we're going to be doing any shooting, wouldn't it have been better to invite a few more people?'

And bring some servants, I might have added. We'd had to lay our own fire, and a sorry job we'd made of it. The October chill had soaked into the bones of this house and though our blaze had finally caught, it was not yet doing much to warm a room that hadn't been inhabited for some weeks at least, by the looks of things. I didn't want to think about the state of the bedlinen upstairs; we were, I suspected, in for a clammy night.

'We're not here for the shooting,' Morgan said, taking out his cigar and examining it for flaws, 'though it is said to be excellent here. And there are trout in the river. Perhaps next time, Thorpe.'

'Then what are we here for?'

He'd told me next to nothing so far. We'd left London under

a pall of secrecy, without notifying anyone or leaving any clue as to where we'd gone. We'd driven to the Welsh Borders and arrived under cover of darkness, without pausing at the village inn for the recuperative tipple or the blazing fire that I was rather in need of after such a long and chilly drive. All I knew was that our location was Morgan's own country residence; he'd made me read him directions from the hand-made map. The house was called Levingshall and was ensconced in a bend of the River Lugg – or possibly one of its tributaries – and though there'd been neither tenant nor servant to greet us, Morgan had the front door key in his possession.

'We're here because I'm thinking of living here after I get married.'

I nodded, not much the wiser. 'You think Cicely will like it? I suppose it's good for gardening. Very ... damp.' My recollection of the grounds was that they were substantial but overgrown. We'd crossed a stone bridge to get here and the river ran round three sides of the garden. If the shutters had been open I didn't doubt we'd be able to hear it. 'Good for her Japanese azaleas or whatever it is she's keen on at the moment.'

'It's an excellent house. And there are good neighbours: the Torrington-Henrys over Ludlow way; and the Milburns have a place further up the valley. Cicely won't be bored.'

Cicely, in my opinion, would find it terribly remote. But one doesn't criticise a friend's marriage plans. Besides, I was interested in the dark inward look on Morgan's face; in what he so obviously hadn't said yet. 'But there's something wrong?' I hazarded.

He raised one eyebrow. 'There's a ghost.'

'A ghost.' I blinked, and without thinking looked around us as if one of the palely sheeted lumps of furniture were likely to raise shrouded arms and moan eerily. 'Is that why there's no one here?' Why the place was shuttered fast? Why there were no staff? Why Morgan had never lived here nor even, so far as I could tell, visited the place?

'Not at all. The tenants never had any complaints. Their lease ran out, that's all, and given the timing of the wedding I thought it convenient.'

'It's a quiet ghost then?'

'Nobody has seen hide nor hair of it in three hundred years, Thorpe.'

I was slightly disappointed. 'Not much chance of us spotting it then, is there?'

'Ah.' Morgan looked smug. 'It's a very particular ghost, they say. It only . . . manifests . . . when the owner of the house spends the night here, which is why we haven't ever lived in the place. My father regarded the whole thing as a joke, to be perfectly honest, but it's a family tradition: the taboo of the Morgans.' His eyes glinted.

'And what does it look like?'

'It's a woman, apparently.'

I tilted my brandy glass towards him. 'And?'

'And the story is that if the master of the house stays here overnight, she turns up and . . . he dies.'

I flicked ash off my cigar into the hearth and remarked, 'Not terribly friendly then.'

'That's why we're absentee landlords. Nobody's risked it in generations.'

I ran my tongue around my teeth. 'How does she kill them?'

Morgan shrugged. 'Not sure. One is said to have thrown himself from the bedroom window and broken his thigh.'

'You believe that, old man?'

'I aim to prove it one way or another.'

'Ah. Tonight.' I leant back in my armchair, affecting a nonchalance that was not entirely sincere. The glimpse I'd caught in the car headlights of the house exterior had been disheartening: a solid building part farmhouse and part fortification, very ancient in parts but with big leaded windows that had been added in later, more peaceful times. Though picturesque, I suspected that even by daylight it would have a sombre feel to it; at night, camping upon the parlour rug as the cold and empty rooms yawned about us and the draught flitted in under the oaken door to chill our ankles, it was somewhat eerie. 'I can see why you didn't tell Cicely we were coming.'

Morgan shifted in his seat. 'Cicely would have been terrified for me. You know she takes all this spiritualism stuff seriously. She knows the legend of Levingshall from Mama, and wouldn't countenance our living here. So,' he sighed, 'I have to disprove it before our wedding.'

'What if you don't?' I wondered. 'Disprove it, I mean.'

Morgan raised an eyebrow. 'Are you worried, Thorpe? No need for concern. The ghost is only dangerous to the master of Levingshall, they say. You shall be perfectly safe whatever happens. Which, most likely, will be nothing worse than a cold and uncomfortable night in bed.'

In point of fact I'd already decided I was going to stay down by the fire and doze in my armchair, but I was stung by his mocking tone. 'I don't know,' I murmured. 'You might be better not to be too sceptical. When I was living in Paris –'

'Ah, here we go with the Parisian stories!' Morgan rolled his eyes.

'– there was an *appartement* in my building that simply couldn't be let. They say a young man, an artist, had hanged himself there, and all the tenants complained that their possessions would be moved about while they were out, or go missing while their backs were turned.'

'Sounds like an infestation of chambermaids to me,' he chuckled. 'French girls with their light and dextrous little fingers ... You should know all about that.' His verdict ended with a wink and a grin, and I had to shake my head in protest, smiling wryly.

'Still, I was no keener than any other man to rent those rooms, Morgan. It seems to me that where we are most ignorant, there we should be most wary.'

Morgan looked both amused and exasperated. 'Oh, I am wary. I told no one, not even the land agent, that we would be here. I wanted no one to prepare for our arrival. No one human, at any rate. If there is no ghost then I shall have proved the house safe, and if there is a ghost – see, Thorpe, I am not the dogmatic sceptic you would think me – then I am prepared to greet it as cordially as it treats me.'

'Her,' I muttered.

'Her, as you say. Of course one should never be ungracious to a lady visitor.'

'You're not the slightest bit nervous?'

'Of course not.' His manner was disparaging. 'The kind of thing that might have frightened my rude ancestors into apoplexy will have no such effect on me, I assure you. We are not so burdened by fears and superstitions in this century. And we have rather better resources at our disposal.' Leaning forwards, he pulled from under his chair a long slim box that I recognised. I'd seen its morocco binding at many a house party up and down the length of Britain, and counted it as a travelling companion abroad too on a number of occasions. It had been the bearer of fatal tidings for more grouse, pheasant and assorted wildfowl than I could enumerate.

'If there is a ghost,' I said dryly, 'what good do you think a shotgun will do you?'

'I dare say that dry bones are quite as susceptible to a

twelve-bore cartridge as living ones. And as for anything immaterial – what would I have to fear?'

I had to hand it to him: Morgan was never lacking in confidence. As for myself, I was less sanguine about the situation, but not yet unhappy. My curiosity was piqued, certainly, and with it my sense of adventure. And if I have rather more imagination than my friend, I was determined not to let it get the better of me. I rose, throwing the stub of my cigar into the fire, and started to stroll about the room, stretching my legs. We'd uncovered only the two chairs we'd dragged to the hearth; now I twitched the dust sheet off a couple more pieces of furniture, discovering a high-backed oak settle and a coffer that turned out to be empty.

'Looking for ghosts?' asked Morgan, spreading his legs indolently.

'In hostile territory, secure your immediate surroundings,' I replied, quoting the cadet officer who'd taught us both at Winchester. We shared a grin. I bundled up another sheet and added, 'Hello!'

It was species of large chaise longue or day bed I'd uncovered: very heavy looking, carved of the black oak so typical of Welsh farmhouses. The counterpane was of Indian cotton, but looked clean enough. 'Bags the bed here!' I said smartly.

'Too nervous to go upstairs?'

I shot him a pointed look. 'It will be as cold as Erebus up there, and I don't suppose the mattresses will be aired.'

He nodded. 'Well, I intend to sit up. If we stay down here, we can take turns to watch and to sleep.'

'Sounds fair.' I turned to the nearest wall and pulled down the sheet draped over a frame there. I was expecting to find a painting; what I uncovered was a mirror, its glass a little spotted at the edges, its depths grey. I paused, struck by the play of firelight on Morgan's face. His handsome aristocratic features and sandy moustache contrasted with my blunter, darker countenance and my pensive expression. 'Why is it that the ghost seeks out the master of the house?' I asked suddenly.

'Mm?' He looked up from inspecting the swirl of brandy in his glass.

'Is it revenge?'

'Isn't it always revenge?' He laughed shortly. 'The story is that there was this girl ... Hm. I was told her name but I forget the details – Alyse, was it? She was a daughter of border gentry around here. Not sure how long ago, but I believe it was around the Civil War. Something like that. She grew up a proper little hoyden, allowed to run wild, but very beautiful too. She was wilful and wouldn't marry any of the men her father lined up for her, but one day she was out riding – on her own, mind you, and astride the saddle – and she met one of the neighbours, the Lord of Levingshall. My ancestor.' Morgan smirked, and watching his reflection in that glass his expression struck me as oddly unpleasant. 'Now, Lord Price – he wasn't a Morgan back then – was a very handsome man and quite the charmer. She fell for him, head over heels, out there in the greenwood just like in the old songs. He laid her down on the grass so green and lifted her skirt and with a hey-nonny-nonny ...'

At that moment there was a draught down the chimney and the fire flattened, shadows leaping across the room. I spun to face my friend in mock alarm. Well, perhaps it was not all mockery. He'd stopped, lips parted over his next word, eyes glinting. He bared his teeth in a grin.

'Well, let's say he taught her a few things about riding she hadn't learnt at home. Gave her a good churn with his cream stick, as they say out here in the country. The lucky lass thought she was in Paradise. And when she slipped off back home that night she couldn't help thinking about him, about how kind he'd been to her and how helpful and how handsome ... And how big was his prick.' Morgan patted his crotch fondly. 'The upshot was that next day she got on her horse and rode from her father's lands to his, all the way to the house here, desperate for a repeat performance. But when she got to Levingshall she found the place was in the midst of wedding preparations. Lord Price was to be married that day to another lady.'

I pulled a face, bracing myself.

'Of course, if she'd have had the least sense she would have scuttled off quickly and kept quiet about the whole thing and salvaged some dignity. But the silly wench had just lost her maidenhead and was wildly in love and she made the most terrible scene, demanding that he marry her instead, and then begging him, and then cursing him for betraying her – which he hadn't done, never having promised her anything. Lord Price laughed her out of the place. Alyse jumped on her horse in the end and rode away from the hall to the bridge, where in her rage she threw herself off into the waters. It was spring and the water was icy cold from the hills. Servants dragged her out but she was already stone dead. They buried her in unconsecrated ground of course, being a suicide as well as a whore.'

Poor girl, I thought.

'A month later, Lord Price was found dead in his bed, as cold as ice and wringing wet – and a look on his face like he'd seen the Devil himself. Luckily he had brothers, but the next one went the same way before they worked out it wasn't safe for the landholder to stay in his own house.' He sighed. 'It's come down to us through cousins and younger sons. No one in the family wants the damn place, and though the rental income isn't bad it's no fortune.'

'I can see your problem.'

Morgan stretched ostentatiously. 'And you can see why I'm going to get it sorted out.'

'Why can't you keep renting it?'

'What? And have Cicely in my London house all year round?' His nose wrinkled. 'That wouldn't do, you know.'

I did know. Despite Cicely's cornflower eyes and Alpine slope of creamy bosom, Morgan had a penchant for other company that would only be hampered by her presence. I shook my head wearily. 'Then sell this place and buy her a new one.'

'It's legally entailed within the family, I'm afraid.'

I almost felt sorry for him. 'You've inherited a bit of a white elephant, haven't you?'

'I hope not. I sincerely hope not. And with luck we shall know by the morning, eh?'

'Mm.' I wasn't sure what species of luck he was courting here. I turned back to the mirror and considered re-covering it, rather disliking the shadowy room reflected in the tinted glass. Common sense – or pride – got the better of me though. Discarding the sheet, I turned to the fire for something to keep me occupied, but the blaze had steadied and was burning bright and warm. 'I'll go get another basket of logs, shall I?'

'Shh!' Morgan held up his hand.

I froze. For a moment there was silence except for the pop and crackle of the flames. 'What?' I ventured at last.

'Shh! That!'

This time round I heard it: a low squeak. In the time it took me to turn and face in the direction of the noise I'd identified it as the sound a wet fingertip makes upon glass. I took a deep breath. The interior shutters in this room were closed and barred, but I knew from the front elevation that the tall rectangular windows were made up of leaded diamonds of glass.

Quietly, with a look of grim satisfaction, Morgan opened his gun case and bent to the weapon within. Breaking it, he slipped in the first cartridge. 'Open it,' he said in a low voice.

I barely hesitated. Dropping the steel bar that held the central panel, I pulled the shutter wide open. A multitude of diamond panes reflected the firelight at my back, but the cold draught was immediately felt. The night outside was moonlit and filled with the soughing of the unseen river. Bushes pressed right up to the house; beyond them I could make out the grey wash of a lawn.

Squeak.

'It's a branch rubbing on the glass.' I glanced back triumphantly at Morgan and caught him stood with gun readied but pointed down and away, for which I was grateful.

He cracked a grin. 'Of course it is.'

I reached out to grasp the shutter again, but stopped mid-motion, puzzled by something half visible through the shrubbery. 'I say, what's that on the lawn?'

'What?' Morgan grabbed the oil lamp and started forwards, but I waved it away: the more light around me, the less I could see outside the house.

'Out there – something white on the grass.'

Side by side, we peered out through the thick bubbly glass and the criss-crossed branches, trying to bring into focus the pale object lying out there at some indeterminate distance. I wasn't even sure it was an object: it might have been a patch of light or a litter of stones. There was no telling how big it was or even if it was moving.

'What the hell,' Morgan muttered, really irritated.

'We'll get a better view from the landing window,' I suggested. We would be higher than those damned shrubs up there, and able to look down on the lawn.

'Good idea.' Turning decisively, he strode from the room

and I followed, bringing the lamp. It was a good thing I did: the hall was in darkness otherwise and the big oak staircase would have been near impossible to negotiate because the moonlight did not fall further than the half-landing. The ancient treads creaked beneath our feet as we ascended. Shoulder to shoulder again, we stared out on to the back garden lawn.

There was nothing out there. The lawn was a sweep of unbroken grey, the trees beyond as black as India ink.

'Can't see a damn thing,' Morgan complained. 'Are you sure there was something out there?'

'I thought so.' I felt chilly all of a sudden, though I attributed it to moving from the only room with a lit fire.

Behind us, the front door knocker crashed. We both jumped like someone had run a galvanic current through us, and spun round to look down the stairs. The ground floor was in impenetrable shadow.

'Who is it?' Morgan called. 'Who's there?'

There was no answering shout, but the door knocker slammed again.

'Someone saw the car as we drove through,' I suggested. 'They've just come to check what we're doing up at the hall.'

Morgan nodded his emphatic agreement. 'Most certainly.' But he lifted his shotgun to his shoulder and pointed it down the stairs.

The knock sounded one last time. Silence fell, as if the house were holding its breath.

'I'll go down and answer the door, shall I?' Straightening my shoulders, I advanced step by step down the oak flight until my feet met the flagstones. I had the lamp in my hand and I turned the wick up to cast as much illumination as possible. One glance behind me told me that Morgan had come down a few steps, but only so that he could cover the front door with his shotgun more effectively. 'Careful with that,' I said as mildly as I could.

'See who's there, Thorpe.'

I put the lamp upon a table and advanced with every intention of looking outside. I didn't reach it; a few paces off I stopped, blinking at the dark stain spreading from under the front door. 'Good Lord.'

'What,' said Morgan harshly, 'is that?'

It was a pool of liquid, seeping out upon the flagstones. In this light and on the dark slate it was impossible to tell what colour the liquid was. I squatted on my heels and dabbled a finger tentatively. It was icy cold. I couldn't bring myself to touch it to my tongue, but I sniffed at my wet fingers, discerning nothing.

'It's ... water, I think. Just water.'

'Then where's it coming from?'

I couldn't answer that. As far as I recalled the river had been well within its banks and below the level of the house. It could hardly have risen so rapidly. And the water was spilling out across the slates still, making them as black and reflective as obsidian. I realised I'd have to retreat to keep my shoes dry. Shivering, I turned my back on the door. 'It's rather rum, Morgan. Do you think the river has burst its banks?'

His eyes met mine angrily. 'Since we crossed the bridge?' Then I saw his face change as his gaze switched back to over my shoulder, and his jaw dropped. The gun jerked in his hand.

Directly at my shoulder, barefoot in the pool, stood a young woman. She had not been there a moment before; she was there when I turned. My heart nearly flew out of my mouth. She wasn't looking at me; she was staring up at Morgan, her eyes wide and unblinking. She was soaking wet. That was what you noticed about her first of all. She wore a sleeveless white linen shift of some sort and it was so sodden that it clung to her body and had turned half transparent on her pale skin. Her long dark hair was plastered to her shoulders.

'Oh my good God,' I whispered to myself.

She was shivering visibly. Like a dog that's spotted a squirrel. Or a young woman soaked to the bone on an October night.

'Can you see her?' Morgan demanded.

'Good grief, yes.' She looked completely solid, completely real. I could see pearls of river water tracking slowly down her marble cheeks.

'Where did she come from? I looked up and she was just there!' His voice was screechy with shock and outrage, but the shotgun was aimed straight at her, unwavering. I was far from confident that at this distance the spread would not catch me too.

'Morgan –'

'What in damnation do you think you are, miss?'

It was hard to blame him; her sudden appearance, her utter motionlessness, her fixed glare directed on him alone, the legend of the Morgans' nemesis . . . If it had been my own self in his place I'm sure I would have been just as alarmed. As it was I was stupid with shock. I just stood looking, transfixed.

She took a step towards the stairs. Instead of leaping out of the way of any blast I put my hand out to her and touched her shoulder. She was as cold as a stone from the bottom of a Welsh river, but perfectly present to my hand, her skin soft and smooth. And at my impetuous touch her legs folded beneath her and she slithered into a swoon, falling against me. Without thinking I caught her into my arms, my instinct to save her from the wet flagstones. And suddenly there I was, standing speechless with the slender limp form of a maiden from beyond the grave in my arms, looking up at my friend almost apologetically as he gaped back at me.

'Thorpe!'

I shrugged helplessly, a Gallic mannerism I had acquired and often been berated for by my friends.

He ran down the stairs to me, lowering the shotgun at last. 'What are you doing?'

'She's cold,' I said. My shirt front was already soaked through from her. 'We should ... should get her to the fire, should we not?'

He laid one hand on her head, not without trepidation, to check for himself that this was a real girl and not some figment of his imagination. Her dark eyes were half open. She moaned faintly at his touch, the first sound we'd heard from her. Looking down I could see the sweep of her lashes, the pallor of her full lips, the peak of a hard nipple jutting against the wet linen. If this was not a real woman then I had never known one that was.

'Well then.' Morgan sounded dazed. 'I suppose we should.'

I carried her through to the parlour. She was a slender slip of a thing, hardly any effort to hold. I knelt with her in front of the fire. 'Get the counterpane.'

'Oh. Right.' He brought the quilted cotton throw from the chaise longue and we wrapped her in it. She did not struggle, even though she seemed to regain consciousness at the first lick of firelight warmth. She put her hand on Morgan's as he arranged the folds and when he snatched it away she watched him with yearning eyes.

'Ghost my arse,' he huffed. 'This one's real enough.'

I was supporting her head with my hand and most of her

slight weight was leaning against me. 'Real, perhaps,' I said, and my tongue felt numb as I spoke. 'There's no warmth in her, Morgan. And I can't feel ...'

'What, man?'

'I'm not certain she has a pulse.'

'Rubbish.' He put his hand to her throat. She stirred, arching her neck, reaching up to take his hand and draw it down her breastbone. He let her guide him for a second, then pulled from her grasp and sat back hard, his eyes as wide as hers and his face very nearly as pale. 'Good Lord.'

I was feeling dizzy. 'Morgan ...'

'What's your name, young lady?' he asked her, his teeth showing under his lifted lip. 'Who are you, by God?'

She lay back against me as if exhausted. There was a profound vacancy in her eyes. Morgan lurched forwards and grabbed her face. I tried to protest; he ignored me.

'Who the devil are you, you hussy?' he shouted. She only whimpered. His fingers were biting into her skin.

'Morgan, I'm not sure she can talk –'

'Really? Let's see.' He released her, only to slap her across the face. 'Found your tongue yet?'

'Morgan!'

He looked at me as if I were a stranger. She moaned, then reached out her hands to him. He recoiled, jumped to his feet and began to pace about the room. Her gaze followed him, as if he was the most fascinating man on earth. There was no blush of blood to her abused cheek. There was no fear or anger in her expression, only a formless longing.

'Morgan, I think she's mute and a bit ... simple.'

'You think so?' All his confusion and frustration was coming out as temper, as usual. 'And dead?'

I became aware that the counterpane bundle was sodden all the way through. I couldn't answer him directly. 'She's still soaking,' I muttered. 'We ought to find her a blanket or something dry to wear.'

Morgan laughed.

I unfurled a corner of the quilt in order to expose her arm to the fire. The skin was still wet. Droplets stood up in the delicate crease of her elbow. Water was still running out of her hair. I bit my lip. The counterpane should at the very least have blotted up this moisture. This was not natural.

'Want my jacket?' Morgan asked with ill humour.

'She's still soaked. I think the water's coming *from* her.'

Cautiously, he circled back for a better look. 'We could get her out of that wet dress.'

My mouth was dry, to make up for the cold water wicking into my clothes from the girl. Her linen shift was translucent where it adhered to her skin and tented over the pebble of her nipple. That detail had not escaped Morgan either; he hunkered in front of her and ran his fingertips down the inside edge of her shift's deep neckline. 'What do you say, Alyse? Like to get out of your nasty petticoat?'

She didn't respond to the name. But she took his hand and laid it on her full teardrop-shaped breast, and a hungry breathy noise issued from those pale lips.

'Well, ghost or no, there's no doubt what sort of a girl she is,' Morgan murmured, his voice thickening to hoarseness.

'I don't like this,' I stammered.

'Really? You should get a handful of what I've got.' He squeezed, and she moaned and surged into his grip, her shoulders writhing against my chest.

'Morgan!'

'Stop being such a bloody prude, man.' He sniggered, and I could see the doubt and the nervousness evaporate from him. 'She's frantic for this, can't you see?' He grinned foxily. 'Maybe this is what she wanted all along, all those years. Think about it – she came to the house desperate to make the beast with two backs with Lord Price, and died unfulfilled. Maybe all she's needed is for someone to give her what she wants. Maybe she just needs the master of Levingshall to give her a good, hard seeing-to.'

'So now she is the ghost?'

'I don't give a damn what she is, old chum. Except that she's wet and wide for it.'

'Think about Cicely!' I protested, as the girl rolled her head back on my shoulder, her lips parted, little breathy pants shaking her breasts as Morgan played with them. Her aroused nipples poked through the wet linen like accusing fingertips.

'I've thought about Cicely until my balls are blue,' he growled. 'Don't you dare reproach me Thorpe. I've had enough of waiting for what's mine. Now the Lord of Levingshall is going to do his duty.' He took hold of the wet cloth. 'Let's get you out of those wet things, shall we my girl?'

With a good hard pull and a twist, he tore her shift open down the front. Unnecessary, I thought. But I said nothing. I have always been weak compared with Morgan. And despite my protests and my misgivings, it would be dishonest to pretend that the darker part of me was not moved by that girl moaning and writhing in my lap.

'Take a look at those beauties!'

Her pale skin was marbled with blue veins and her nipples were only tinted with colour, but they stood stiff and responsive to his touch, beaded with running droplets of water. She reached out for him, her slim hands stroking his face, but he slapped them away, grimacing.

'Your hands are like ice! What about the rest of you, girl?'

Cold hands: warm heart, my mother used to say. It was one of her store of comforting adages such as *Unlucky at cards;*

lucky at love. But I was by no means certain that the heart beneath those pert, ripe breasts was either warm or beating.

Morgan threw back the counterpane and completed the sundering of the dress with swift movements, laying her bare all the way to her pubic mound. She was as slender and as pallid as I'd anticipated, her private fleece curled to ringlets by water. He slipped his hand between her thighs and she writhed her hips as she parted them willingly for him. Then she uttered a moan – a real moan, a soft, thrilling sound – and arched against me. Despite my soaked and freezing clothes my cock stiffened at the unmistakable noise of a woman's desire. Morgan had gone still. His eyes met mine.

'What?' I demanded, my voice unsteady.

'Cold all the way through,' he whispered, and his lips curved cruelly. I could see the muscles working in his wrist. 'But wet there too. Gloriously wet. And she's no virgin.'

Alyse's hands reached for him again, pleadingly. He pulled back in annoyance.

'Hold her arms out of the way, Thorpe.'

'What are you going to do?'

'What do you think? Hold her tight.'

I am ashamed to say I obeyed him. The pressure of his will – his will, his lust, hers, mine, I could no longer distinguish them – was a force I could not resist. I took the girl's wrists and pinned them back out of the way, while Morgan unbuttoned his trousers and released his straining length. His face was flushed but the crown of his member was plum purple, the colour of rage. I remembered that back at school I had always admired the size of his masculine equipment and the confidence with which he had handled it. But now, looking down the body of this slender girl, it suddenly seemed to me monstrously ugly and threatening. How could such a solid thickness fit into such a slip of a lass?

I was about to find out. Pumping his rod a couple of times as if to charge it, Morgan settled his knees apart, then pulled her up towards him, lifting her onto his thighs. With me holding her arms, she was stretched between us, her breasts and belly taut. He guided his prick as he pushed into her quim, as if it were his fist that were pressing home. I heard her gasp. Morgan's movements were deliberate and slow.

'Cold to the core,' he said through clenched teeth, eyes rolling. Then: 'God but it's good.'

He began to pump into her, pushing deep then pulling back all the way. I could see the gleam of her juices on his shaft. I breathed deep, thinking that I should be able to smell her, but as she had no heat she had no sexual musk, as cold and scentless as a river-washed rock. Yet she was capable of sensation. She struggled a little against my grip and gasped at every thrust, eyelids fluttering closed over glazed eyes. Her lips were parted and moved silently as if pleading. And as if in a trance of my own I watched Morgan's merciless plundering of her body with a look on my face that I knew was only partly pity.

'You like this. You like watching me fuck, don't you, Thorpe?' His eyes were narrowed, his throat as red as if he had a rash.

'You should be gentler,' I whispered, registering the way his fingers were biting into her flesh. Would he leave bruises? Was she *able* to bruise? Did she feel pain?

'You think so?' He laughed in his throat, his rhythm slowing. 'I suppose there is no hurry. We can take our time. We can do what we like with her.' That thought seemed to evoke others of interest, judging by the glitter in his eye. 'Ever fucked a girl in the arse, Thorpe?'

I opened my mouth. He didn't wait for my reply.

'Yes, of course you have: Paris, eh? French girls will let you shovel around in the coal hole, won't they? Not like good English girls.' He slapped Alyse's thigh thoughtfully. 'I could fuck this one up the arse though. She'd love it.'

'You don't have to behave like a barbarian, you know,' I complained weakly.

'What? Am I embarrassing you?' His hand indicated his crotch.

'Just show some ... restraint.'

'You don't like what I'm doing then? Really? Isn't your cock hard, watching me fuck her?'

'Morgan ...'

'Is your cock hard?' he rasped.

'Yes,' I admitted. My erection was a burning brand pressed against the frigid, soaking cloth and body.

Morgan jammed himself in to the hilt and held himself there. 'Get it out. I want to see it. You can't just sit there pretending to be holier-than-thou.'

I was shaking, but I obeyed, wriggling back a little from our prisoner and lowering her to the rug, then using my knees to pin her arms down as I divested myself of my lower garments. My cock sprang out stiffly, delighted to be free of its prison. My conscience and my body were at war, and my body was by far the stronger.

'That's better. Now put it to her mouth. See if she'll lick it like a good girl.'

I moved in, pressing my erect length to an angle where she could reach it.

'Lick his cock.'

She gaped, her expression as mindlessly carnal as ever.

'Lick my friend's cock, you little whore,' he ordered, his fingers closing cruelly over her left nipple.

She gasped, then tilted her head back, tongue presented to lave the underside of my shaft.

I writhed inwardly, in shame and pleasure. Her mouth was cold, of course, but that was no discomfort by now. Her slick chill sent shivers up my spine.

'Good girl. You do speak the King's English then.' Morgan gave her an encouraging stab with his weapon. 'By God, you're a real find.'

He slapped her breast, making it quiver, and the noise of skin on skin was loud and satisfying. She did not protest. Then he did it again, harder. The third time he raised his hand I saw it clench to a fist, and I grabbed his wrist as it swept in.

'Morgan!' I shouted, shoving him backwards.

He dumped the girl from his lap and lurched to his feet furiously. Only the fact that I rose to face him made him hesitate about striking me back, I think.

'What? What have I done wrong now, you milksop?'

'Is that your idea of how a gentleman fornicates? With his fists?'

'I'll do what I damn well like!'

'Not in front of me you won't. What sort of a friend would that make me?'

He squared up to me. 'You blithering idiot, Thorpe. Don't you understand? We can do anything we want to her – she's the perfect harlot. She's not a real person. She doesn't have any feelings.' There was the slightest hesitation before the word 'real', I noticed.

'But you are,' I countered, 'and *you* are supposed to have feelings.' I was breathing hard. 'You are supposed to be a gentleman.'

His knotted brows rose. I think he was as shocked by my standing up to him as by my rebuke. His mouth opened, and then he looked down suddenly. While we stood shouting the girl had crawled between us and now she was sucking at the semi-turgid length lolling from his open trousers, her eyes closed in rapture.

'Oh,' Morgan groaned.

She was completely naked now. I had a perfect view from behind of the viola curve of her ivory back. The wind went out of my sails.

'I suppose she's willing enough . . .'

'She loves it,' Morgan said in a much more moderate voice, as she climbed the length of his body, pressing her pale flesh to the dark tweed of his clothes. 'Can't you see that, Thorpe? She wants it badly. She needs what I've got.'

Alyse kissed his throat, squirming her hips against his, her white hands delving up under his shirt.

'Fine. Just, there's no need for . . .'

He took a handful of her dark hair and pulled her head back so he could gaze into her eyes. If there was anything there except hunger, neither of us could see it. 'Do you want me to give you a good fucking,' he asked softly, 'my pretty little whore?'

She mouthed at the air as if her lips missed the shape of his cock between them. Morgan's gaze slid to me. There was implacable intent in it. 'Stay or go,' he said grimly. 'But if you stay to look after her then you're having some too, Thorpe. This isn't a theatrical revue.' He pushed her from him, straight into my arms. 'Now put her on the bed.' He began to unbutton his jacket.

There was only a mattress with blue-striped ticking now that the counterpane had been stripped from the daybed. I'd taken two steps towards it with the girl before I thought to question what I was doing. I stopped, crushed by the moment, and as I did so her hand drifted over my prick and sent the blood surging through my frame like a tidal bore. Her fingers furled about my shaft, stroking the sensitive skin. I looked back at Morgan, who was stripping off his damp shirt.

'What position do you want her in?'

He smiled. 'Hands and knees. I'm going to make a sally through the postern gate, old chum, like I said.'

So I drew Alyse onto the bed and arranged her on hands and knees. She was completely compliant. Morgan came up behind her.

'Stick your prick in her mouth, Thorpe. I saw this in a Rowlandson cartoon once, you know. I've always wanted to try it.'

'You should wet your cock with spit beforehand,' I muttered, as I fumbled my own aching prick to her mouth, 'and use your fingers to open her up first.'

She took me without complaint, of course, her throat cool and clinging.

'Not to worry,' he laughed. He found the furrow he'd ploughed once already, rubbed his cock-head up and down in it vigorously, then struck home with a single thrust. Alyse was pushed up on my member all the way to the root. When Morgan withdrew his shaft was shiny with her juices. 'Well greased, you see.'

Then he grabbed her bottom and bored straight into her nether passage with the efficiency of a navvy driving a piling into its socket. If she'd been a normal girl she would have shrieked, I swear, even though my member was filling her mouth. She only moaned a little and her throat clenched around me. I discovered over the next few minutes something I should have guessed: that she did not need to draw breath. The import of that might have given me pause, had I not been fixated on the sight of her dark hair under my hands and her white body with its soft splayed bottom lifted to view, and my friend Morgan thrusting between her cheeks with that darkly flushed cock. He was a sand-pale man, but his hands looked swarthy on the pallid swells of her buttock cheeks. His face was locked in a grimace of concentration until the end, when it opened up wide-eyed as if he saw all the glories of heaven. Yet his language was far from holy, as he thrust and spat and mashed her body beneath his. At that I felt his climax entering her and racing through every channel of her body until it reached my cock and ignited my crisis too, and we both filled her simultaneously from front and back.

I forget what happened in detail after that, except that we forged on to make use of her willing passivity in every way that we could think of. Perhaps there is that darkness in every man's heart; that powerlessness makes it crueller. Perhaps I'm worse than other men, though I do not think so. Mere orgasm became a side issue to the dredging of Morgan's carnal imagination. We rooted her together and separately, at every conceivable angle, without respect or subtlety.

And we never conquered her. After every bout she would crawl over for more, little moans of need fluttering pitifully in her throat. Until finally, as she lay supine with her head tilted back right over the edge of the mattress while Morgan shafted her throat in weary wonder, I slipped down exhausted between her thighs and parted the folds of her labia, burying my nose in the wet ringlets of her hair, while my tongue sought her pearl.

'What's that?' Morgan mocked me. 'Something your Parisian mistress taught you?'

I ignored him, and felt Alyse rise beneath me like a river in flood, her body undulating under my hands, her thighs first opening wide so that she could press me closer then clenching around my head until the blood boomed in my ears. For a moment she did not feel cold at all. And as she bucked and twisted and shuddered and her wetness filled my mouth and nose it seemed to me that I was being swept away by a current, wrapped in weeds and tumbled among stones, into the deep.

When I woke it was almost dawn, that time when the light is dim and grey. It shone in through unshuttered windows. I opened crusty eyes and tried to swallow, but my mouth was parched. I'd fallen asleep at the edge of the bed and the wooden frame was denting my cheek painfully. Something passed in front of me: white cloth, hanging in folds. Someone walking past the bed. I reached out and my fingers brushed linen. She'd worn a linen shift, I remembered blearily, and Morgan had ripped it.

But this cloth was dry to the touch.

I clutched the fabric, felt the smoothness of a thigh beneath my hand. Then, in silence as ever, Alyse knelt down by the bed so that her face came down on a level with mine. I stared. I wanted to apologise, but was too ashamed.

She smiled, faintly.

I became aware then how cold I was, in the unheated room on a bare mattress, wearing only my shirt.

Her dark eyes no longer spoke of hunger. They were no longer vacant. A knowingness haunted her smile. She laid a single cool finger on my lips, as if bidding me to keep a secret. Then she stood again, and her white shift and pale face faded away into the light of morning, becoming one with the panes of the window where the dawn mist was pressing up against the glass.

With a shudder I rolled over. 'Morgan!'

But Morgan did not answer. He lay on his back beside me,

his eyes fixed on the ceiling overhead. He was quite cold. There was a hole in his bare chest where his heart should have been – a black bloodless hole with withered edges, filled to the brim with water.

The Scent of Hawthorn

Northern Italy, Autumn AD 695

The villagers were paying more attention to his horse than to him, noted Herrick as he rode in. He wasn't completely surprised. Around here in the butt-end of the mountains strangers were few but horses of Bastion's size and mettle were fewer still, and Herrick himself was wrapped in a hooded leather travelling cloak against the wet sleet, which had only just ceased for the first time that day, and it hid his armour and his sword. He looked, he supposed, fairly nondescript except for his height, but there was nothing nondescript about the black stallion he rode. So they judged him by the horse.

They looked worried.

By the time he reached the heart of the village there was quite a crowd. Herrick looked for a church among the stone huts – priests could be useful if co-operative, or trouble if they pinned him for an Arian and not an adherent of the Church of Rome – but couldn't see one. He noted, though, that the houses seemed to be in poor repair, and some were obviously empty. He laid the fold of his cloak back over one shoulder to reveal the chain-mail hauberk beneath and a wave of consternation and fascination rippled through the watching villagers. Without a word he dismounted, patting the horse's shoulder. For the briefest of moments he felt the urge to lay his head against Bastion's neck and just give up on the entire enterprise, but it was too late for that. Besides, deep down in his belly the old embers still burned. This was his time. He straightened his shoulders.

Three paces brought him to stand before the horse, facing the small crowd. Herrick was taller than any man in it. He removed his helmet and ran his hand across the close-cropped mat of his hair, sending a mist of condensation droplets dancing over his head. He was letting them get a good look at his face, at the blunt features and the commanding eyes. Then he folded his arms. 'Where is your priest? Or your *capo*?'

A middle-aged man neither more nor less damp and grubby than the other villagers pushed to the front of the audience. 'We have no priest here in Estoli. I am Antonius, the headman. What do you want?'

'I am Herrick of Turin. In lands to the south of here that name is well known. But whether you have heard of me or no, I am a knight of the Court of Pavia and a Companion of the King's Household. I've fought in eighteen battles since my fourteenth year. I've slain a manticore upon the shore of Dalmatia and fought alongside comrades to slay a hydra in the ravines of Arcadia. I have come here to kill your monster.'

The village had no inn for travellers; wedged up against the mountains' feet it was not on the route to anywhere else, nor did outsiders come to trade – and if they should, Herrick doubted that they would find anything worth buying in bulk. But there was a stable to shelter Bastion alongside the miller's gelding, and a hall set aside for meetings and for drinking in after the long work in the fields, and they led him there. The beer was cloudy, barely fermented and flavoured with sage, which made everything taste of regret.

They had heard of Herrick, or at least professed to. He was famous. They wanted to know everything, their appetite for vainglory immense. Because it was a part of his duty he obliged with stories of war and triumph, with an account of the battle of the Adda River and the subsequent re-ascension of King Cunicpert to his stolen throne, then a description of the victory over the renegade Ansfrid outside the walls of Verona. Nobody thought to ask why, if he was a favoured companion of royalty, he should be here in the dripline of the mountains taking an interest in their woes.

'Now tell me your story,' he instructed from where he sat in the best place by the fire, a wooden flagon of beer in one hand. He hadn't removed his armour, though the straps of his greaves were biting into the backs of his calves. Their faces swam in front of his eyes, indistinguishable one from another in the firelight. He was twice the bulk of some of the village men and seemed to himself twice as solid, sat there under their avid stares, all in iron. He wondered if it was only his armour that made him real. 'In Pavia we heard there was something in your area slaying men. Tell me about your monster.'

'You mean the dryad.'

There was muttering then. Some of the people thought it was bad luck to name the demon at all. Herrick was a little taken aback.

'A dryad? A tree-woman?'

'You think that sounds harmless?' Antonius raised his hand to quiet the chatter. 'This used to be a prosperous enough place to live. There was farming, as now, and mining of lead seams in the forest on a small scale, and animals to hunt and timber to send downriver. Then ...' He looked around at his people.

Herrick waited, biting down on his impatience. To him this was only another challenge but to them this was the central drama of their lives, and all their little passions and rivalries and struggles were worked out in its shadow.

'Then,' continued the *capo*, 'things changed. We went too

deep. There had always been stories about the forest; that a dryad lived in its heart and should not be disturbed. But we heard the King was building his new church, and that good oak joints and angles were being paid for in gold coin. We went deeper in, looking for bigger trees to fell.' He shook his head. 'Something woke her. She came out one evening, and killed everyone right up to the field margins: the charcoal-burners and the miners and the woodcutters. They all died.'

'How?' said Herrick.

'They were torn to pieces. The flesh pulled from their bones.'

'A *dryad* did that?' The old monsters had emerged again in remote places since the devastation of the Gothic Wars, but Herrick had never heard that a dryad was something to be feared.

'Believe what you like, Lombard. I saw it.'

He switched his attention to the new speaker: an elderly beldame shawled in black. Her eyes were full of challenge. 'Go on,' he told her.

'I was in the church the night she came. It stands on the mound north of the village, nearest to the forest.'

'Yes?'

'I was praying for the soul of my youngest grandchild, given to God and the earth that winter. That tree-witch threw down the doors and marched in, and all the wooden furnishings in the church – the rood screen, the tables – they broke out in blossom. I remember the smell of hawthorn.' Her voice faltered as her eyes focused on the memory. 'Then she went up to the priest and embraced him. And he died in her arms. The scent of hawthorn is the scent of death, you know.'

She fell silent.

'What did she look like?'

Her black eyes rested on him. 'Beautiful.' There was contempt in her voice; it took a moment for him to realise that it was directed at him. 'Be careful, Lombard. The priest hesitated too long and let her act.'

'But she let you live, I see.'

The woman's head drooped. 'I ran while the priest screamed. And she came no closer to the village.'

'And since that night,' Antonius continued, 'we have not been into the forest. Not even to gather dead wood. There's no priest in Estoli, and no wealth. Did you hope to be paid for this, sir knight?'

Herrick waved the question aside. 'Tomorrow I will go into the wood and hunt down your dryad, and return your forest to you.'

They cheered him then. If there were any doubts they were drowned in weak beer and the excitement of the moment. The whole village celebrated on into the evening, until the barrels were empty and heads were drooping with sleep. Then, because this was not a proper inn with rooms, Antonius invited Herrick to sleep in his own house: 'You will have the best mattress my wife can find.'

They went out into the darkness together and Herrick stopped by the miller's stable to check on Bastion. The big black stallion was eating hay steadily.

'You won't be riding up into the wood, will you?' asked Antonius. 'The ground is steep and broken.'

'No. I'll go on foot and leave Bastion here.' Herrick cast him a sideways glance. 'He'd better be well when I return, *capo*.'

Antonius's fingers interlaced. 'He's an expensive animal to look after, I'll be thinking. He'll need oats, a groom ...'

'Let him run free with your village mares,' answered Herrick shortly. 'You'll make profit enough by him next year.'

The headman's house was two storeys high and stone-built, the lower floor consisting of stores and tool sheds and winter byres, the upper where he and his family lived. Instructions to his wife caused a flurry of rearrangements as family members and servants were shifted about and worked to make their guest comfortable. Herrick accepted a draught of ice-distilled apple brandy from Antonius's daughter, served in what looked like a glass from Imperial days. It must be a family treasure, he thought, no one made glassware like that any more.

Then he was shown to his chamber, which had a stone hearth and just enough clearance under the roof beams for him to stand without stooping. A servant brought him a bucket of heated water to wash in – a bit of luxury he was genuinely grateful for – and once he was alone Herrick unbuckled the plates protecting his limbs and bent double to shuffle his mail shirt off over his head. He arranged the armour carefully on the lid of a wooden chest; the accoutrements of war were his most precious possessions. The mail links were fine and neat, each one riveted in bronze. His bow was strongly built of yew. The sword, embossed with a lion's head at the pommel, was a gift from the King. He ran his fingers over the tiny snarling face.

He was naked and scrubbing his thighs when the door opened and a girl came in with a second bucket. It was Antonius's daughter – Fosca, he remembered dimly. She put her bucket down, leant back against the door to close it and looked him up and down. Herrick had made no attempt to cover himself. He stepped out of the bucket, damp and dripping, the hair on his shins drawn in dark stripes by the runnels of water.

'My father said to see you were comfortable tonight,' she said, one hand playing with the hem of her overtunic. She had a plain peasant face but the smile on her full lips gave it character. 'What would you like me to scrub?'

It wasn't that unusual an offer in Herrick's experience,

especially in remoter communities. Farmers knew what the tradition of hospitality demanded, and weren't averse to acquiring grandchildren with noble blood. And the girls . . . The girls usually found the change from the local boys exciting. And Herrick was not off-putting in his person, not judging by the way Fosca's eyes lingered over his body. Herrick knew he was one of those few men that look better without the adornment of clothes; his muscles were bulky and defined, sculpted by years of campaigning. His prick hung long and dark between thighs like hewn wood.

'Anything you like,' he said, throwing her the rag he'd been rubbing himself with. Her presence neither disconcerted nor delighted him. She was not attractive enough to pique his interest so he merely accepted her as a simple courtesy, like the bucket heated with stones from the fire, and an aspect of his duty. If he turned her down the headman would be insulted.

Fosca started with his back, seeming to think some sort of niceties were to be observed – or perhaps, Herrick thought with a flicker of distaste, that she needed to flirt with him. 'Have you really been in all those battles you were talking about?' she asked, rubbing his broad shoulders.

'I have.'

She slopped water over his buttocks. It ran down the crack between, tickling him pleasantly and dripping from his balls. 'And you've been to Rome?'

'Yes.' He'd been part of a delegation sent by King Cunicpert to the papal duchy.

'What was it like?' Her fingers traced the indent of his spine and he felt his scrotum tighten.

'Magnificent.' And heart-breaking, he thought. The ancient capital of the Empire was in ruins, sacked repeatedly over the centuries. Broken aqueducts, burned-out buildings of almost unimaginable size, shattered temples littered with excrement and the desecrated statues of pagan gods: those were his memories of Rome. Its insignificant population was only a fraction of that which must have teemed the streets during its prime, and he'd felt like he and his fellows were ghosts haunting the broken corpse of the city.

'And what is the King like?'

'Cunicpert? He's a wise man, and a courageous one, blessed by God.' What else was he supposed to tell her – that after being deposed by the Arian Duke Alagis for nearly a year the King was now foul-tempered and erratic, mistrusting even his most loyal noblemen? That he was pushing those following the Arian form of Christianity to convert to Catholicism, and that Herrick was better off away from court now that 'heretic' was a word being plied freely?

'You've really killed those monsters?' Her fingers traced the scars across his ribs.

'Really.'

She looked down at his crotch slyly. 'I've never seen the pizzle of a famous hero before.' She grinned. 'It's big enough, isn't it?'

He smiled. 'I hope so.'

Thoughtfully, she draped the rag over his prick. It was full enough to hold the cloth up without dropping it, a solid elegant curve beneath the wet linen. 'Getting hard too.'

The wantonness in her eyes filled his stones with heat and stiffened his cock until it twitched. He flicked the rag away and ran his fingers up his hot length. She was no beauty but she'd do, he thought. He hadn't had a woman in weeks and his seed was curdling. And he was tired of her questions. 'Suck it,' he suggested.

'What?' Her eyes flashed. 'Is that how ladies do it in Pavia?'

With a sigh he pushed her unceremoniously to her knees, and when she opened her mouth to protest he slipped his prick past her lips. Her mumbles turned to chokes. A few strokes made it obvious what he wanted, and once she'd got that clear she became quite willing.

Not her fault, he thought, gripping her hair, his cock luxuriating in the hot wet grip of her throat. He could see her eyes watering. She was just a village girl, as stolid and unimaginative as one of the cows she herded down to the meadow of a morning. She'd been handed to him as a gift, and if she wasn't and never could be what he needed then how was she to know?

Her lips looked good around his girth though. Herrick warmed to her just a little. She sucked nosily, gasping for breath, almost slurping. The sight and the noise were at least as arousing as her inexpert movements. When he was good and erect – really erect – he pulled her off him, hearing her gasp. His cock was shiny with her spit and a dull angry red at the bludgeoning head. Her breath washed round his wet glans like a memory of her mouth. He wished she'd tease at the split of his cock-head with the tip of her tongue, but she only gaped.

'You want to make me comfortable, Fosca?'

'Yes.' She was as eager as a puppy, eyes shining.

'Show me your breasts. I'd like to see them.'

She struggled to peel down the layers of her dress, but he was disappointed. Her breasts were flabby and there was a distractingly large mole next to her right nipple.

'Stand up.' He lifted her to her feet and turned her, lifting her skirts. Her rump was much better than her front, properly plump with a good wobble on it when she staggered forwards, pushed to the bed. He was relieved. But she could have had the most bountiful breasts in the Kingdom of the Lombards and he still would have swived her from behind; he didn't want to look at her face. He arranged her face down, bum in the air, throwing her skirts up over her back. Her pink slash gaped at him from between her rounded thighs. Her white buttocks cushioned his hard body as he entered into her, relishing the tight hot grip. She squealed under her breath.

This was part of being a hero, he thought, as he powered into her. There were expectations to be met; an aura of over-weening masculinity to be maintained. He was the monster slayer, the weapon bearer, and now his weapon was stabbing the furry beast between her legs over and over, burying itself to the hilt. Fosca squeaked enthusiastically, pushing back against him as she grew accustomed to his size.

A hero, he thought, watching his shaft pump into her tight slot, smelling her sex. A veteran of wars in which he'd seen courage debased to savagery and ideals soaked in blood until the face of God Himself ran red. A slayer of monsters; a banisher of ancient pagan horrors; a defender of the weak. Showing the lowly some of the greatness of those that ruled them. Showing a slattern how a knight fornicated. The contradictions swarmed in his head.

'Yes, yes, yes,' she gasped, her dangling breasts wobbling wildly as he battered at her frame.

The bed creaked like it was cheering him on. Her buttocks shook and he grabbed them with both hands, spreading them to get a look at the little knot of her anus. He should stick her in the arse, he told himself as his sap rose. He should stick her in the arse because that's what peasants were prob-ably used to, living like animals, living in shit, fucking in shit . . .

With that thought he loosed his seed, pulling her rump up hard into him and gasping. When he let her go she collapsed onto the mattress and rolled over so she could look up at him.

Herrick slumped beside her, his long limbs spilling over the edge of the bed, and ran his hands over his face.

'That was ... so good!'

Herrick couldn't help staring. Fosca's eyes were shining. No it *wasn't*, he wanted to say, it was boorish and brief and I paid no thought to your pleasure. If I am unsatisfied, how bad must it have been for you? Out loud, he only grunted.

She snuggled up against him. 'You're wonderful – like one of the old heroes in the stories.'

Had she climaxed? he wondered, not recalling any sign to that effect. Did she even know that anything was missing?

'Will you take me back with you to Pavia?'

'What?' His heart sank.

'I could be your mistress.' She kissed his bare shoulder hopefully. 'I wouldn't expect you to marry me, you know.'

That was too much. He disentangled himself from her, trying to be gentle, and began to pull on his discarded clothing.

'What's wrong?'

'Nothing. I'm going to the privy.' Maybe she would be asleep by the time he returned, he told himself; maybe she would have left.

He did go out into the yard, but he only pissed on the dung heap. His cock was still fat, loaded with a strange frustration. He was heading back to the outside stairs when a shadow detached itself from the wall and intercepted him.

'Looking for a bit of something more?'

It was the servant girl who'd been carrying the bedding about as sleeping arrangements were made. Dear God, he thought, is there no end to it? She was considerably prettier than Fosca but as plump as a suckling pig, so he steered her to the sty wall and bent her over that to swive her. The pig grunted softly at having its sleep disturbed.

This is what I do, he told himself, staring at the roofline as he thrust patiently. I fulfil the same role as Bastion: injecting new blood into an inbred backwater. I am a farm animal servicing other farm animals.

Her bottom bounced under his hands, warm and soft and infinitely eager. Stars shimmered in the sky; the clouds had evaporated and the night was now still and chilly. He fixed his eye on one bright one whose red tint identified it as the planet Mars. The star of warriors, he told himself. He'd been a great knight once; forged in war, looking always for the moment of heroism, the cause that would be worth dying for and the leader to whom he could pledge himself wholeheartedly. It wasn't fame that had drawn him, but the quest for something greater than himself. He'd remained loyal to Cunicpert through his exile even though the King was a Catholic, because he'd believed the man was a better monarch than the Arian who'd deposed him, and Herrick's lifelong quest was to find a man worthy of his service.

But Cunicpert was no longer loyal to the men who'd been loyal to him – and rulers of the duchies further south had proved no better, not in Friuli or Spoleto or Benevento. He'd met monarchs and dukes and popes, and all had fallen short of the true standard, so now he roamed the Lombard duchies and lands even further afield, killing bandits and slaying the monsters of a pagan past. This was what he'd reduced himself to, he told himself bitterly: swiving peasant girls in murky villages, garnering the acclaim of people who lived one notch above their animals and two steps from starvation.

'Harder!' moaned the servant girl, and Herrick obliged. His cock made a wet noise in her with every thrust. She spread her big pale cheeks with her hands and squealed. 'Fuck me! Fuck me!'

By the good Christ, yes, he'd tried. He'd saved lives and brought hope to people who hardly recognised it. The star seemed to burn into his eyes as he focused unblinking upon it. His body was a dull beast heaving beneath him, disconnected from his mind.

I want ... he thought. I want ...

But he could not articulate what he wanted except that it was the star, the point of light, the beacon far overhead. And as the girl began to moan and jiggle her hips he became aware that he was not going to come this time, that there would be no face-saving end to this exchange, just a shamefaced acknowledgement of failure. He slid his hand surreptitiously down to his crotch. The root of his cock was hard still, but he felt almost numb. Pinching a fold of his own skin between thumb and forefinger, Herrick dug in his nails. Pain lanced through his groin, like life returning to a dead thing. He inhaled quickly, tasting the night air. His cock jumped and his spine prickled with sweat. His nails bit in harder, shearing the skin. There would be half-moons of blood when he took his hand away, but for now there was only pain. Pain bright as a star. The Mars-light poured through his veins and down into his cock and there, at last, was the climax he was reaching for. It boiled through him into the sex of the girl, and it didn't matter that she didn't know what was making him spend or that he didn't want her, it didn't even matter whether she was there; his whole being was fixed on that blazing star.

In the morning, when he was alone, Herrick made his prayers and donned his armour. Preparing for battle was a ritual thing. It focused his mind, leaving no room for his doubts. The last act of the ritual before lacing on his vambraces was to kneel by the fire slab and pull out the dagger whose tip had been resting in the hot embers. Baring his left forearm, Herrick pressed metal to flesh. Pain flashed through his nerves, bright and fierce. He gasped in welcome.

His forearms were smooth where the burning over the years had seared the hair follicles.

If he ever found himself flinching from this moment, he'd told himself, that would be the day he would turn from questing and retire to court, because he would no longer be able to confront an enemy. Pain was the companion of the soldier and a knight could not fear it. He had to accept it, even embrace it, and Herrick's relationship with pain was long-standing and intimate. Not fearing pain was what raised a warrior over a civilian; it was what raised men over women. Pain was the keen edge of life; it was the only time he felt his life in him as a tangible thing, to be cherished.

When he was dressed he descended the stairs and met the crowd of villagers waiting outside for him. A hard frost had settled overnight and the ground and rooftops were painted white. People huddled in their winter cloaks and stamped their feet. Antonius made a little speech to which he hardly listened. Then Fosca rushed up, flung her arms about his neck and pleaded, 'Come back safe to me!'

Without looking her in the eye Herrick extracted himself from her grip.

Antonius and a few of the other men accompanied him out of the village as far as the old church on the knoll; no one else cared to go that close to the dryad's wood. The tiny windows of the building were broken through and choked with the black stems of briars, the doorway likewise impassable. It didn't look like anyone had been in the building for a century, though Antonius told him the attack had taken place less than three decades ago. Beyond the church the hills rose, and the forest that spilled down their flanks was advancing on the village; young birches and hawthorn and elder had turned the rank grassland to scrubby wood. They didn't even dare graze their livestock this side of the village, Antonius said bitterly.

Herrick left them at the church wall and went on alone. Sheathing his sword and slinging his shield across his back, he nocked an arrow to the bow, carrying it across his body with deceptive casualness.

The *capo* had been right about this land not being suitable for horses. The slopes were steep, falling away to deep gullies, and the footing was made treacherous by fallen trees and dead wood. But there were the remnants of trails; people had been here once, unmistakably. He came across what looked like a lumber yard quite soon, the piles of rotting timber furred with moss, and there were small houses hidden here and there, with roofs all broken by sprouting trees and floors thick with autumnal litter. Miners' huts, he guessed. There were bones lying about here too, among the broken pots and rusted trivets and fallen beams: just skulls, which are always the last to disintegrate when left out in the open. Not all the skulls were adult-sized. Herrick turned one over thoughtfully with his foot and passed on into the deeper forest.

Away from the village the chill seemed fiercer, the frost thicker. The day was quite still, as if it held its breath. All but the oak trees had shed their leaves and frosted twigs hung like a froth of lace against the black trunks and the iron-grey sky. Every long weed stalk was turned to a feathery plume by ice. He was crossing a stream on a fallen log when a deer stepped out from the frozen undergrowth, glanced at him curiously but without fear, then paced gracefully away. He watched it go without raising his bow, thinking that it must have been generations of deer lifetimes since the last human dared hunt in this place.

Another beast gave him greater pause for thought. Upon one stag-headed oak sat a large bird with bronze plumage. Not just bronze-*coloured* plumage he noted; the heavy individually discrete feathers and the metallic clinks as the bird preened them made that clear. It was a Stymphalian bird, a type he'd thought extinct. They were dangerous in flocks, he knew, but this one seemed to be alone and indolent. Herrick gave it a careful berth nonetheless.

The going was steep. Despite the weather Herrick was starting to feel uncomfortably hot in his arming jacket and mail hauberk. Then he heard singing.

It came from a valley steep enough to be called a ravine, and when he'd descended carefully through the trees he found a level floor and a river that was probably ferocious in spring, but now only half filled its bed, lying in dark pools between stretches of moving water and broken rock. It was markedly warm down here; no frost lay on the ground and there was a steam in the air and a scent of warm earth. Primroses bloomed unseasonably in drifts among new spikes of grass. In one of the pools the singer was bathing. Her song was gentle and wordless.

It was as it should be, he told himself with a half-smile, as he edged forwards: nymphs and goddesses of old were always discovered at their bath. He raised his bow, the arrow aimed straight at the pale glimmer of skin in the shadows under the trees.

It was a narrow target; she was slenderly built. Her long hair was the black of ash buds in winter while her skin was a pale uncanny green, like the flush on the petals of snowdrops. Defying the season overhead, white petals of hawthorn were drifting down in the still air from trees on the cliff face, and lay on the pool's surface or clung to her damp skin like snowflakes that refused to melt. The water must have been gelid, but she washed herself slowly, with great concentration, as if enthralled by her reflection or the slim body under her hands. The surface of the pool cut across her form at the exact point at which the cleft of her gently curved rear started, and Herrick's keen glance found that precision peculiarly frustrating.

The smell of the may blossom was heavy and sweet, like honey. *The scent of hawthorn is the scent of death*, the old woman had said – but hawthorn blossom at different times may smell alluring, or of sex, or of corruption. It depends on the tree, and the time, and the man.

Her song faded away. She lowered her hands to the water. 'Why don't you shoot?' she asked, without turning. Her voice was low-pitched.

He didn't answer. He stepped forwards out of cover though, the bow at full draw, the arrow tip aimed unwaveringly.

'You don't shoot deer or birds,' she continued. 'Do you shoot unarmed women?'

That hurt. 'I've never shot anyone in the back.'

She laughed. 'What about in the front?' she asked, turning. Her face was triangular and delicate, with slanted green eyes under angled rows; a hungry face, not beautiful by any courtly standards but entirely arresting. And her body – oh, her body made Herrick's heart thud against his ribs, so he dragged his eyes back to her face, away from those breasts upon which the water droplets sat like pearls. Her lips, like her nipples, were the dark red of ripe haws. She smiled. 'Well? Will you shoot me now?'

Then she walked forwards out of the pool, up onto the spit of sand and grass where he waited, and as she did, her hair changed colour, blanching to the blond of new-cut pine, and her skin warmed to the cream of peeled willow strips. Her expression with its mocking smile did not change though.

'No,' he said with resignation, dropping his bow to one side. But he put his hand on the hilt of his sword.

'Your mistake,' she told him. She was nearly as tall as he

was when she came up close, with long clean limbs. 'How are you going to kill me now, man of iron? You are here to kill me, aren't you?'

'I'm here to stop you.'

'Stop me doing what?' Her hair moved about her like a live thing, undulating softly. It reminded Herrick of the twitch of a cat's tail before the beast pounces.

'Killing innocent people.'

'And when have I done that?' She looked him up and down. 'You don't look innocent to me.'

He raised a brow in acknowledgement. 'The people of Estoli. The woodsmen and the hunters and the miners.'

Her eyes narrowed. 'They were innocent, were they? Felling the trees? Killing the animals? Raping the earth?'

'They were just trying to stay alive.'

'So am I.'

'There were children,' he growled.

'Ah.' Her eyes glittered with ire. 'There is no end either to the greed of men, or the begetting of their children. They will fill the earth and take everything.'

'A child is of more worth than a tree!'

She laughed. 'Says you, human.'

'Says God.'

'Not this one!' Her arm lashed out, faster than he would have believed, and she backhanded him stingingly across the face. Herrick felt his blood surge in his veins. He blinked hard, meeting her mocking eyes, but his sword did not leave its scabbard and his hand did not leave its hilt.

She shifted on her toes, clearly frustrated by his lack of reaction. 'Well,' she sneered, 'aren't you going to fight me? Shall I strike you again? Will you turn the other cheek?' She raised her fist again, but this time he saw it warp, changing, and as she swung at him he jerked back out of the way. Her hand swung past his face and he glimpsed six-inch thorns jutting from the knuckles. She'd have ripped his throat out.

Without needing to think he was in the fighting stance, his sword out in his hand. She danced around him, laughing, her damp hair swirling, her feet barely seeming to touch the ground. Herrick's face burned, not just from the blow she'd struck him but from shame that she should scorn him. He was a knight and not used to being treated to lightly. When she feinted at him he slashed back, meaning to catch her knuckles on the flat of his blade, but her hand was not where it should have been and he struck only empty air.

'Faster than that, man of iron,' she mocked. She stabbed at his eyes. As he swiped back she slid past beneath his guard and ripped her other hand across the exposed underside of his arm, just at the edge of his mail sleeve, drawing blood.

She was inhumanly swift, he realised. And her nails were now as sharp and thick as lion claws. A duel that should have been hopelessly one-sided – armed knight against naked nymph – turned instead into a twisting dance of slash and dodge, both combatants proud and angry, she grinning but he grim-faced and increasingly discomforted. He had the armour and the sword and the reach on her; she had a litheness that would have put a cat to shame. They circled each other frantic-ally. Herrick took a moment to unsling his shield, but it was hardly in his hand before the wood warped, burst into leaf, turned sear and then withered to dry sticks that fell apart. The iron boss and rim fell uselessly to the ground, and she laughed.

Then a raking blow from her snagged her curved claws in his mail, trapping that hand long enough for him to seize the wrist. His grip was harsh enough to grind her wrist bones together, but she responded by growing thorns from her skin like the spikes of blackthorn, long as fingers and narrow as awls, which punched clean through his palm and out the other side. He gasped, but didn't let her go – not until the points emerging from her hand pierced his hauberk and the padded cloth beneath and drilled into his abdomen. Then he wrenched away and released her, scattering droplets of blood as he staggered out of her reach, and cursed in shock.

'Come on. You aren't trying!' she spat, closing for another bout.

He was aware at the periphery of his vision of the trees moving, of the landscape flexing as the forest warped into an arena for their combat. Water hissed as it boiled away, rocks groaned and shivered into sand. Grit and leaves and pieces of bark whipped around them, stinging his eyes. Even worse was the knowledge that she was right: killing her was not his heart-felt goal. He was not putting everything into it. He wished she were armoured, or even clothed. He wished she wasn't so fast. He wished he wasn't starting to pant for breath.

He took the decision and swung a killing blow at her. Somehow she side-stepped, the tip of the blade scoring her ribs, then whirled and kicked out at him. Her foot connected with the side of his knee. In her movements she'd been so swift that she seemed almost ethereal, but she was solid enough when this blow slammed into him. Herrick felt the joint break, even heard the crunch, and then the afterwash of pain took his breath away. He collapsed to a crouch, his head full of a white roaring agony that swamped everything else. He was only vaguely aware that the dryad was still there, that his mouth was open, that he was retching emptily as his body tried to vomit out the pain.

'Get up.' She impinged on his consciousness. He swung his head to focus on her, wondering if she would step within reach of his blade. But she stalked in a half-circle well beyond the swing of his arm, her back arched proudly, ignoring the thin red trickle crawling down to her hip. 'You can't give in just yet,' she said. 'It's much too soon.'

Herrick tried to get his gasping under control. Every nerve sang with strain and the blood was roaring through his veins. He didn't trust himself to speak out loud. He had to get upright, he told himself, get his back to something solid. It was his only chance; down here on the ground he was finished.

'You must be in a lot of pain.'

He nodded once, his lips clamped shut. Her hair was dry now, a dense dark cloud the green-black of yew leaves, her skin flushed all over to the russet of an autumnal beech crown. But her eyes were the same, and her piquant, cruel face.

'I know what pain is.' She touched the nick on her ribs. 'Not this. But seeing my trees felled, my land invaded, my shrines overturned . . .'

Herrick got his good leg under him, trying to rise, but that was not part of her plan. 'I'll heal you,' she announced. 'We've hardly started, have we?' Taking up a handful of soil from between her feet she threw it contemptuously upon him. Herrick jerked his face away, shutting his eyes. Then he felt his broken leg twist beneath him, and a warmth flare up his thigh and down his calf.

'Get up,' she repeated.

He stood straight, testing his knee, dizzy with shock. The joint was whole, as was his pierced hand, the pain nothing more than a memory. His awe must have shown upon his face, because she made a spitting noise.

'In this wood, man of iron, I am a goddess. The earth hears my whispers; the oak moves to my commands. Do you think you can kill me with that little blade?'

He was beginning to doubt it. 'I can try.'

Her smile widened. 'You learn too slowly. Shall we have another lesson?'

Then she threw herself at him. Herrick had no time for anything except to thrust the sword straight out at her breast, braced in both hands. She struck the blade full on, dashed up its length and all over him – a hail of autumn leaves and stones, no more solid than that. The moment she was behind him she took form again, whirled, smashed the helmet from his head and kicked him in the back of the knee, folding him. He caught himself as he went down, but even as he turned and slashed there was movement in the grass all around him. Bramble tendrils whipped from the earth, tangling his feet and hands. In moments he was dragged over on his back, a spiny loop tight around his throat. Fragile in themselves, in numbers they pinned him to the ground. Then new tendrils grew and slid up his sleeves and under the edge of his hauberk, their passage like lines of fire drawn on his skin, emerging at the neck. Dozens and dozens of living strands, binding together into stronger and stronger cords. They tightened and flexed – and tore his mail shirt open. The bronze rivets first corroded and then stretched and snapped.

Herrick had seen thistles cracking marble slabs in Rome, or else he would not have understood that a living plant could be so strong.

Then the ground heaved beneath his back, a huge boulder thrusting him up until he was raised and spread and nearly snapped in half, the pressure against his spine almost unbearable. The brambles did not let go, but having ripped open his armour and shredded the cloth beneath they did nothing but tighten against his skin, a thousand tiny thorns speckling him with his own blood. He felt the air against his stinging flesh. He saw the tree branches tossing overhead and the white petals of shed may blossom fluttering down upon him, and he wondered if this was the end.

The dryad jumped up onto the rocks and straddled his hips.

He couldn't even raise his head to look down at those naked thighs.

'So, does the guest bed suit you?'

He groaned.

'A little hard on the back? What a pity.' She bent and licked the blood streaks on his chest; he was surprised to learn that her mouth was warm. 'Still, you did arrive at very short notice, without invitation. You must make allowances.'

His heart was racing; she must be able to feel its thud against her lips as she sipped from him. 'Don't blame yourself,' he said through gritted teeth, as the world spun around him.

She chuckled, surprised. 'Do you enjoy this, man of iron?'

'Herrick.'

'What?'

'That's my name.' It seemed important to him that she should know it. He did not want to go nameless to death.

She mouthed the foreign word with distaste. 'Is this how you expected it to end, *Herrick*?'

'One day.' And he was horrified to find that his strongest emotion was relief.

'You've fought my kind before?'

'No. No dryad.'

She circled his nipple with the tip of her tongue, making it harden. 'Monsters ...'

'Yes.'

'The last children of Rhea. So that the children of the stones may inherit the earth.' Her teeth closed cruelly over his left nipple and he groaned from deep in his chest. Then she released the crushed nubbin of flesh and crept forwards up his chest, breathing the smell of his sweat and his fear until her lips were against his ear. 'Do you wish to hear the good news?'

He managed to swallow, and she took that for assent.

'This isn't the end, Herrick. Not yet. You are not going to die until I tire of hurting you. And in this place I can take you to the brink of death and bring you back again, over and over, for my pleasure. Until your pain has brought me ease.'

Fresh damp sprang from every pore. His insides seemed to turn liquid. She raked claws down his chest and stomach, testing every patch of skin between the criss-crossed bonds. He rolled his eyes back and tried to call upon the mercy of God, but it came out sounding completely wrong somehow.

'What's this?' Her voice was low with surprise.

He strained to look down at her and found she'd reached his lower garments, had been sliding about on his crotch, had found something that should not have been there at all: his massive, stony erection, pushing up against the cloth, the swollen head seeping with such eagerness that it was making a damp patch. Herrick was washed by a crimson tide of shame.

Dear God give me strength to resist her, he begged.

She ripped his clothing to shreds, delicately. His cock thrust out blasphemously through the rent fabric, and jerked with eagerness as she traced the veins with the tips of her deadly claws. Like a dog rising to greet its mistress, he thought, sick with humiliation.

'Oh Herrick. Now I know.'

'No,' he groaned.

'This is a gift, isn't it? A phallus like this, and a man like you, in my power?'

'You're wrong ...'

'Wrong? No. Men may lie, but this does not. It makes plain what it wants, Herrick.' She slapped his prick with first one hand then the other, like a cat playing with a mouse. He burned with shame. 'Slattern,' she mocked.

He twisted in his bonds uselessly, driving each pinpoint of pain deeper.

'Lick me,' she ordered, looming right over him, lowering her breasts to his mouth.

He put out his tongue to her nipple but she snatched it away, giggling, before he could touch her. He groaned, scoured by her glee and his weakness. Then she wriggled back down and crouched over his prick, laying her lips to the underside of the shaft and nipping her way delicately right down to the root, never quite hurting him but threatening all the way. She took his balls one after the other into her mouth, rolling them between her teeth until sweat ran down his temples. Spitting out his slippery ball sac she then found the silken skin stretched between his soaring cock and his scrotum, and took a fold delicately between two eye teeth. She held it for a moment, letting him realise what she was going to do.

Herrick quivered, choking out incoherent prayers.

She bit down. Two sharp teeth met through a thin fold of skin and he opened his mouth in a soundless roar. His cock jerked twice, and clear fluid bulged at the slit and, welling out under its own volume, ran down his hard length, testament to his need.

'Herrick,' she chided. 'Look at you.'

'Oh God, no!'

'Shh. Stop pretending.'

With her tongue she traced the path of his overspill back up from his balls to the head of his cock, where she lapped his ooze. He groaned again and shook like a man with the ague. His world was in flames. Could there be any defeat more shameful than this – to be beaten in combat, then abused as a whore, his body a treacherous accomplice?

And her mouth was exquisite comfort now after the hurt she'd inflicted, as tender as a mother hugging her child after smacking it. The pleasure was overwhelming; he knew he needed more. More hurt. More solace.

Her lips, wet from painting his glans, left it bereft and straining. 'Pain,' she whispered, straightening and kneeling up astride him again. 'Your pain is my pleasure, I thought. But your pleasure too. Don't worry, Herrick, I will give you what you need.' She guided his erect cock between her thighs, into her tight slick grip, her eyes rolling back with the effort of taking his girth. Then she refocused on his face. For the first time she sounded a little breathless.

'You will not spend, Herrick. You will hold it back. Because if you let spill before me I will walk away and leave you here and never return. You understand that?'

'Yes.' Oh my God, yes.

'But if you give me my heart's desire, I will give you yours.' She reached behind her, down between his thighs, and sank her nails into his scrotum. He gasped and nodded, water running from the corners of his eyes. 'I'm going to hurt you.' Her voice was cold, her eyes green fire. 'I'm going to hurt you badly and there is nothing you can do about it. You are mine to play with. Your strength will not save you. Your God will not save you. Your life is mine now, and it is over.'

'You are beautiful,' he rasped, 'my lady.'

She began to move upon him, stirring his cock within her, and he lost all words in a groaning out-rush of breath. Helpless, he could only watch as her hair undulated about her, as her breasts shook and swayed, as her splayed thighs framed his cock. With one hand she touched herself, with the other she scored whatever of his skin she could reach. When her fingers brushed a piece of the living rope that held him the thorns upon it grew longer, piercing into his muscle. He could hear himself moaning softly with the pain, and with the exquisite friction of her grip upon his cock. She bared her teeth in a grin at first, but as her cheeks flushed and her eyes darkened her expression smoothed, becoming the blank mask of need. Her chest rose and fell more sharply and her back arched, thrusting her breasts forwards. He wanted to touch her. He wanted to fondle those wonderful breasts, to stroke her taut belly, to knead the straining thighs. He wanted to plunge his hand into the folds of her sex and feel himself pumping in and out of her, the sticky slipperiness of her juices, the way he filled and stretched her hole. He wanted to make her whimper to the rhythm of his fingers and cock. He'd always been able to touch the women he swived; now he was bound tight, his muscles bulging between the green cords. He'd let women ride him before, but never like this. Whatever their physical positions, he'd always been the one in control.

Not now.

Now he was truly mastered. Now he was at her mercy, and she had none. She had beaten him, humiliated him, mocked him. She was going to kill him. And deep in the welter of his pain and fear Herrick knew a wild joy beyond anything he'd ever experienced in his life.

Her head began to roll upon her shoulders. Her hair bleached as white as hawthorn petals and whipped at him like striking snakes. The smell of may blossom, musky and sexual, clogged his nostrils so he could hardly breathe. The bramble rope about his throat was tightening. He strained against his bonds, thrusting up into her, even as the margins of his vision grew dark. She tore the skin down his breastbone. She struck at his face. The thorns at his throat swelled and lengthened, biting deep. Soon he could no longer breathe even if he had wanted to, even if his whole soul had not been focused on her parted lips, the flash and flutter of her eyes, the shudder rippling through her frame. Blotches danced before his eyes, like yellow and black leaves chased by the wind. In that moment before the darkness closed in on him he clenched and jerked and flooded into her, feeling her thorns pierce him to the core, seeing the leaves turn red.

There is a wood at the foot of the mountains that no one dares enter. They say that it belongs to a dryad, but she has not been seen in years. To get into the wood one would have to get past the tall swordsman who patrols the edge, driving away all intruders. The guardian of the wood is a matchless warrior, devoted to his duty. For Herrick of Turin has finally, after all these years, found the one he can serve with his whole heart.

Chimaera

I first see him the night we go to visit the Chimaera.

It's the fourth day of our honeymoon in Turkey, heading east along the Lycian coast before we double back overland to finish in Istanbul. We've been scuba-diving in Kas and we've kayaked over the sunken city at Kekova, Keith's been up parascending – though I had a dodgy stomach that day and cried off – and we've waded the Saklikent Gorge and explored Lycian tombs in groves of gnarled olive trees almost as ancient as the stone sarcophagi themselves. This night, after a long day on the water, we arrive as darkness falls at the Chimaera. Other tourists are here too. In legend, this was the home of the fire-breathing hybrid monster, part lion, part goat, part snake. Like pilgrims, we climb the footpath up the hillside, and it's long and steep enough to make my legs ache a little. We see the flames before we reach them: first one distinct patch then another, on a pale bare hillside.

Flame from the earth.

There's no eponymous monster in the vicinity now, and the flames that used to be visible to passing ships in the bay below have diminished over the centuries, but still it's a little eerie. From cracks in the bare limestone the flames issue, in about a dozen places. Some of them are tiny, blue and liable to disappear for long moments; others burn yellow, with a soft roar. We can walk among them, careful not to roast our sandalled feet. We find our own little patch of flames and sit around it like it's a campfire. People are bringing out chunks of sausage and toasting them; I can smell the fatty meat over the whiff of gas. There's laughter and chatter. Keith opens a bottle of local wine and pours some into our plastic camping mugs.

We've been told that if you extinguish the fire it re-ignites spontaneously; the next group over is trying just that, covering a jet up, then oohing when the gas gives a little pop and bursts into flame once more. I wish they'd keep the noise down. It seems disrespectful of such a unique place. In ancient times, I know, this whole area was sacred to the god of fire. I dip my fingertips in my wine and flick droplets into the flames. An apology of sorts. An offering.

Maybe it's a mistake. This is an Islamic country, and fire worship has traditionally been regarded as the epitome of forbidden heathenism. Because it's then that I see him, standing a little way off, staring at me. He's a tall, dark-haired man, and certainly looks Turkish. His black brows are knitted over a hawkish nose. I feel suddenly embarrassed, as if I've been caught doing something wicked. I look away, pulling my face into a mask of indifference. Keith hasn't noticed; he's kicked off his sandals and is examining the sunburn pattern on his feet.

By the time I glance back, the man has disappeared into the darkness.

I see him again the next day, while I'm swimming at the beach near our *pansiyon*. The setting could not be more idyllic or more evocative: turquoise waters and an arc of beach backed by steep, verdant cliffs through which ravines descend to the sea – and on the banks of the nearest river valley the ruined site of the port of Olympos which we've spent hours exploring this morning, its aqueduct and tombs and rock-cut theatre hidden away among the fig trees and oleander and carob, the yellow plumes of spurge and the long reeds. No modern build-ings or stalls have been allowed on the beach so the scene is unspoiled. The bay is sheltered and the sea almost still. I rise from the clear waters where I've been hovering over pink sea slugs and slender trumpet fish and, as I pull up my snorkel mask, I happen to glance towards the shore.

He's there on the sand: the man from the Chimaera. I'm not perturbed; he likely works at one of the *pensiyons* nearby. He's wearing loose red trousers and a long-sleeved white T-shirt which glows against his skin. He's watching me. The heat reflected from the sand makes the air around him dance.

I pull my mask off completely, smoothing back my wet hair. I'm aware that now I'm standing my breasts, cupped in their pink bikini top, are clear of the water. They feel heavy in their Lycra sling, and the sea is cool enough to have hardened my nipples to points. Water droplets pearl my bare skin. There's no mistaking that he's looking straight at me, though it's not possible to be sure of his expression.

Then Keith explodes out of the sea behind me, hurls wet arms about me and drags me under, kicking and thrashing. By the time he pulls me to my feet again and I've coughed out salt water and slapped his chest and squealed my outrage and he's kissed me hard, laughing, the stranger is gone from my mind. Keith puts his hands down my bikini bottom under cover of the water. 'Want to fuck you,' he groans in my ear.

I'm instantly self-conscious and try to squint over my shoulder at the beach. 'Stop it! We're being watched!'

Keith grunts. 'So? Anyway, no one's paying any attention.'

I press up against him, letting him play with my bum cheeks, slip a finger between them and tease my crack. 'There's a guy been watching me ...'

'Really? What's he look like?'

'Um ...'

'Talk, dark and handsome?'

'Uh-uh,' I admit, nibbling his ear.

'You'd better tell him you're taken, Mrs Everts.'

'Tell him yourself. He's just on the beach there.'

'Nope. No one there.'

I pull out of his arms enough to turn, putting my shoulders to his chest. His hands rise from the water and cup my breasts, but I'm distracted, searching the shingly sand and the little knots of tourists for a figure like the one missing. It takes a good hard nudge from Keith's cock against my bum to bring me back to reality. And I'm impressed because despite the cool water that erection means business.

'I've had enough swimming,' I purr, grinding my hips in a circle to stir his interest. 'Let's go back to the room.'

We're still damp from the sea when we reach our bed and Keith tumbles me onto the coverlet.

'Are you happy, Mrs Everts?'

I am. I am gloriously happy. He discovers that for himself as he pulls down my bikini panties and slips his fingers inside me. I am beach-wet in there and carry the aroma of the sea. Then he moves upon me like a ship taking to the waves, ploughing the Aegean in long rolling stokes. His skin tastes of sunblock and salt and there is sand in his hair. He looms over me as he surges into my wetness, gilded by sunlight. My lover, now my husband: I want him so very much. My body aches, stretches, blossoms for him. I touch his face and throat and chest as if seeing him for the first time. His hair is shorn as close as fine turf to compensate for the fact it's retreating – he'll be bald by the time he's forty but I don't mind, I like the blunt masculinity revealed. At this moment he is all golden stubble dusted with sand and skin tanning to a ruddy bronze. I'm not used to seeing his skin, his muscle, his tight lines; back home everything is covered up except for that flash before he dives under the duvet. Here I discover him all over again.

And as we heave and crash upon the bed, through the open window swirls a cloud of petals. I couldn't say what flowering plant they come from, but they are orange like flame and they flicker in the breeze, falling on us like the confetti at our wedding fell. They cling to the sheen of my hot flesh, brushing my face like fingertips, and lie strewn upon the coverlet in glorious flaming disarray as if someone has thrown upon us a bucket of red-hot coals.

When I doze off, I dream of fire.

Three days later we are in Istanbul, hundreds of miles from the Lycian coast, in another world. The city is everything I've imagined. My head is filled with blue tiles and minarets, exhaust fumes and aromatic smoke, steep streets lined with wooden Ottoman houses, apple tea and calligraphy, carpets and concrete. We tour everything that tourists are supposed to: the harem in the Topkapi Palace; the Blue Mosque; the vast Byzantine church of Hagia Sophia; the Kapali Carsi covered bazaar; the spice market. But it's in the darkness of the Yerebatan Seray that he finds me again.

This place is a pillared cavern beneath the streets of the city. In my imagination, an underground lake for the phantom of the Paris Opera; in prosaic terms, a covered Byzantine water cistern rediscovered after being forgotten for centuries. It is still flooded to a depth of a metre or so and the mismatched pillars, looted from ancient temples, rise to the brick arches of the roof. It is enormous; you would not believe that what is effectively a cellar could be built so big. Subdued lighting shows concrete walkways snaking away into the gloom. In several places the roof drips, sending ripples rolling across the black waters.

Keith is playing enthusiastically with the settings and lenses of his new camera. Leaving him by the carved Medusa head which is the most striking piece of stonework, I wander away. There aren't too many tourists here today. I amuse myself by watching the grey fish gliding beneath me and wondering what they live on.

Then the lights go out.

Instantly it is pitch dark. The piped classical music dies and I hear the annoyed and anxious wails of other visitors, but it sounds very faint, as if they are a great distance off. I grip the wooden railing hard; I have no other connection to reality. I feel the chill air move damply against my cheek and cock my ear to the plash of a falling water drop. The air seems colder, though I know that's only suggestion. Suddenly the awesome but peaceful space yawning around me is quite horrible: a Stygian darkness in which anything could be moving; a chamber of Hades. I bite my lip, determined not to squeal as the others are doing. Their muffled cries of distress only add to the illusion of an underworld of tormented souls.

There is light. Just a spot of it, but it's approaching. I think it's a man carrying a torch, but as the shape resolves from the utter darkness I see no torch. Just the man. His tread is steady and confident and he is coming straight towards me. It is the man from the Chimaera, dressed as he was that day on the beach: red cotton trousers, white shirt, bare feet. He is carrying no lamp – yet *I can see him*. He glows against the velvet blackness, like a paper lantern carrying its own flame. When he gets close enough I can see that he faintly illumin-ates the pathway, the railing and finally me by his light. At this my brain locks down in shock, unable to deal with anything except minutiae.

It's disconcerting how familiar his face is, and how hand-some, though he doesn't smile in greeting. His expression even now is one of intense scrutiny. He comes in so close I press myself back against the rail, holding my breath. He's taller than any of the local men I've met, and his tight T-shirt clings to sharply defined muscle. He looms over me. His gaze eats me.

'Stop this.' My voice is weak and husky but I say it, aware how stupid I sound, as if he were an ordinary man who had for no very good reason decided to follow me across the breadth of the country. 'You have to leave me alone. I'm married.'

He lifts a brow, and there is a hint of challenge in his enquiry. Keith is not here to defend my honour, and the man's eyes defy me to wish that he were.

'I'm married and I love him,' I repeat, brandishing my wedding ring, wondering if he even speaks English.

He takes my hand. His skin is warm, his fingers long. I can see the gold of my ring shining in his unnatural effulgence. I don't dare to wrench from his grasp but I avert my eyes momentarily and it is then that I notice the water puddled on the walkway retreating from around his naked feet, steaming a little. I think I might scream if I had breath for it. My lips gape, my eyes are wide.

He spreads my palm, weaving his fingers with mine. His eyes never leave my face. He lifts my hand to his mouth and touches the tip of my little finger to his lips. They are full, dangerous-looking lips, and his breath is warm. He really is shockingly handsome. He puts one fingertip at a time to his mouth, sometimes touching with the tip of his tongue, sometimes his teeth, finishing with my thumb. Then he exposes my palm and bows his face to kiss it, those glittering dark eyes veiled by black lashes. He kisses my palm tenderly, yet with unabashed hunger. Then, lowering my hand but not releasing it, he steps into me until the whole length of his body is against mine. He's not crushing me, not even pressing against me properly. Just sharing the sweep of my tingling flesh.

My better self is demanding, *Why aren't you stopping him?*

In this chilly, lifeless place he is so warm. He slides a finger under my chin to lift it and my breath catches in my throat with a noise like a sob. His lips stoop to mine.

At that moment the lights flicker back on all around us, but I am paralysed by his touch and unable to react. He makes a small frown – regret, resignation – then bends to brush his lips against my ear.

'*Selamün Áleyküm.*' Peace be upon you. His voice is deep. It crawls under my skin and sinks into my bones.

Then he steps away, his look a lingering promise, and walks off. He leaves me breathless and squirming in my skin, my hands moving without volition to my tingling breasts, my eyes fixed on his figure and then, when he has vanished into the gloom, on the line of bare footprints he leaves behind: dry footprints pale on the damp slabs.

We dine, on the penultimate day of our honeymoon, in a small restaurant near our hotel, in the old Sultanahmet area of the city. It's a traditionally dressed room, so we've taken off our shoes and sit on low couches in our alcove. The wooden walls are dressed with geometric-patterned rugs and oil lamps burn on every table. There is one modern painting right inside the front door, of the creature after which the restaurant is named: the Chimaera. It roars, triple mouths open.

I wish I hadn't let Keith pick this place. I can't keep my mind off the painting. It seems too reminiscent of the man I am trying not to think of: the lion symbolising magnificence and strength and pride, the goat denoting lust, the venomous snake tail suggesting ... What? Wisdom? The Underworld? Evil?

I know what the snake would symbolise in Western art.

We eat our way through platters of *meze*. Our lips shine with olive oil, our eyes with playful lechery. Keith takes advantage of moments when the waiters' backs are turned to stroke my inner thigh, sliding his fingers up under my skirt to flick and tickle me through my panties: impolite in any society, indefensible in one as strait-laced as this. But I'm restless, twitchy and eager for transgression. I only giggle when he leans in to whisper in my ear.

'When I get you back to the hotel, do you know what I want to do?'

'No.'

'I'm going to bend you over the foot of our bed and slip my cock into you from behind. And I'm not going to close the curtains before I do it. You know our window looks out the inner balcony ...'

Shivers chase up my spine. 'Yes.'

'So anyone in the rooms on the other side will be able to look across and see me humping you. Anyone passing in the corridor will get a look in: cleaners; hotel guests; that cute guy from reception. My butt slamming away, giving you a proper stuffing. Something to remember us by.'

'You can't,' I giggle, squirming, both mortified and horribly aroused. This is not the sort of thing we'd dream of doing back home. My knickers are sticky under me as I move on my cushion. We sit back, flushed, doing a very poor job of looking innocent as a waiter deposits another couple of plates before us. Butter beans swim in a tomato sauce. Little filo tubes ooze white cheese. Then I press against Keith's arm, meaning to whisper in his ear, *How about if you tie me to the bed?*

I never get a chance to speak. The air bursts around us in an ear-splitting roar and the whole building lurches. As the lights flicker out I grab Keith's arm and we're slammed back into the cushions.

It's a bomb. These days, it's the first conclusion we all jump to. It hasn't gone off underneath us though; when I open my eyes the only window in sight is gaping wide, wooden shutters and glass alike shattered, but the room looks intact. People start to scream – some out on the street, some here in the restaurant with us – but my ears are ringing so loudly I can hardly hear them. There are flames. The oil lamp from our table has been knocked to the floor and the carpet has caught fire.

I touch my face with my hands, trying to convince myself I'm still here. There's a cut on Keith's forehead, but I can't think what to do. The room's too dark to see anything properly, though the red flickering is gaining strength.

Fire. Fire in a wooden building.

Keith's lips move, but I can't hear him swearing. He fumbles for the rug on the wall behind us. After a moment's stunned inertia I help him drag it off its hooks and he throws it over the flames, smothering them. My limbs feel like puppets, operated by remote control. But though we stamp on the carpet it is not enough. Our flames vanish, but in other parts of the dining room fire is licking up the walls, people are flailing uselessly or stumbling away. Already thick smoke that smells of burned wool is billowing across the ceiling. I paw at Keith.

'We've got to get out!'

We stagger from our alcove, but our heads are spinning with shock. I can't remember which way to turn for the stairs down. I make a decision, then remember too late it's the route to the toilet I'm taking. Keith blunders in to me as I stop. We turn back, but there are flames as tall as us curtaining the archway, and there's no one else in the room now. The smoke is making it hard to breathe. I can hear Keith shouting. He drags me towards the broken window.

Then he walks in, through the flame, my Chimaera, straight through the fire without so much as blinking or shielding his eyes. He looks absolutely calm. He's not scorched; he's not even sweating. Sparks land in his thick black hair but they wink out. He walks up to me, takes my wrist, then turns away. He's heading for the flame-wreathed doorway. I don't resist, but I scream for Keith, and when his flailing hand catches mine I drag him in our wake.

And I see the flames shrink and recoil from my abductor, guttering back to scorched wood. We walk unharmed down the stairs, and we're out into the cloud of brick dust that fogs the street before I know what to think.

Then he releases my wrist and walks away. Keith grabs me and crushes me to his chest, and all I see for many long minutes is his filthy, blood-streaked face twisted with anguish.

It was a bomb, it turns out, though next day they are still arguing on the TV whether it was the PKK or fundamentalists who'd taken out the government offices over the street from our restaurant. We were lucky; two people died in the blast and several were badly hurt in the fires it started.

It's the last day of our holiday. We fly out tonight. Though the cut on his head was superficial and the worst injury either of us sustained, Keith has been badly rattled, I think. He won't admit it but he opts to stay in the hotel for the day, packing our cases and hanging out on the sunroof with a book.

I can't hide indoors. Unlike Keith, I don't see our escape as a random thing, a piece of luck. I know we were under protection, and that the man who led us out was not just some brave waiter as Keith assumes. I feel the pressure under my skin, writhing in my belly, forcing me onto the streets to confront this city once more. I am in his debt. Keith doesn't want me to go, but he accepts that I am determined not to waste the one day left.

I head out alone, on foot. I wear an ankle-length skirt. Perhaps it's not having Keith's six-foot blondness marking us out for tourists, or perhaps the city is subdued by the incident last night, but this day for the first time no one tries to lure me into any carpet emporium. I pass through Sultanahmet without being accosted. I take a tram down to the waterfront and cross the Galata Bridge on foot, past the ranks of rod-and-line fishermen hauling even the smallest tiddler out of the water, to the steep streets of the old European diplomatic quarter. It's a bit of a hike, and I'm glad to take a drink and a baguette full of *kofte* in a café. I admire a few mosques and the Pera Palace hotel. Then I pay to ride up the lift in the Galata Tower to the observation gallery.

The view is breathtaking. Under an orange fug of pollution, the old part of the city masses on the facing hill, over the glittering waters of the Golden Horn. The boat congestion in that inlet is so busy I cannot believe I won't witness a shipwreck. The skyline bulges with domes and is punctuated by minarets. I know I should hate this city; it is humid and overcrowded, filthy and incredibly loud, with lethal traffic. But I don't. Istanbul has gripped me; simultaneously ancient and modern, Western and Middle Eastern, it has so much presence, such charisma. It is a place where history is still immanent; time here does not seem linear.

Then the voice of the first muezzin wails out from a minaret and others join in, in a staggered cacophony: the mid-afternoon call to prayer. I feel the hairs stand up on my neck and tears prickle in my eyes; it's like the whole city is shouting at God.

The walk back down from the tower and over the bridge is a lot easier, so I decide to make my way back to the hotel on foot. It should be easy enough to navigate by the minarets of the big mosques, and I'm in no hurry. I head up a long straight street, through the crowds of shoppers. This is the overspill area from the Kapali Carsi, but it's no tourist market. The stalls either side are more likely to sell cellphone covers, cheap plastic toys, bread and vegetables, than the amber necklaces and embroidered slippers and water pipes of the Covered Bazaar. I press on uphill, enjoying my anonymity in the crowd.

Then I look behind me, down the slope, wondering if there is a view back over the Golden Horn from this side. And there he is trailing me, a head taller than anyone else, his eyes fixed on me as he cuts through the press of shoppers. My heart lurches in my chest, but that is not my only physical response. Suddenly I want to cry because it is so unfair! I already have the man that I want, the man that I love – why should my sex react so helplessly, with such heat, to this uncanny stranger? Why should I feel a sudden slipperiness, an ache in my pelvis, the beat of my pulse at my wrists? Am I so faithless? Am I such a slut?

I turn away and keep walking, but I know he's gaining on me. My mouth is dry but the skin between my breasts is damp. I wonder what Keith is doing. I wonder what will happen when my Chimaera catches up with me. I tell myself there is nothing he can do in a public place. I tell myself I will be a good and irreproachable wife, not the slut that Western women are reputed to be.

It goes quiet.

Like someone has switched off the soundtrack, it goes silent. The traffic, the voices, the screech of gulls – everything snaps off. I lift my eyes and see that everyone around me has stopped in their tracks, frozen in place. Hands are lifted, but do not fall. Mouths are open, but no words come out. A cloud of smoke from a wayside snack stall hangs motionless in mid-air, like a puff of candyfloss. I swing on my heel.

He's almost at my side; the only moving thing in the whole city, apart from me, for all I can tell. He looks just as he did every other time I've seen him – still barefoot, even among the mess of the market. In sunlight his hair looks almost blue, it is so dark.

Still he doesn't smile. He reaches out and lays his hand on the railing of the building at his right, and the iron gate swings open soundlessly at his touch. Let me get this straight: *he doesn't push the gate, but still it moves.* I am distracted enough to glance at the structure beyond the rails. It's the ruin of some traditional-looking building, not too big. You see them around in the city, usually mosques that have for some reason fallen into neglect. This one doesn't have a visible minaret though it does have a dome, so I assume it is a bath-house. Grey swathes of plaster hang from the stonework. The crumbling walls are overgrown with some sort of creeper that has withered to dried sticks in the Turkish summer. Back home kids would take one look and deliver the verdict: *haunted.*

He lifts his hand in a gesture of invitation.

I must be out of my mind. I must be begging for trouble. I walk past him through the gate, under the archway of the outer wall, into the derelict *hamam*. I hear him follow me, his feet quieter on the rubble than mine. We pass through an antechamber. We're inside a room that must have been domed and tiled once, but is now open to the sky. Most of the tiles have fallen and are loose underfoot. I'm dreading the sort of squatter mess you'd find in any abandoned building, but not even a plastic bag defaces the artwork of time. It is absolutely silent in here too. My heart is in my throat as I turn to look at him.

He moves upon me with grace but with a terrible eagerness, gripping my arms and pressing me back against a pillar so he can kiss me. He tastes of cardamom. He tastes of sin. He's more beautiful than I have words for, and my guilt at betraying Keith is no more than paper in the flame of my hunger for this man, burned to ashes. His body presses against me, just at the groin so that there is no mistaking his intentions, and I feel like I'm going to melt or explode or both. His hands find my breasts, pushing up under my respectable long-sleeved blouse, fingers closing over the nipples jutting through the rough lace of my bra. I moan into his mouth, covering his hands with mine to make him squeeze me harder. He pulls from my lips so he can look down at me, his eyes alight with pleasure. We're both panting.

'Who are you?' I ask.

He nuzzles my ear, licking the lobe, teeth teasing my skin. 'Ifrit,' he breathes.

It doesn't occur to me that this is not a name.

I don't have time to think about it, anyway. He pulls me away from the pillar, scoops me up bodily and plants my bum on the top of a block of masonry. I'm almost at eye level with him now. My feet dangle.

Now he can afford to draw breath. He stills me with a touch to my cheek, then unpicks the buttons down my blouse, his big hands incongruously delicate, just far enough to reveal my bra. He scoops my breasts out of their cups so they lie displayed on the taut fabric, pouting at him. I think my nipples look ridiculously pink against his brown hands, but he doesn't seem to mind. He plays with them until I gasp and wriggle, drawing them out to stiff points then punishing their temerity with obvious delight.

'Harder,' I moan. 'Please.'

His eyebrows rise but he obliges with a long, cruelly judged pinch that has me seeing stars. Then he arches me over backwards, supporting my spine so he can get his head down and suck my nipples and bite me softly. I hang in space, trusting myself to his hands and his teeth, tears burning in my eyes, feeling and hearing his hot sucking kisses. I must be mad, I think, but my thighs are apart and he's standing between my knees and his free hand is pushing my full skirt right up; it's warm on the smoothness of my thighs, it's probing into the moist flesh between them.

I gasp: 'Yes! Oh yes!'

With a good strong pull he sets me upright in my seat again, breathless and wide-eyed. He needs both hands to help me wiggle out of my panties, and when he holds the little piece of cloth up for inspection it reveals that I may have come out looking outwardly sober and sexless, but I've worn my bronze and pink might-get-lucky knickers, the ones reserved for special nights with Keith. My desire is laid bare. I blush, biting my lip, and crooking his own in a dark smile he wraps his arms around me, crosses my wrists at the small of my back and loops the elastic and lace of my panties over and over them, until I am bound with the evidence of my guilt.

Now I have to trust him. Now I'm helpless to catch myself if I overbalance. Now I can't fend him off, even if I want to. He kisses me again, lingeringly, but it doesn't work to distract me from the advance of his fingers up between my thighs, parting my inner lips, delving into my wet welcome. Like his kisses, his touch is expertly invasive. He works my wet flesh with every finger until I'm so slippery I feel I'm going to slide from my perch, until I'm flushed and gasping and splayed. Then he steps back just enough to be able to loosen his cotton trousers and scoop his cock and balls out over the waistband.

He's both circumcised and shaven, which is a bit of a shock to my English sensibilities. Framed by red cloth, his erection looks enormous and desperately impatient, his balls bulging in a smooth, loose scrotal sac. I strain against my bonds, wanting to touch them, but all I achieve is making my breasts jiggle. He slides his fingers deep into me again, then strokes my juices over his cock, working up a bead of his own lubrication. Then he picks up one of my feet and drapes it over his arm, holding me to stop me falling. His hand snakes around my waist as if we are about to dance – and it still feels like a strange waltz even when he shrugs my raised leg right up to his shoulder. He kisses me again, his mouth slow and hungry. He's still kissing me when his big cock rampages up my slit and, discovering the gate it's looking for, slides home.

God, he *is* big.

He stretches me to the limit. He fucks me slow and hard and deep. He knows what he's doing. He knows what he wants, and I have no choice but to give it to him: in this waltz, he leads. And what he wants is to make me come, so I do it: on his pumping cock, on his wicked fingers. I shriek as I come, my voice echoing under the sundered dome.

When my surrender is complete he pulls out, shimmering with my juices, and plops me onto my belly over the stone. My toes barely reach the floor and it's far from comfortable, but that doesn't matter to either of us. My wrists are still captive at the small of my back. He pulls up my skirt, spreads my bum and fucks me from behind, leaning in low so he can embrace my torso in one arm, his cock ramming my open slot, his thighs slapping against my arse and his balls bouncing on my sex. All dignity gone, it seems to me that a hundred dismissed and disappointed purveyors of carpets and taxi rides and antiqued souvenirs are being avenged all at once. I am moaning in counterpoint to his grunts, gathering to a second storm. He is quickening his pace, no longer slow and easy but urgent.

Fire erupts from the stones.

All around us, flames burst from every joint and crack of the ancient masonry. I feel the heat, though nothing actually burns us. All the air seems to be sucked out of my lungs. He is hammering into me like he would split me in half, and I can feel it happening, I can feel my whole body cracking into pieces, opening up, and the fire bursting out of those splits too, whirling me away in a storm of flame. I am aware of his roar as he slams his way to orgasm, but I am already alight and flying away on the conflagration's updraught, spinning like ashes and smoke up into the blue skies overhead.

It's hard to act my normal self when we return from our honeymoon.

Back home in England, I do what any normal woman would do: I Google him. It takes a little while; misunderstanding and ambiguities of spelling handicap me. But I find the reference in the end:

> *Afrit, Ifrit, Efreet: The tribe of evil Djinn who followed Iblis in refusing to bow down before Adam upon God's command. According to the Qur'an, Iblis explained to God: 'I am better than he. Thou createdst him of mud, while me Thou didst create of fire.'*

Scratch

When the berries on the rowan tree in the yard turned black and withered overnight, Maarten Gansevoort's wife, Mercy, knew it for a warning. She read omens like Pastor Arne read his big black Bible: she knew whether a cow was about to calf a bull or a heifer by the patterns of licked hair on its flanks, when a summer storm was on its way by the flight of birds and whether the river ice would hold solid by the squeak of snow-laden branches. She had been full of warnings before her marriage to Maarten Gansevoort.

'What do you want to marry me for?' she'd asked, knuckles on the jut of her hips, one eyebrow raised. 'I'll bring you no luck: a red-headed woman never brings luck.' Her hair was the bright colour of newly poured copper, and escaped from under her sober bonnet in kinks that would have been becoming on a young girl, and on a grown woman looked quite indecorous. 'And am I not to old for you?'

'Too old for what?' Maarten Gansevoort had said, turning his hat over in his hands for fear that if he left them idle they'd reach out and pull her to him so he could plant a kiss on that wide and luscious mouth.

'Too old to mother you any children, I'd have thought.'

'And so? I have a son and a daughter already by my Ingeborg, God rest her soul. What need have I of more children, Widow Lafferty? But I have it in mind that I need a wife.'

She'd done her best to put him off, turning his suit aside with good humour, sending him away with a bottle of elderberry cordial or a twist of dark toffee in his coat pocket as if he were an urchin importuning her for treats. But he'd persisted. Maarten Gansevoort was a big, vigorous man with a strength of will that had seen him hew a prosperous farm from near-wilderness and establish a dairy that supplied cheese and butter that was sent into Albany and as far down-river as New York itself. He was used to getting his own way in the end, and nothing would satisfy him but to take the Widow Mercy Lafferty to wife, because he saw in her a similar strength of will. He wasn't interested in her money either – though she seemed to have a fair private income, and had rented a house on the hill where the richer folk lived. He liked her ready, conspiratorial smile, her wit and her confidence. What had brought her out alone to this little country town he did not know – no more than did any of the local gossips so frustrated by her serene indifference to their curiosity – but he did not care that her accent was different from that of the farmers thereabouts, or that her clothes were cut in a different fashion to the stolid goodwives', or that she had unlucky red hair.

So he'd got his way as he was determined, wearing her down with his wooing until she'd submitted, laughing. But still she'd warned him, even as she'd accepted. Her green eyes had grown dark as she looked up into his face, her hands slipping into the compass of his, her mouth turning down almost for the first time.

'I have a past, Maarten Gansevoort. If I am to marry you, you must promise never to ask me about it.'

Besotted by her eyes and the curves of her body, and knowing himself so, he'd answered, 'So long as you have no husband alive somewhere to make this marriage void, I swear I do not care to know.'

She'd smiled at that, but her smile seemed a little bleak. 'No husband, I promise. I will be an honest wife. But ...' She hesitated. 'It is possible my past may return to touch upon me. If that should happen, promise you will be guided by me. Promise that you will let me deal with it in the way I know best, so that neither of us will come to harm. Promise me that, Maarten, or I cannot wed you.'

It had seemed a strange thing to say, and a dark omen for their marriage, but he had promised. And so they had been married, and happily enough, until the day the rowan berries blackened even though there had not yet even been a frost. Mercy came to him then with the news, and more warnings.

'Someone is coming to visit.'

He pulled out a plug of cheese from the round he was inspecting and sniffed it. He was used to her knowing that a stranger would soon pass by the farm; she would say she could see it in the watermarks left on the stone threshold when she scrubbed it on a morning. And she was always correct. 'Right, then.'

'Someone important.'

He looked over to see that his wife was as pale as new curd, her freckles standing out across her cheeks and nose like ground peppercorns. 'Is something wrong?'

'Husband ...' Mercy's hands twisted at the belt of her apron. 'Before I came here I was ... indentured as a servant. To someone very ... very powerful. I left his service. And he did not try to constrain me at that point. But he made it plain that he might call upon me at any time. He's coming here.'

'Do you owe him money?' It was the only thing Maarten could think of to say. He'd never seen such an expression of dread upon her face.

'No.' Her eyes looked sunken, but burned like green coals. 'Money is not what he is after.'

'Then if he is intent on hurting you, I will not let him through our door. I have my musket, Mercy, and my axe.'

'No!' Her eyes widened. 'You mustn't do that! You must not confront him. Maarten –' She broke off to put her hand on his breast. 'Remember you promised that if this happened you would let me deal with it?'

'Yes, but –'

'You must do what I say. You mustn't anger him, or cross him. He is capable of destroying us all. And ... I owe him. I gave my oath in service. If you do what I say then he will be happy and go away again.'

'I see.' Maarten was trying to hold down the mutiny in his breast. 'And what do you want me to do?'

'Go stay with your sister tonight; take the children. I've told the servants to leave the farm and not return till dawn.'

'And I'm to leave you alone with this man?' He wanted to shout, but he kept his voice low.

Mercy nodded mutely.

'And what's his name, this master of yours?'

She looked away, as if she could not meet his hot gaze any longer. 'He goes by a number of names.' Then she took a deep breath and admitted: 'Nicholas.'

'Nicholas what?'

'Nicholas ... Scratch.'

For a long time Maarten did not answer. 'Salem,' he said at length, thickly. He'd heard the rumours. 'You came here from Salem.'

Mercy bit her lip and dipped her chin.

'Oh.' Maarten blinked hard, trying not to feel the skin crawling on his spine. 'Shall I fetch Pastor Arne?'

Her voice was only a whisper. 'That will make it worse for us all. Let me deal with him on my own.'

He felt as if all his joints had seized and he could hardly move. 'As you wish.' He groped his way to the shed door, then paused. 'But I'm not leaving you.'

'Husband –'

'Enough. Do what you must, but I'm not running away. You're my wife. I will stay with you.'

It was a good thing that the servants were all away that day, because there was nothing for them to do. The hens had stopped laying. The cows refused to come into the milking shed, and instead clustered up at the top end of the pasture, facing outwards like buffalo sensing wolves. Kindling which had been dry the day before refused to catch and no fire could be lit in the house. Crows circled overhead, but no birds flitted down to pick through the chaff in the yard or steal from the feed bins. In fact the only animals that behaved with bravado were the frogs in the pond, who kept up an ascending chorus of croaks all day – and even that was unnerving, because frogs call in spring, and this was the fall of the year.

There was no breeze all day, just a thick breathless warmth.

At sunset, as the golden light lay across the stubble of the meadows and glinted through the trunks of the red oaks, the frogs fell silent. And up the track to Maarten Gansevoort's farm came a man riding on a black horse.

They stood out on the porch to receive him, the two of them by then the only living souls on the farm. Mercy looked more composed now, Maarten noticed, and he wondered if she had been dreading his reaction more than the news she'd given him. She was still pale, but there were two spots of colour high on her cheeks as if she'd pinched them. She'd been silent all day. The rider drew closer until they could see him and his mount clearly. The horse was a tall stallion as black as charcoal. The man was dressed in a long black coat too, and his unruly hair was the same glossy jet as his mount's, but he was pale of face. He was tall and slim and rather young, with wicked arched brows and dancing violet eyes. He swung down from the saddle and spread his hands. 'Mercy!'

She bobbed a curtsey.

'*Meneer* Scratch,' said Maarten, not bowing or nodding or holding out his hand. Just letting him know.

'And this must be your husband. How pleasant to meet you, Goodman Gansevoort. Mercy, it's been twenty years. Have you missed me?'

It struck Maarten that this handsome young man did not look old enough to have met anyone but his mother's teat twenty years back, but he said nothing.

'I have been happy, sir,' said Mercy faintly.

'Little Mercy Martin.' He looked her up and down. 'Then Mercy Lafferty. Now Mercy Gansevoort. You look better than ever. Don't say I don't look after my own: you've prospered.' He winked broadly at Maarten Gansevoort. 'Only the innocent hang.'

Maarten would have replied sternly, but he was distracted by his wife's reaction; she'd flushed and then moistened her lips with the tip of her tongue. He'd never seen her look so disconcerted, not even on their wedding night. It made the hair on his neck prickle.

'Now, will you not ask me in to sit with you?'

'Do you need to be invited?' Maarten Gansevoort growled.

The stranger arched a brow, amused. 'Strictly speaking, no. But you should be pleased when I observe the social niceties.'

'Please, sir,' said Mercy, her voice a little husky, 'do us honour and enter.'

'How hospitable of you. I'd be delighted.' The stranger followed Mercy over the threshold and Maarten brought up the rear. He could not help sneaking a suspicious look at the other man's feet, but only polished leather boots peeked from under the ankle-length hem of his coat.

One last glance overhead showed him that the crows were wheeling about the building in a tight circle, in silence.

Maarten Gansevoort's house was a big, comfortable one, every board pegged and sound, with a kitchen hall for cooking and eating, and beds and stores kept in the rooms beyond and overhead. Mercy directed their visitor to the high-backed oak settle by the fire, and Maarten sat himself awkwardly at the head of the table. 'Will you drink, sir?' she asked in an odd voice. 'We have buttermilk and small beer.'

'I'll take a hot cider.'

She shrugged, helplessly. 'I'm sorry, sir. I haven't been able to light the fire today.'

He shook his head and waved one hand negligently. Flames leapt up in the hearth, filling the room with light, and Maarten jumped before mastering himself. The logs spat, shrank and turned to glowing embers; in a moment the fire looked for all the world like it had been burning all day. He could feel the heat fill the room. The stranger leant forwards to ram the poker into the heart of the embers. 'That'll do it.'

Sweat trickled down Maarten Gansevoort's spine, but Mercy didn't seem surprised at all. She turned away to the cider keg and filled an earthenware flagon. Then she wrapped her hand in her apron and pulled out the poker; its tip was already, impossibly, starting to glow. Carefully she lowered the metal point into the drink, and Maarten heard the liquid hiss and bubble.

To present the drink to their guest, she went to her knees before him, proffering the vessel with both hands, head bowed and eyes lowered, her full skirts belling out around her. Maarten felt shock pulse through his body at that sight. She's so graceful, was his incongruous thought. He knew his wife as a capable, boisterous women who took no nonsense from anyone. To see her behaving so submissively, so out of character towards another man made his guts twist and his blood race.

'She's beautiful, isn't she?' said the stranger, accepting the cup. 'Oh, Goodman Gansevoort, you should have seen her in her youth, under moonlight, as naked as Eve.'

Maarten felt the blood charge to his face. Mercy made not a sound, but watched their guest from under her lashes.

'Her eyes wide and her lips inexpertly rouged,' the stranger reminisced. 'The slick of five women painting her face and the pearls of six men strewn upon her spread thighs. Oh, you should have seen her face, Goodman Gansevoort, as I revealed myself to her for the first time. Such dread and such eagerness as she abased herself, spreading her pert and pretty buttocks with her own hands –'

'Enough!' Maarten groaned, slamming his open palm on the table. 'Stop shaming her!'

'Shame?' The stranger cocked an eyebrow. 'Does she look ashamed?'

She did not. The lambent, poised expression on her face made jealousy coil in Maarten's guts like a nest of garter snakes.

'Mercy, kiss my boot,' said the stranger gently, and without hesitation she bent to press her mouth to the foot he presented to her. Her lips parted, her pink tongue licked at the dark leather. She kissed eagerly, without restraint. He sipped his cider and watched her coolly. She lapped at his instep; then he tilted his foot. His boot was rather more pointed at the toe than was fashionable in these parts, Maarten saw, and she opened her mouth to take it in as far as she could, working her lips around the width. His sole must be resting on her tongue, Maarten realised. He'd walked across the farmyard in those boots but she showed no distaste. Her eyes in fact were lifted for the first time to gaze steadily upon her erstwhile master's face, in perfect openness and surrender.

Maarten Gansevoort's heart felt like it would burst his ribs at that sight.

'Now tell him, Mercy,' said the stranger, 'why you signed yourself to me.' He withdrew his foot from her mouth, and the momentary gape of her lips was obscene before she licked them. 'Tell him.'

'When I was young,' she whispered, eyes once more down-cast as if focused far away, 'there was nothing but toil and fear. No frivolity, no indulgence, no joy. Even their God was dark and bitter, and I hungered for colour and delight. And some came to me and whispered that there was a master who would promise those things. So I went with them. I knew what I was doing. They debauched me and I was their willing whore. It was the first time in my life I was not a dull drab thing, not just a servant, not just a girl-child. And then he came to me.'

Maarten tugged at his plain linen collar, releasing some of the heat.

'You see?' the stranger asked his host pleasantly. 'Such memories she has. And one of the few things I have in common with your kind, good people, is – let us say – nostalgia. A capacity to regret what has been lost. I miss my sweet Mercy.

So with your permission, Goodman Gansevoort ...' He stood, setting his flagon aside.

'What?' said Maarten thickly, as the stranger held out his hand to Mercy, who placed her fingers in his.

'I intend to make a cuckold of you, friend.'

Maarten opened his mouth but no words came out.

'We will retire to the bedchamber to spare your feelings, Goodman. Of course you will hear her scream her pleasure; I can hardly prevent that. She was always most vocal, I remember.'

Maarten gripped the table edge as if he would overturn it.

'Maarten,' said Mercy swiftly: 'Be at peace. Please, my husband.' For a moment her eyes focused warningly on him, pinning him to his seat, but then he seemed to slip her mind. Her gaze turned back to their guest and she led him away to the inner room, and the door closed.

Maarten Gansevoort was in agony. He felt as if his stomach was full of knots. The room with its blazing fire was suddenly too warm, so he stood and flung off his woollen jacket and paced about the floor. He went to find his flintlock musket, and even got so far as to reach for the lead, but his hands fumbled uselessly with the box and he gave up. He scratched at his sweating chest and rubbed angrily at his crotch, sickened to find a most disloyal tumescence which he immediately put down to anger. He could not believe he was permitting another man – or anything in man's form – to take his wife from under his nose like that, no matter that man's status or puissance. He could not believe that she seemed so willing, when their marriage had been so warmly content. He could not bring himself to face the confession she'd made, though it rolled around the margins of his mind painfully. He put his head in his hands and groaned, tried to pray but recoiled from the words. How could he pray when he had let such a guest into his house?

Without intending it, he suddenly found that he was holding his breath, listening. Nicholas Scratch had been right about Mercy's tendency to cry out in the throes of rutting; often he'd had to stifle her noises with his hand or the corner of the quilt, lest she disturb the whole household. When she fornicated she did it without restraint. It was one of the things that made his blood burn for her.

Reaching a decision, Maarten Gansevoort slipped off his blunt-toed shoes and crept on stockinged feet towards the inner door. He knew every board in the house he'd built, and not one of them creaked under his weight. He reached the bedchamber door and crouched down. The handle was only a smooth dowel that ran through from one side of the sliding latch to the other, and hadn't been pegged in place. With much hesitation and care, he pulled the stick clean out of the door, leaving a round hole to which he applied his eye.

He could see quite clearly. The chamber with its shuttered windows, lit by candlelight. The big bed that he had made himself for his first marriage, spread with the cream quilt that Mercy had brought as part of her trousseau. Mercy standing at the side of the bed, facing the door, the stranger's bare arms about her from behind. He had evidently removed his clothes, though Maarten could see little of him. Mercy's own clothes were in disarray, her bodice unlaced, her shift pulled down from her shoulders, her big freckled breasts bare and cupped in the stranger's groping hands, her plump brown nipples being plucked and flicked and pinched. Her neck was twisted at an angle and there was a look on her face of such painful need that Maarten Gansevoort caught his breath. Her mouth formed a quivering 'O' as if she were moulding it about some virile member. She writhed her sumptuous hips, grinding her ass cheeks into the stranger's crotch, and covered his hands with her own as he mauled at her.

Nicholas Scratch licked at her white throat, chuckling, then turned her in his hands and pushed her to her knees. Suddenly his body was visible, the unblemished body of a muscular young man, perfect in every way. His stiff stood up rampantly erect from a nest of black curls, dark with blood against the paler skin of his thighs and belly. He took himself in hand and laid the other hand on Mercy's head as if in blasphemous blessing. But all he was doing was pressing her lower. She put her face to the fat pouch of his scrotum and kissed it fervently.

Maarten Gansevoort loosed the drawstring of his breeches and slipped his hand inside his clothes, ashamed beyond words, yet aroused so much he could no longer wait. His own member was hot and sticky and as hard as smoked meat. He stroked himself, feeling his balls clench, feeling the length in his hand grow thicker and longer with every beat of his heart. To see his wife kneeling obediently before a stranger, to see the plump out-thrust of her skirted behind, the eager caresses of her hands upon his hard thighs, the flash of her tongue as she licked all the way up his cock and then took it in her mouth, slipping it deep into her throat – it was unbearable. The slurping noise she made as she sucked him, the look of satisfaction on the stranger's face, the way his hand twisted in her hair, the bob of her head as she rose and fell upon him with unholy appetite ...

The stranger's eyes lifted to the door. His expression slipped from pleasure to triumph. Then the door cracked its latch and slammed wide open, back against the wall, splintering its hinges. Maarten Gansevoort was revealed kneeling in the doorway with his breeches open and his stiff in his fist.

Mercy's eyes opened wide, and for a moment she detached from the false idol to which she was giving worship, leaving it plum dark but shining with her spittle. Maarten felt as if the floor must open up and plunge him into the fiery pit of hell at that very moment.

'I see you've come to lend us your blessing, friend,' said the stranger, greatly amused. He gestured. 'Enter.' Then, when Maarten only gasped and goggled, his voice hardened to a silky command. 'You must be half a witch already, Goodman Gansevoort. There is a broomstick between your legs and I see by your face you have been riding it hard. Join us now. On your knees.'

His dignity gone, without any other recourse, Maarten shuffled forwards on his knees almost to Mercy's side. His whole body was aflame with shame.

'See now. Your wife was just about to take Communion,' said the stranger, directing her back to the glistening plum of his cock.

With deliberate showmanship he delved deep down her throat, pumping long and smooth, pulling out to show his full length all wet from her suckling, then plunging in once more, all the time Maarten watching, unable to tear his eyes away. He knew when the stranger came off because Mercy nearly choked, eyes watering, nostrils flaring, struggling for breath as her throat worked frantically to receive his outpourings. When Nicholas let her go her mouth came away as milky and sticky as a nurseling's.

'Kiss her,' the stranger ordered in a voice both quiet and implacable.

Maarten leant in, his lips finding hers. She was still gasping for breath. Her mouth was soft and wet, her tongue slippery under his, and he was shaking so hard he felt he might collapse. He could taste it – the stranger's spend – sharp and salty, and he wanted to die for shame. Then her hand fumbled past his and found his cock. She stroked it as if comforting a frightened and frantic animal, and he groaned into her mouth even as tears spilled down her cheeks.

'Now stand up Goodman Gansevoort, and prepare your wife for me. Remove her clothes and lay her upon the marriage bed.'

Maarten's eyes met hers. He read in them regret and fear, but above all a terrible selfish need. It was too late for her to hide her desires from the man she had pledged herself to. Her promise of faithfulness was worthless. She nodded almost imperceptibly, urging him on in the debauchment of their vows. So he rose and drew her to her feet, and completed the unlacing of her bodice, the discarding of her petticoats and shift, revealing to her master the full curves that he had thought belonged to him alone, the creamy swells of hip and buttock, the copper tangle of her puss. His hands quivered as he caressed her warm skin, feeling her gasp and heave to his touch, all for another man. Then he pressed her back and laid her upon the bed, climbing up beside her.

'Touch her,' whispered the stranger. 'Touch her slit.'

Her thighs were already loose; when he slipped his hand over her mound they parted wantonly. Her eyes were not on him; her attention was raptly fixed upon the stiff of the stranger, which stood as engorged as ever. It had not drooped for a moment after the man's first crisis. Maarten parted the petals of her puss with his fingertips.

'Is she wet?'

'Yes.' Maarten cleared his throat. 'She is, sir.'

'Put your fingers in her quim. Tell me how she is.'

He obeyed, half closing his eyes. 'She is soft, and wet and

hot. She sucks at my fingers.' Mercy moved under him, moaning. His own cock, a goodly length by most accounts but meagre fare against his guest's weapon, was as hard as wood.

'Is she ready for my quimstake, Goodman Gansevoort?' The stranger ran his hand lovingly up his beam. 'Push your hand in deep. Is your wife ready for me?'

'Ah. Oh yes.' Mercy's wet grip undulated around his fingers. He could smell her sex.

'Then go kneel behind her head and hold her wrists.'

Maarten took his place as he was told, drawing out her arms over her head. Her big firm breasts heaved, the nipples pointing at the roof beams. He wanted to touch them, but he had not been given permission. So he watched as the other man knelt between her splayed thighs, scooped his hands around her waist, lifted her backside from the bed and impaled her slowly upon his cock. Her back arched almost beyond endurance, Mercy wailed. Maarten pinned her wrists to the coverlet, keeping her stretched, sweat running down his temples as he watched her take her pounding. It was a display of such strength and endurance that his heart was in his mouth. That length of meat rammed into her, deep and rhythmic, pushing her body to its limits. Nicholas Scratch's face was wreathed in a triumphant smile, candle-light dancing in his eyes, every stroke both a master's punishment upon a runaway servant and a reward for her shameless concupiscence.

She was more beautiful in that moment than he had ever seen her, and that realisation hurt him to the core. It was as if he were seeing the real her for the first time, as if she'd kept the best part of herself hidden from him. He would have liked to have spent his seed in her open mouth or poured it out as an offering on her wobbling breasts. He would have liked to have done it as the stranger filled her with his cream, but he knew himself unworthy, so he only watched as Nicholas Scratch showed his appreciation with a facility that no mortal man could ever possess. He came with teeth bared and his throat stretched, barking his triumph, and he did it over and over again, as often as Mercy did, jetting into her wet cauldron and laughing with satisfaction as she was reduced to heaving, wailing, incoherent exhaustion. Then he dropped her to the bed and stood back, stroking a cock that stood as proud as ever. 'Turn her over,' he said. He hadn't even broken a sweat.

'What?'

'I wish to sodomise your wife. Have you ever tried that, friend?'

'Of course not,' he whispered. 'It's a sin.' His heart was hammering.

Nicholas Scratch smiled. 'Roll her.'

So Maarten did, and Mercy did not try to resist. She buried her flushed face in the rumpled quilt. Her behind was as pale and round as a full moon.

'Spread her thighs.'

He did. The smell of sex was thick and heady and made him want to plunge himself into her swollen slit. Shame and lust roiled in his ballocks, threatening to spume forth.

'Now kiss her brown eye for me.'

Maarten looked up, startled.

'Do you think I'm going in dry, friend? That's hardly the action of a gentleman. Get her wet and open. Use your tongue.' His smile had not lost its menace.

So Maarten obeyed, bending to press his face between her cheeks and kiss that which he'd never touched before, tasting her sharp meatiness, testing the muscular pucker of her hole. He had no masculine dignity left to guard now, after all, having given his wife up to the stranger. He had only shame and submission and a wild, sickened arousal. Still he was shocked by how easily she opened to his tongue, as if she had been waiting years to surrender her most filthy self to invasion. He could not push his tongue in far enough to fill her. He rose gasping from her slippery cleft.

'Good. Now, Goodman Gansevoort, you must moisten me too.' Nicholas Scratch ran his thumb over the turgid head of his cock. 'Come here.'

Maarten's head swam. If sodomising a woman was a sin for which one might burn, turning to a man would be to invite the very wrath of God. And to suck this fiend for the purpose of buggery and adultery combined ...

Maarten's cock twitched even as his stomach roiled. He wet his lips. Eyes burning, he crawled into position and opened his mouth, for the first time in his life, to another man's member. It was solid and hot and slightly sticky; he tasted first his wife's familiar tang, then the alien taint of a man's seed. He shut his eyes and sucked. His stiff throbbed.

'Good.' The stranger's voice was almost tender. 'This is what you are good for, is it not? Now, friend, put me to your wife. As if I were a bull to a virgin heifer: you have done such things before, I'm sure. Guide me to her with your own hand.'

Turning to Mercy, Maarten saw that she was watching over her shoulder, taking in all his humiliation avidly. Nicholas got up behind her on the bed and Maarten took that thick length in his unsteady hand and angled the cock to the dark well of her anus, prick and ass cleft both lubricated with his saliva, her hole pliant and receptive, blossoming open under his duress. She wailed as the stranger's cock penetrated her, and the sound made his heart soar.

'Now watch, friend. See how it is done.'

He would have given anything to have been the one fucking that upturned ass, gripping those pale hips, shafting that tight forbidden hole. At that angle her bottom looked as round as a pumpkin, her waist tiny, her hair a tumbled harlot's mess. But he could only watch. She was all receptive femininity, but she was responding to a greater male than he.

'Yes! Yes!' she screamed in her ecstasy.

He watched as Nicholas fucked her then pulled out, leaving snail trails of pearly spend upon her quivering ass. Mercy collapsed face down.

'May I?' he whispered, bewitched by the pink gape of her still-dilated hole. His cock was a rod of iron in his hand.

Nicholas shook back his hair. 'No. But you have one last task. One you are worthy of. You may clean her up, Goodman. Clean my seed from your beloved wife, with your tongue.'

Eyes blurring, he bent to his appointed task. His wife oozed another man's cream from both orifices, and he could do nothing else than lap it up. His tongue got lost amongst her deep soft folds. The taste and the slippery mess of it were unforgettable, burning his mind. It disgusted and excited him to the depths of his soul. He could not understand his arousal or bear to think about it, but nonetheless it was stronger than his Christian conscience. When he felt Nicholas's hands on his backside, pulling down his loosened breeches, he sobbed in relief. Of course this was how it had to end; this was the ultimate humiliation. Having already surrendered his wife without a fight to another man, having lusted over her dishonour, having helped that man in plundering her body in the foulest of ways – this was the deepest sin that was also its own chastisement. He felt his buttocks being parted by firm hands. He felt the wetness as Nicholas spat onto his anus. He felt the blunt probing of that cock – that perfect, inhumanly virile cock – and he did not clench against it as it bored into him. He groaned out load, not bothering to disguise his pain or his surrender: he had no pride left. On hands and knees, sweat springing out from every pore, he yielded, deep rhythmic groans issuing from his chest. He was aware that Mercy had twisted over beneath him and was staring.

Of course, he told himself, it must be most gratifying to her, to see her wretched husband fucked by her lover. His prick jerked, dripping.

He was aware that she had reached to grip the stiff prong of his hanging cock and fondle his balls. The tugging on his stiff was an immense relief. He felt himself opening out internally, the rush of blood through his veins, and – even as a part of him was appalled that he should stoop so low as not just to be buggered, but to enjoy his sodomisation – he let loose in a gush, spurting over his wife, adding the sin of Onan to every other.

Then he collapsed forwards over her, his legs too weak to hold him against the pounding from above. Nicholas Scratch bore him down, thrusting ruthlessly, then erupted inside him, his semen as cold as the icy depths of hell.

She looked into both their faces as the two men came. Her husband's face was twisted, almost unrecognisable, his eyes closed as if to hide his soul, but her master's face was wide-eyed and exultant. His participation in the pleasures of the flesh would always be halfway to a joke for him, she thought, an ironic critique of his original nature. But they were both wonderful, and the sight of them together made her sorely used quim tingle. In their spasms they pitched forwards over her, and as the weight of both men slammed down they were so heavy that Mercy thought the breath would be crushed from her chest.

But then her master threw back his head, laughing, and turned to light: a cold blue celestial light that filled the room, illuminating in that brief moment *everything*. The cobwebs hanging in the corner. The rat droppings by the skirting board. The knobbly knuckle on her left hand where a cow kick had broken the bone years ago. The slackening billows of her belly, and the dirt in the ingrained lines on Maarten's flushed face. Every dust mote hanging in the air; every particle of their frail mortality.

Then in another heartbeat her master was gone and they lay once more under kindly candlelight, alone in their marriage bed.

Maarten made a noise of shock and tried to look over his shoulder, but Mercy threw her arms around him. 'He's gone, husband. Gone.' He let out a long breath. She held him tight to her, talking softly and slowly as she might to a frightened child. 'Away over the black tree tops and under the moon, gone to fright the sheep in the fields and curdle the milk in the byres, gone to pinch the flesh of maidens black and blue, gone to whisper in the ears of sleeping men and find who will listen to him and open their eyes. He dances under the full moon on the hilltops among the stones raised by the Indians, and comes at the call of those who dare face him. He is here, and then he is gone. He opens our guarded souls like a man prising oysters. For he is the light-bringer, and what he illuminates is our secret selves, our hidden dreams, those things we do not admit even to ourselves. He takes away our pride and gives us truth in exchange. Not shame, husband, truth. It is up to us whether we can live with it.'

She paused, her heart pounding in her throat, but Maarten did not reply. He lay slack and heavy against her, his breathing slow. She bit her lip. He had fallen asleep, taking the easy plunge into darkness, fleeing from the light and the shock. It might not last long, but at least he had neither sprung from the bed, nor struck her, nor raged against himself, nor fled in horror and recrimination. He had fallen asleep, exhausted. And that, she told herself, was a good omen.

The Red Thread

When I awake the boat and all its sailors have gone. I am completely alone. I scramble up the scrubby hillside behind the beach and look out across the dark waves. Yes, there is the black sail, diminishing into the distance. I wave my arms and scream and call him back, but it's no use and I know it. They haven't forgotten me; I was in full view on the sands all the time. The Prince of Athens has abandoned me on this island.

I put my head in my hands and weep.

I had grown up with the fact of Asterion's imprisonment. It was an unquestioned part of my small world: the monthly presentations of the tributes, the nightly feedings, the sudden muffled sound of him roaring in frustration or fury from beneath any random floor of the palace. It was not something that seemed strange to me as a child, or that moved me either to fear or to pity. In fact I liked it. People tell me that even when I was very small I used to lean over the edge of the central well, the one point in the palace where one could look down into the basement below, and watch for him. It was the one place he could look up from too, to see the blue sky and the sun, or the stars after which he was named. Everywhere else, the Palace Below was in darkness. So he would often be visible in the crescent shadow, squatted on his haunches, gazing back up at us.

I would giggle and reach out to him even as a baby in my mother's arms, they tell me.

When the oracle first advised my father to lock Asterion up for the protection of us all, he had his finest craftsman design the place of incarceration. The rock-hewn cellars beneath every palace room, where grain and fleeces and water were stored safe from the burning sun of summer, were all knocked together to make a single basement. Everything of value was removed. Cisterns were sunk. Trapdoors were nailed shut and plastered over. By the time the workers had finished Asterion had a palace all to himself, as extensive as the King's own palace above it, but one that existed in eternal night. Only two entrances were left open: the central light-well in an inner courtyard, which had once been a pit in which dogs were set on bears, and a door at the back of the palace compound that opened onto a steep stair. That is still the route down which prisoners are driven.

There is one other entrance to the Palace Below, but I'm the only one who knows it.

They had to force Asterion into his new realm with spear points and torches, they say. Even then, when he was only entering into the full strength of his youth, he was too dangerous for any one man to control, and he harboured a particular aggression towards the King. They shut the door behind him and threw oaken bars across it and set guards, yet for days if you passed that door you could hear him thudding his head against the wood.

This was all before my time, of course. I've only picked up palace gossip.

Every night the royal family assembles about the central well. It is my father's one act of contrition. A rope has been run over a roof beam and with this is lowered a basket containing bread and wine and cheese, and a bushel of whatever fruits are in season. Asterion has a hearty appetite. Sometimes he will speak, asking for things he desires: a blanket, a lamp, a songbird in a cage, a wreath of the wild roses that grow on the hills, more straw for his bed. His voice is deep, as you might expect from such a broad chest, but surprisingly melodic. My father is not unkind, though he never agrees to send down any palace slave. He learnt that lesson long ago, and if Asterion wishes to be entertained with the lyre then the musician stands at the top of the well and Asterion must stand beneath, out of reach. The only humans who enter the Palace Below are the youths given in tribute by Athens, which was laid siege to years back by my father's armies and capitulated rather than burn.

I too go below, of course. I have no memory of the first time it happened, though the story is familiar from countless retellings. I had as a very small child been in the habit of lying upon the edge of the pit and talking to Asterion, or singing to him, or recounting the stories of gods and heroes that our tutor had had us learn. Asterion did not deign to speak to me, but that did not seem to matter. I was never in the least afraid of him. One day my nurse turned to find me gone. There was panic, and a search, and eventually guards were sent into the basement in a squad, armed to the teeth and bearing torches. Asterion has always been wary of fire, though impervious to so much other pain. They found him and me together in an antechamber under a guttering lamp. I was sat upon his broad knee, singing to him the song of Europa. I must have thought, in my naivety, that the theme would appeal to him. The guards stopped, aghast. One swipe of Asterion's huge fist would have been enough to kill me outright; they could not snatch me from danger. But Asterion only glowered and lifted me from his knee, setting me on my feet before he shambled away into the darkness.

My nurse was torn apart between horses in the *agora*, for that carelessness.

I must have fallen, or jumped, that first time. He must have caught me. Later on I know I used the rope to shin down.

I'm certain that that was the time the King realised that I was my mother's true child, as wilful as she. According to the family historians she was a daughter of Helios the sun god, and that thread of divinity has come down the bloodline. We are not constrained like other people. We are not afraid. My father was only a king, and knew better than to set himself against the gods. He consecrated me to Artemis, thinking that would save him from finding me a husband, and let me grow up how I would.

So the years wore on. Nothing changed in Asterion's world. Every year a ship with black sails would arrive from Athens and the tribute would be offloaded, seven young men and seven young women a part of it. Every full moon one of those captives would be taken to the back stairs and sent down into the Palace Below. The noises they made would be covered up by the playing of musicians. It made no difference to Asterion what time of year it was, because where he lived it was always dark and always cool.

Upstairs, of course, things did change. My father remarried: a mousy woman from Thera whom I despised. I grew taller and stronger and changed in other ways. And I discovered another entrance to the Palace Below – a cupboard around the corner from my room that had once been a stairwell. It now contained old masks and props from the Bull Festival and was rarely entered, but at the back, I discovered, was a badly mortared brick wall and when I pulled out enough bricks I found a descending shaft choked with rubble. Surreptitiously, one piece at a time, I removed that rubble, enough to make a narrow slot I could squeeze down into the dark below, where it came out in an obscure corner of some abandoned storeroom, behind a stack of roof tiles. It became my private entrance and I never told anyone, not even Asterion, that this was how I gained access.

You will note that I never had any plan to clear the stair completely. I did not want to release Asterion into the world; I knew his capacity for violence. And, though it shames me to acknowledge it, I was proud to be his only link to the world above. Beneath the innocence of my pleasure in his friendship was a more selfish pleasure in having him all to myself.

And we *were* friends. It might seem impossible to believe that such a man could crave company of more than the most basic sort, but Asterion was lonely. He was gruff and short-tempered, but he tolerated my girlish chatter and my teasing and even my clambering upon his frame. He listened to my stories and complaints, and when I grew older I passed on to him palace gossip and news of the outside world. I treated him carelessly, only visiting when the mood took me, blind to his feelings. Until one day I tried to sit on his knee and he brushed me off.

'No. Stop that.'

'But I want to sit there!'

'You are too heavy now, Ari.'

'Too heavy?' I was outraged. I slapped his huge thigh, as hard as a slab of oak. 'You mean you aren't strong enough to take my weight on your skinny legs?'

He shifted uneasily. 'Don't be silly.'

'Don't you like me sitting on your knee?'

'No, I don't.'

I put my fists on my hips. 'Why not?'

'You wouldn't understand. You're too young.'

I glared. 'I'm too heavy *and* too young?' That made him growl deep in his chest, but my pout gave way to a smile. 'Don't you like my bottom, Asterion? Isn't it soft enough for your lap?' I turned my back briefly, pulling my skirt tight so I could wriggle it at him.

'Ari!' His warning rumble was like distant thunder.

But I was all heavy-lidded eyes and sly smile now. 'Why don't you want me sitting on your lap, Asterion? Are you scared I might touch something I shouldn't? You scared of my soft little bottom pressing against your naughty –'

'Ari. You are too young to play this sort of game.'

'Too young?' I repeated, cupping the curve of my breast. My tight bodice nipped in my waist but left both of them bare and enticingly framed, and I knew it. 'Have you not noticed these?'

'Stop this. You are just a child.'

I bared my teeth. 'I am not! If it wasn't for this stinking vow to Artemis I'd be married by now. I'd have a husband and a baby!'

'Don't mock the goddess. She will hear you.'

'She won't.' I cast a disparaging glance at the ceiling. 'She walks the hills and doesn't come down beneath the earth. I think she's scared of you.'

'Don't. The gods are merciless, Ari.'

I stuck my bottom lip out. 'Let me sit in your lap. I want to.'

'Why?'

'I like it. Go *on*.'

He glared at me, his exhalations loud. But he didn't stop me moving in to his knees. This time I didn't sit demurely on one knee, though; I picked up my long skirt and straddled both of them, facing him. His legs were hard under my thighs and bottom.

'Don't you like this?' I asked in my meekest voice.

'You shouldn't be doing it.'

'I'm not a baby any more, you know. Look.' I gathered the

flounced linen folds in my hands, drawing them up my pale thighs. Asterion looked down between us and seemed to stop breathing, as I revealed the dark delta at my groin. 'I have fur.'

His brown eyes widened.

'Would you like to touch it?' I asked softly.

Very slowly, he shook his head.

With a *moue* of disappointment I let the cloth fall again, veiling my immodestly spread thighs. 'Can I see yours?'

He groaned. 'Ari ...'

'It's not like it would be the first phallus I've seen, silly,' I chided him. 'I've been to the games, and seen the bull-dancers. And Cholios, when he's on guard outside my room, he always touches himself when I walk past. And his sticks out under his chiton. He rubs it like it itches, but that just makes it stick up harder.' With great daring I put out my hand to touch the bulge beneath Asterion's tunic. He was wearing the simplest of short chitons, under one shoulder and pinned over the other, with no belt. Undyed linen, it had the labrys pattern of the royal household worked in red thread around the border. It might even have been a piece I'd woven myself; weaving was after all the principle duty of the women of the palace. 'I just want to see.'

'Why?'

'To see whether you're the same as other men.'

It was easy to pull the cloth aside; he did not stop me. A sigh escaped my lips. His phallus lay flopped in a curve on his upper thigh, smooth and soft-looking like the finest kidskin, but stirring restlessly even as I watched. His foreskin pouted, wrinkly.

'Am I the same, then?' He sounded a little bitter.

'You look bigger. Can I touch it?'

'No.'

'Why not?'

Strain was audible in his voice as he said, 'Because if you touch it, it might get angry, and then I will hurt you.'

I bit my lip. 'Will you hurt me *with* that?'

His chest heaved. 'Yes.'

'Oh.'

'You are only little.'

I fiddled with the edge of my bodice, stroking my breast. 'What if I were to stroke it very gently – would it get angry then?'

'I fear so.' His phallus stirred, straightening as it filled out. It trailed a smudge of wetness across his thigh.

'But I can stroke you here.' I ran my hands down his chest. 'You like that, don't you? It doesn't make you angry?'

'Ah,' he grunted.

'And I don't mind you stroking me, Asterion.' I took his hands and placed them on my breasts. They were warm, and they cupped and enfolded me. They felt so strong that I was washed with dizziness, and pressed myself into his caresses. 'That feels nice, see. Just stroking.'

'Yes.'

'Shall I tell you a story?' I wrapped one hand around his phallus. It was definitely bigger now, and almost standing upright, and as I squeezed experimentally I felt it harden under my hand. Asterion did not object; he seemed mesmerised by my breasts, which he was playing with. I'd never touched a man's phallus before. I was delighted how warm it was, how silky to the touch, how alive. My fingers could not quite circle its girth. It was difficult to take in all the new sensations and to talk at the same time. 'This is the story: back in the Golden Age, when the gods had first made human beings, men and women were the same as each other and everybody was happy. There was lots of food. There was no fighting. But there were no babies either and although everyone lived for hundreds of years, people started to die eventually and the gods got worried. So they took all the people one night and Hypnos put them to sleep, and Hermes cut a piece out of every woman and stuck it onto a man. Since then people have been able to make babies, but the wounds have never healed properly – women still bleed sometimes. And *everyone* is unhappy. Women miss the flesh that used to be inside them and long to open their legs and take it back; the phalli are desperate to return to the bodies they came from, so all men want to do is stick it into any woman they meet.'

'Who told you that story?' he rumbled.

Both my hands were now sliding up and down his length. He was big – really big – and his ruddy helm was poking from its cowl. 'Just the servant women, while we were weaving. They always talk about that sort of thing.' I didn't tell him that this stroking motion was one that had been demonstrated with much ribald laughter on a wooden shuttle. I was most gratified that it seemed to be working, and that the column of flesh in my hands was no less hard now than the wood had been.

His voice, when he spoke, was oddly thick too. 'Well, they are wrong. Women do not welcome the entry of the phallus.'

I licked my lips. 'No, they're right. I can feel it inside me: an emptiness. A wanting. Sometimes it's so horrible I want to cry. I have put my fingers in that hole just to make it feel better. Would you put your finger inside me now, Asterion?'

Without a word he slipped one hand between my open thighs, cupping the fuzz of my mound in his big palm. His middle finger slid between the lips of my split.

'You are wet, Ari.'

'Yes. The first time I played with myself I got so wet I thought I had brought on my bleeding. But this feels good, Asterion.'

'Good?' He seemed bemused. One finger, seeking the source

of the moisture, plunged into mouth of my sex, sinking deep. I whimpered. 'Am I hurting you?' he breathed.

'No! Oh, that is good! It feels nice when I'm filled up like that.' I had to whisper my next words: 'I know what you do to the Athenians.'

His eyes widened, showing rims of white.

'I would like to feel your phallus inside me.'

'No ... If I did that it would hurt you. I am too big.'

'I know.' I was squirming on his hand. 'But I want it anyway. Do you want to put it in me?'

He made a funny noise in his throat. 'Squeeze harder,' he ordered, 'stroke faster.'

I increased my efforts until I was actually tugging his phallus. 'If I tell you something, do you promise not to tell anyone?'

He moaned assent, his eyes rolling. Sweat was springing up on his chest.

'I like to have something inside me. Fingers or a weaving shuttle. But what feels best of all is when I do that and touch myself at the front here at the same time. There is a piece of flesh the size of a pea ... and when I do both those things I am taken by the gods, Asterion. I come.'

'Women do not come.' His big frame was shaking.

'We do. It is like a wave curling over and crashing on rocks. And I can do it over and over. Once I tried to see how often, and I got to a score before I fell asleep exhausted. But – this is the bit you must never let my father know – Do you promise?'

'I promise.'

'I needed something the right shape and size to put inside me, so I took up the statue of Artemis from the shrine in my room, the one made of olive wood from Delos, and I fucked myself with it, Asterion. It was all knobbly, and when I pulled it out it had my blood on it. I promised her my maidenhead and then I gave it to her.'

'Oh gods ...'

'But that's not the worst thing. After that I wanted to come again so this time I stuck that statue up my bottom and I came with the goddess in my *arse*.'

With a bellow that made the room ring, Asterion spurted seed between my fingers. It slopped on my belly and the undersides of my breasts in big wet splashes. I was completely taken by surprise, and all I could do was hold on while he strained and quivered beneath me, his head thrown back and his throat distended. I rubbed the slippery gooey stuff over the head of his shaft.

He seemed to take a long time to come back to me.

'See,' I said, unable to stop my voice shaking. 'I should have taken my dress off; now you've got it all messed up.' I scooped at the gobbets on my breasts, trying to wipe them off but smearing them instead.

His chest heaving, he held me with his glare. Sweat glistened in the hollow of his throat. 'Show me,' he demanded. 'Show me how you come.'

I nodded dumbly. Then I licked his seed off my fingers. It tasted grassy and sweet. I was pleased I liked it so much, and he seemed astonished that I would lick it up so eagerly. Plunging my wet fingers obediently between my thighs, I began to stir myself. Asterion pushed me further back on his knees and laid me back in his hands, holding me safely over the floor. Working my flesh, I felt the first gathering of my storm, and over my own gasps I heard his harsh breathing and little grunts. Soon I felt him reach between my parted legs and manoeuvre the head of his spent but still heavy phallus to the split wet flesh beneath my moving fingers. As my inner waves rose to mountains he pushed his helm into my tight slot. His sweat dripped onto my shaking breasts and he stooped to lick me, making me gasp with pleasure. He was right; his phallus was too big even for a deflowered maiden. He could only press in an inch or two, even when I fought to accommodate him. But I came squealing and kicking, my sex clenching around his fat girth.

That was only the first occasion, of course. In time he taught me to accept his whole length, administered with full vigour, in every position. My visits were sources of sustained and bruising mutual pleasure. And he had a particular liking, almost a compulsion, for licking me; he seemed to go almost into a trance while he was doing that, even when I was straining and shuddering to climax.

I worried for a while that I might fall with child to him, but perhaps it was not surprising that he, like a mule, sowed parched seed.

Then one day the ship with the black sails came from Athens as it did every year, and everything changed.

I was waiting along with my father and stepmother and brothers on the quayside as the cargo was offloaded. My father by this time was elderly, and even under the awning he found the heat of the day a trial, but the ritual is always the same; we are there for the payment of the tribute. It's no small thing to hold the Athenians as vassals, all the way from our island. We watched as the seven young women were led down the gangplank, followed by six youths, all of them looking pinched with fear and all dressed in plain white chitons – but followed by one young man dressed in the Hellenic style, which is to say in no tunic at all, just sandals and a saffron-dyed himation draped around his shoulders. From feeling bored and weary I snapped to focus: the body of the youth was well worth displaying. He walked with an arrogant strut. His skin was tanned to the colour of polished amber and covered long taut planes of muscle. He wasn't bulky like Asterion, but all of it was good. The first growth of beard graced his cheeks, but there was no hair on his chest. His phallus and scrotum were of goodly proportion and size. And his eyes were blue.

'Who is this?' muttered the King under his breath.

So the young man was revealed to us: the Prince of Athens, son of Aegeus, come as part of the tribute so that he might pit himself against our monster. He was a champion wrestler in Athens, he boasted, and had slain single-handedly many brigands and rebels. He was not afraid because he carried the blood of Poseidon in his veins as well as that of his mortal father, he said. His demeanour was not respectful.

'Prove that boast,' said the King sourly, taking from his finger a gold ring and tossing it into the harbour. The Prince marked where it plopped into the blue waters, then shed his cloak without a word and dived down between the anchored boats. For as long as I could I held my breath, willing him to endure. I had to yield and draw air though, before he reappeared and raised his hand over his head. Over his thumb was the ring, glinting in the light. A frond of seaweed was wrapped about his dark head like a victory wreath. And when they pulled him from the water back onto the dock, the salt droplets shone on his sleek golden body like gems.

It was at that moment that I lost my heart to him, for his beauty seemed to me as unearthly as that of Narcissus or of a god.

They put the Prince in the same wing of the palace as the other Athenian prisoners, but in a separate room in deference to his rank. That meant that I had to wait until the right guards were on duty who could be bribed to keep their silence. I laid it on thick that the goddess Artemis had moved me to confront him, and by now I had such a reputation for my strange moods and unconventional ways that they probably believed me. Nobody understood why a prince should volunteer to be part of the annual sacrifice when there were plenty of other youths of no importance available, so the muttering of the soldiers was that we were as mad as each other. When I entered his chamber he was sitting upon his bed, sharpening the edge of his sword. He looked surprised to see me, then pleased. My heart bumped about painfully at the sight of his smile and I felt my limbs weaken.

'Ariadne, isn't it?' he asked, standing and approaching me. It gave me a better look at his perfect body and I could feel the heat soaking through my own. As for his eyes, they could not help falling to my bare breasts. I think our island style of dress is disconcerting for mainlander men, who cover their own women in shapeless draped sacks. 'I'm honoured, but what is the daughter of the King doing in my chamber?'

'I came to let you know that the steward has agreed that you will be the last to be sent into the Palace Below.'

He frowned. 'Why should he do that?'

'Because I asked it of him. It is only courteous, as you are of royal blood.' I didn't add that I'd given the steward the use of one of my maidservants in return for the favour. 'There is every chance, if the other Athenians remain well and the ship next year arrives on time, that you will not be required at all.'

'No. That's wrong.' He slapped the leaf-shaped blade across his palm. 'I am going in first. I will demand the right!'

'Why?'

'Why do you think? It is my intention to slay the monster.'

I could feel my face twisting. 'Do you think you'll have the chance? They won't let you take your sword in with you – Asterion is of royal blood!'

'Then I will wrestle him and crush his throat.'

Words nearly failed me. 'He is a cubit taller than you,' I said with difficulty. 'He will break you like a green stick. Oh please, don't be foolish.'

The Prince snorted, flung himself away and paced about the room. 'You've seen the monster then?'

'Of course.' I didn't like his language and I know I sounded petulant.

'Then . . .' He dived for his bundle of belongings at the foot of the bed, and from a folded piece of cloth extracted a slip of pottery. He came close to show it to me, his hand touching mine, and I tried to hide my sudden trembling. 'Is it true? Is this what he looks like?'

It was a piece from a broken dish he showed me, with black figures silhouetted on a brown background. Depicted there was the hunched form of Asterion, braced for combat. 'Yes.' I ran my fingertips across the clay. There is no depiction of him allowed on our island, because my father is ashamed, but this seemed a precious object to me. 'Just like that. This is wonderful.'

'All my life I've heard of the monster and of the shame of Athens. Truly, he is real? How did he not slay his mother by being born?' I could hear the excitement in the Prince's voice, an almost holy awe.

'I imagine he was a great deal smaller then,' I said faintly.

'But why was such a foul and ugly thing not exposed at birth?'

'He's not foul!' My confusion made me snap. 'He's not ugly – he has beautiful eyes and he's . . .'

The prince put a hand on my shoulder, quieting me. 'I'm sorry. I didn't mean to upset you. Of course, he is of your house.' Something seemed to stir behind his expression. 'You . . . know his ways well then?

'Yes,' I muttered.

'Would you tell me what you know then? Would you help me?'

'I was trying to help you. You mustn't go into the Palace Below.'

'I am a prince, and the champion of Athens,' he said, quite gently, as if I were a little child. 'All my life I've dreamt of facing this monster and saving my people. Standing up against this creature of darkness and terror. Don't you understand?' I happened to glance down and noticed his phallus twitch, thickening, but the Prince himself seemed not to notice. 'Don't you see how barbaric it is to take young men and women who have so much of life and beauty in them, and give them up so this creature can devour their flesh?'

'He's called Asterion,' I mumbled sulkily. 'And he doesn't devour them.'

The Prince was a little taken aback. 'He doesn't?'

'Of course not.' I gestured at the shard of pottery. 'Look at him – he doesn't even eat meat.'

'Then ... what does he do to them?'

I shrugged. 'He takes his use of them.'

The Prince blanched, recoiling from me. I wondered why. 'Oh great Zeus and Athene,' he said to himself, swallowing a number of times. 'So ... let me get this straight, Ariadne. He doesn't kill them?'

'Well, he kills some of them, yes. He has a hasty temper and he's so strong. And he can't stand the ones that scream; that drives him mad him, he says.'

'He *talks*?'

This seemed so obvious to me that I couldn't grasp his incredulity. I just nodded, wide-eyed.

The Prince covered his face with his hands for a moment. 'So,' he resumed with what seemed like difficulty, 'he does not kill … the quiet ones. Those who submit to him. Not straight away.'

'No. Sometimes the guards open the door and the previous offering is waiting there to be taken out.'

His inhalation was ragged. 'And what happens to them?'

'Oh, they're sacrificed at the Temple of the Sea Bull.' I saw his eyes flash and added hurriedly, 'They are witless by then, they couldn't go home; their minds are broken. It's the dark, I think. The dark under the earth.'

He swung away and flung the pottery piece upon the bed and I watched him anxiously. His movements and his face seemed full of rage, but when he spoke to me it was quietly. 'And this doesn't disgust you? It doesn't seem in any way barbaric or offensive or cruel, what is done here?'

I considered this, dumbfounded. It had never entered my head. Of course the rituals were not pleasant; I did not find any amusement in them. But it had not occurred to me to be upset by them, any more than I should be upset by the temple sacrifices or by the daily slaughter of sheep and cattle and fowl in the kitchen yard. Yet clearly the Prince was upset, and I set great store by his opinion. 'It is unkind,' I whispered cautiously.

His lips narrowed, pulling wider, though it didn't look like a smile. 'So will you help me?'

'I was trying to, I told you that –'

He seized both my hands in his, holding my gaze. 'The moment I saw you I thought to myself, There is one whose heart might be touched by my plight. There is a beautiful young woman who – if I were not doomed to a cruel death – might look upon me with tenderness, whose admiration and even love I might win, if only I could live and be free again. Was I wrong?'

My heart felt like it would burst. I shook my head, helpless before his passionate words and yearning eyes.

'Good. I'm glad I wasn't wrong. Because even though I am under the shadow of a terrible fate, my own heart beats wildly, full of life and love.' He pressed one of my hands against his chest, pinning it to the firm muscle. 'Can you feel it?'

I nodded, wide-eyed.

'Do you know what it is saying?'

'No.'

'It is saying "Let me live, let me live. There is a beautiful maiden I have only just met and I must live ... for her."'

My mouth was dry, my cheeks blazing. When he bent to kiss my lips he must have found them parched, but his tongue was wet and it slid into me like a promise. Asterion did not – could not – kiss, so I must have seemed most inexperienced and maidenly to him. As for me, I was transported. Every particle of my being seemed to be alight with joy and purpose, and I did not resist as he drew me to him, pressing me up against his naked body. I was so overwhelmed with this strange giddy desire that I couldn't even furl my thigh about his as I might have done with Asterion. All the breath seemed to have left my lungs, all the strength my limbs. I was aware of his phallus hardening against me, but I didn't have the presence of mind any more to seize it. I just let the Prince kiss me until I felt I must melt in his arms.

He drew back. 'Do you feel the god Eros here in this room?'

I could feel his erect phallus, certainly, and my sex was slippery with *eros*. 'I love you,' I confessed, touching his unfamiliar lips with my fingertips. 'The moment I saw you rising from the sea ...'

'Ah.' His eyes were burning. 'I might love you properly, if I lived. I might take you from this place and wed you,' he whispered as if it were a terrible secret, 'and upon the bridal bed of Athens we could consummate our every passion.'

'Yes,' I whimpered.

'Will you help me live, Ariadne?'

I nodded, but only a moan escaped my lips as he cupped my bottom in his hand and squeezed me up against his erection.

'Will you help me defeat the beast?'

'Defeat' is such a clean word. I opened my mouth in protest but he caught my nipple at that moment between his fingers and made my breast his willing slave. 'Yes!' I hissed, though it's hard for even me to say whether I was answering his question or not. He kissed me again. This time I opened eagerly to his tongue.

When we finally broke for breath his troubled eyes belied his possessive hands. 'Perhaps you won't come to my aid.'

'My love –'

'Perhaps I will fall in battle, whether you aid me or not. Perhaps we will never have the chance to sail to Athens. Perhaps our only chance is here … and now.' He looked from my face to my stiffened nipples. 'Perhaps it is Eros' will that we take that chance.'

'Yes.'

He took me to the bed and laid me upon it, parting my thighs. He did not expect me to do anything but lie back and accept his kisses and his caresses and, swiftly, his stiff phallus. It was my first glimpse of that weapon in an engorged state and I was so dumbstruck by his facial and physical beauty that at that moment it did not seem to me to be inferior to Asterion's, even though it was patently not so large. I did try to take it in my hand but he captured my fingers and pushed them aside, smiling. 'Don't be frightened,' he whispered.

'I'm not.'

'Good girl. Be brave. Love is the battleground where men and women strive together, and even in submission and defeat you may triumph.'

Then he thrust it inside me and I cried out with pleasure to feel him there. It was the most wonderful moment of my life: his beautiful face lit with rapture, his glorious body slipping and heaving upon mine, my sex opening to him like a gift, his gasps of pleasure – the pleasure *I* was giving him – hot upon my cheek. I wanted it never to end.

But it did. He quickened, shaking my breasts with the rhythm of his climactic thrusts, then shuddered to a halt, falling upon my bosom. I clutched him tight, heaving my pelvis beneath him, feeling myself awash and adrift and suddenly no longer impaled upon his spike but simply enveloping it. Then he rolled away and lay beside me, his face flushed, stroking my breast as he might do a favoured pet.

'Our love is for ever,' he said.

I whimpered. I reached for his phallus but it was softening already. I was confused and somehow ashamed; I'd never failed to reach satisfaction with Asterion and this was beyond my experience. Hadn't I been good enough to keep his interest? 'My love,' I said hesitantly.

'Get me a sword into the depths below for my fight with the beast. Bribe the guards if you must. I need a sword, Ariadne.'

I sat up. My sex ached with hunger and my limbs felt as if they had become detached and no longer belonged to me. 'I don't know ...'

'I have to win! I have to live, Ariadne – for us.'

Straightening my dress, I did not dare look at him. 'I'll see.'

Hurriedly, he embraced me. 'You are as beautiful as Aphrodite, my Ariadne. It was wonderful. I must have you as my wife; you know that nothing else will do.' His kisses descended on my burning cheek and my dry lips. 'You do know that, don't you?'

I smiled and kissed him back, but I was seething with

confusion. As I left his chamber the physical discomfort of my frustration made me walk unsteadily. The sunlight of the court-yards seemed too bright and the people I passed seemed vacant of face and almost inanimate. I considered going back to my room and making sacrilegious use of the statue of Artemis, but there was too much chance of being interrupted at this time of day, and not one of my women could be taken into my confidence. No one could relieve me of this burden that churned inside me, in which desire and doubt and confusion had become a curdled mess. There was only one person with whom I could share my hidden needs, so after pacing up and down the western colonnade in distress for a long time I slipped into the Palace Below.

'I need to talk to you!' I gasped as I found him alone in his sleeping chamber. 'Oh, Asterion, I don't know what to do! I'm torn!'

He rose with a growl. 'A week! It's been a week you've left me here in the dark. You've not even showed your face when I was given to eat!'

'So?' I was confused by his anger – what right did he have to expect me to wait upon him, as if I were his slave girl? 'I've been busy. The tribute has arrived and – oh Asterion, what should I do? I have fallen in love!'

'Love?' he said, idiotically.

'With a man I may not marry. It's wonderful but it's horrible too – nothing seems under my control any more – I feel like I'm being torn open!'

'*Love?*' he snarled. 'You love ... someone? That is a joke, isn't it? Does he know?'

'Know what?' At the time I had no idea why he was so angry. My stupidity astonishes me now.

'That you are no maiden? That you are my whore? That you can't be satisfied by a normal man? That you come down here over and over again, desperate to suck and ride the cock of a *monster*?'

'Shut up!' I squealed, horrified. 'Don't say that to me!'

'Why not?' he thundered. 'It's true, isn't it?'

'I am the daughter of the King!' I spat. 'You may not –'

'The King? Well, let me show you what the daughter of a king is good for.' He seized me bodily and threw me on my hands and knees, mashing my face down into the damp straw with a heavy hand. He tossed my skirt up over my back to bare my upraised bottom, and then he mounted me. I pushed back onto his thick cock, squealing, and he fucked me savagely – first in the hole that had been so recently anointed by the man I loved, then up my arse, filling me with his foaming ejaculate.

I came both times. Bucking, twisting, opening myself to the phallus my body knew best and wanted most, but even as I screamed my rage and my release my true love's face and form were in my mind's eye.

Because of what had happened, I went back to the Prince the morning before he was to be confined to the Palace Below. Down at the dock the black-sailed vessel waited, rigged and provisioned for sailing but refusing to depart for Athens until it might take the Prince's body home to his father for burial. He'd asked to be allowed to make a sacrifice to Athene upon the household altar, and I found him as he was tending the flames. The guards were at the end of their shift and dozing where they stood against the red-painted pillars.

I came in close enough to speak to him in a low voice. 'When they close the door on you tonight, kneel down and feel along on the hinge side of the wall. You will find a ball of woollen thread like this.' I showed him the one in my hand, red as the blood on the altar stone. 'Tie one end to the door – on a peg, a knothole, something. You cannot stay by the door; that is where Asterion will come looking for you. Before he finds you, you must find the sword I have concealed. It is not far, but you will be in absolute darkness, and the rooms are irregular with many exits. You must not lose your way. Unravel the thread as you go; if you reach the end you have gone too far, so return and start again. But be quick! Stick to the right wall. You want the second exit, third, first, third, sixth. Be careful; it is harder to count in the dark than you think. Can you remember the numbers?'

He repeated them to me.

'Good. You will find yourself in a chamber. In it is a … wooden cow, the size of life. It opens up along the side, where it is hinged.' I paused to lick my lips. I'd once when small asked Asterion what the cow was, because it seemed so strange to have a carved effigy, faced in hide to look just like a real creature, forgotten and mouldering in the basement. He had replied 'My mother,' before grumbling off into the dark – which was nonsense of course, besides being a joke in poor taste. 'Inside it is padded but all turned to nests by mice. The sword will be under all the mess. Later I will find you and lead you to a secret way out.'

'What about a lamp?'

'I can't bring you a light, not beforehand. Asterion would find it. You must fight him in the dark.'

He nodded. His eyes seemed to burn. 'Thank you, Ariadne.'

'For this you will take me away with you, back to Athens,' I said. 'You will marry me.'

He nodded. 'Yes. Just as you wish. You will be the heroine of Athens for helping me end this barbaric ritual.'

I still thought he used the word 'barbaric' too freely, but I forgave him for the sake of his smile and his blue eyes. From now on my happiness was twined with his. 'My heart will be with you, my love,' I promised.

He nodded. 'And my life depends on you, beloved. Remember that. Remember that I will love you and take you with me. The ship is ready to sail at a moment's notice. You must not let me down.'

I nodded, tears welling in my eyes. Despite my fear for him I was full to bursting with happiness. Isn't this the most precious gift a girl can receive – the love of the man to whom she has offered her heart?

That night at moonrise we gathered as we did every month to witness the immuring. The Prince acquitted himself better than most, striding to the door with head held high and a confident, easy gait. His skin gleamed; he'd had himself oiled as in preparation for a wrestling match. He glanced over at the royal party coolly – his gaze lingering, I thought, upon me – and refused the draught of poppy-infused wine offered by the priest of Poseidon. The beams of the door were knocked off with hammers, and a cordon of torch-bearing soldiers pushed it wide and examined the immediate interior. I knew the passage well, though I'd only ever approached the door from inside the basement, and knew what the Prince was seeing: from here a flight of steps plunged down into impenetrable blackness. The torch flames fluttered in the draught from the tunnels below.

There was no previous offering to remove this time.

Quickly, the guards urged the Prince to descend and secured the doors behind him. Then we went, as we did every month, to make an offering of a bull calf to Poseidon upon the family altar. It was a duty I could not escape from, but as I stood watching the priests lay the requisite body parts upon the embers I strained to hear any noise from beneath my feet. There was silence. I imagined the Prince groping his way along the wall in utter darkness, the ball of wool turning in his hand, the thread unwinding between his fingers, counting under his breath and dreading to hear the ominous snort of breath or the stamp of feet nearby. I ached to be with him, knowing my place was at his side. Like him I was feeling my way forwards into an unseen future, unravelling the thread of my destiny. Ordinary people may blunder about randomly, but like my Prince I had a path to find, the sure knowledge of a purpose. We are special like that, some of us. History sits upon our shoulders, and as we unwind our days we are brought to the goal the gods have devised for us. Only when we look back along the thread do we wonder at how intricate and winding a path has brought us here.

As soon as I could I took my leave of the family and retired to my room. Taking a lit oil lamp in the palm of my hand I hurried to my secret entrance and climbed down the rubble slope into the Palace Below. The little wick cast only a small light, illuminating the indistinguishable rock walls and the pieces of abandoned rubbish that provided the only landmarks: a pile of worm-eaten timber here, a heap of fleece all gone to yellow mould there, a spill of bones, a basket with the bottom worn through, a broken loom ...

The wooden cow. I reached its chamber, breathless, and cast about. I knew which entrance the Prince should have reached this place from, but examination revealed no sign of him or of the red thread he should have been trailing. Biting my lip I worked the latch on the cow's flank and lifted the lid. The interior stank of mice. I plunged my hand into the mass of fluff that was all that was left of the silk-lined cushioning and my fingers found the cold hardness of bronze. The sword was still there.

Fear made me feel cold.

I pulled out the sword, its blade only a little longer than my forearm, and wrapped it loosely in my himation. I had little idea what to do now, other than knowing it was late, that the

Prince should already have been here, and that it was up to me to find him. I took up the lamp again and stole from the chamber, heading towards the stair.

I found the trail of red thread only two rooms away. It led off in the wrong direction. I caught it up from the floor with my fingers and hurried, my bronze burden clutched awkwardly in the crook of my elbow. Two more low doorways, a dogleg to the right, and there was the end of the thread: a little tangle of wool discarded in the centre of the floor. The room was empty. I stopped, holding my breath and staring into the doorways that gaped black and blind about me.

There: a noise. A groan.

My little circle of light pushed back the thick dark as I stepped over the threshold. Forms blossomed into view: limbs glossed with oil and sweat and bulging with strain, clutching hands, a bowed head of black curls. The Prince had listened to my warnings; he did not cry out, though he raised a face wide-eyed and slack-jawed with anguish as he responded to my light. Asterion's great bulk loomed over his crouched form, hands on his shoulders, ploughing hard between his arse cheeks. His rhythm was regular and inexorable. I stopped, transfixed. The look on the Prince's face was extraordinary – torment certainly, but something more than mere pain and humiliation. This was the moment, I thought. This was what he had dreamt of all his life, the beast that had haunted his sweating nights and ruthless days, the apex of his destiny. This was what the gods had brought him here for.

Slowly I moved forwards, mesmerised by the long fluid strokes, by the sense of power and domination. I could smell them now: oil and sweat and a masculine heat. I could hear the Prince's soft groan at every thrust and the slap of Asterion's flesh against his. I could see the ripple of muscles in Asterion's widely braced thighs and the heave of his chest.

With each thrust he snorted down his nose. The Prince's eyes rolled, half closing in shame. Sweat and olive oil were hanging in droplets from his jawline. I imagined him colliding with Asterion in the pitch blackness and the two of them grappling for purchase, hands sliding over slick flesh, muscle mass against muscle mass, until the inevitable penetration was achieved.

Oh, I knew what it was like to take that huge phallus up my rear passage. I could imagine only too clearly the sensations the Prince must be feeling.

Then Asterion paused in his rutting. His eyes turned upon me. I wondered what he would do; I had never intruded upon his time with others before. Was he still angry with me?

What he did was reach forwards, take the Prince by the shoulders and pull him upright, so that that lithe torso was framed against Asterion's bulkier chest. The change in angle brought no relief clearly; the Prince's mouth shaped an unvoiced cry of shock as that thick root shifted within him. But what it did was reveal the Athenian's own phallus, which was upright and as stiff as a spear shaft. From his new position, holding the Prince immobile, Asterion resumed his punishing thrusts. Completely entranced I dropped to my knees before the two of them, laying the lamp upon the ground. I bent low in worship and offered the Prince's swollen glans my open mouth. It took only my breath, my enveloping kiss, the swirl of my tongue across his contours to trigger his eruption. Crying out, he poured his hot seed over my tongue in such copious quantities that it ran out of the corner of my mouth and, as I pulled away, thinking him done, one last pulse brought the final produce of his testes welling from the eye of his phallus and oozing down his shaft like a milky tear.

He tasted salty, like the sea. Like sorrow.

Then, even as the Prince sagged in his arms, Asterion's

climax was upon him and he came with two savage thrusts and a long roar that made my ears ring and the echoes reverberate through the rooms of Palace Below. I stared in awe, seed wet on my parted lips. Emptying himself into the Athenian's bowels, he shut his eyes and his head sagged. The grip of his knotted forearm loosened upon the chest of the man he held. Seizing that moment as Asterion relaxed, the Prince of Athens reached down and pulled the sword from the folds of my bundled cloak. Raising it over his shoulder, he plunged it down behind him – straight and true and deep between Asterion's collarbone and neck.

His second roar was only a gurgle. Then he collapsed. I put my hands over my mouth and stared and stared and stared.

The Prince took me away with him on his ship, but he did not take me home to Athens. I had seen too much.

This island was named as Naxos on their map, I think. It is uncultivated, so far as I can tell, and there aren't even goats to nibble back the scrub. I am the only human soul on the place, though there are sometimes noises that I cannot identify out there in the undergrowth. Perhaps it's wild boar or bears. I hardly care any more.

There is one building: a small and crumbling shrine dedicated to Dionysus. I worked that out from the friezes depicting grapevines and satyrs. In the inner chamber of the shrine are propped huge sealed vessels full of wine. I think they have been left here over many years because some of the amphorae are unrecognisable under dust.

Last night I dreamt I heard flutes.

Can one survive on wine alone? Perhaps I will live long enough to see the worshippers arrive with their next offerings, in weeks or months to come. Certainly there's more than enough wine to dull my hunger and my hurt, for the moment.

Perhaps I will drink my fill and step off the edge of the cliff sometime soon.

Or perhaps I will continue to lie here and weep, knowing myself cursed. Knowing that I deserve this punishment because I betrayed my family and my King, all for a handsome face and a heart as hollow as the central chamber of the labyrinth. I thought I loved Theseus, Prince of Athens. I thought my desire for him outweighed everything else in the world. For false and unrequited love I betrayed to his death the one man who truly cared for me: Asterion, my half-brother, the Minotaur.

Janissaries

Let me tell you something I know from my own experience. The only way anyone – even the most trusted palace slave or the highest-ranking councillor – may approach the private rooms of the Ivory Empress is through the Court of Janissaries, and through the apartment of the Imperial Elite themselves. The janissaries are the Empress' personal bodyguard, 500 strong, every one of them hand-picked as a child from the slave markets and raised as a warrior. They might originate from anywhere in the empire, or beyond, and without family or caste they owe loyalty to the Empress alone. Everything in their lives is dependent on her favour so they are fanatically devoted to her service. Such unquestioning loyalty is important to her. She is a termagant who leads her armies to battle, a cast-iron virgin who refuses to marry lest she lose her power, and a heartless bitch who keeps her witless younger brother in a golden cage where his only task is to sire a child to be her heir – and only the youngest of these children at any time is permitted to live, because she will not tolerate the existence of a viable alternative for the imperial throne. Her laws hold nations in thrall, the riches and glory of her empire are beyond measurement, and her cadre of assassins are dreaded by those who even imagine rebellion.

The Imperial Elite are the six janissaries picked as the most effective and devoted of all guards, responsible for her safety day and night. Always there are at least four of them awake and on guard about her.

I am the pet of the Imperial Elite.

They call me Kitten. It's not my name. They are not interested in my name. To them I am not a woman, not even a slave, I am an object to be used for their amusement. I am a mouth, a pussy, an anus, a pair of wide eyes streaming with tears. I am a gaping receptacle for their semen. Nothing more.

Whenever I enter the apartment of the Elite I am dressed as they prefer me, which is to say in a long rope of plaited leather, dyed crimson, that loops over and around my body to make a complex harness of diamond shapes. It doesn't restrict my movements, but it makes it easy for me to be seized from any angle, to be strapped down, tied up, immobilised or tethered. Set into the braids at many places are brass rings to facilitate this. The harness conceals nothing: my breasts are bare. Attached to some of these loops is a long skirt of soft crimson hide that hangs down the back of my legs, and at the front a wisp of scarlet silk loosely arranged over my mound. If I stand very still and at the right angle this cloth drapes the shaven split of my sex from view, but I am rarely permitted to retain my modesty in this way.

Certainly not when Captain Teodric inspects me, as he does each evening. He glances over me as I enter the antechamber. 'Present yourself,' he orders.

The first presentation position is standing upright, my feet together, my elbows raised and my wrists crossed at the back of my neck, my head high but my eyes cast down. My straight, taut body has almost the parade-ground stance expected of the janissaries themselves, and Captain Teodric is used to inspecting his men. He circles me, searching for any imperfection. I dare not raise my eyes to look at him, but I know he is a gruff, greying man, still fast on his feet even though he is not as bulky as he once was. He is the least selfish of the Elite; his thought is always for his men and he always makes sure that I am shared around until every one of them is satisfied. He straightens some of the ropes, making the pattern across my back symmetrical, and, hearing the disapproval in his harsh exhalation, I quiver in fear.

'Sloppy presentation,' he growls.

'I am sorry, master.' My voice trembles.

He lets it go, for the moment, and returns to face me. In this position my breasts are thrust out, and because this little ante-chamber is unheated my nipples are puckered. He takes hold of one between finger and thumb, drawing it out.

'Bells for the Kitten,' he says. Jewellery glints in the open palm of his other hand. 'Put them on.'

His gifts are decorative clamps, little gold curls closed and tightened by tiny screws. My fingers trembling, I put one on each of my nipples, tightening them to the point of discomfort. From each clamp hangs a ring and on each ring is a cluster of tiny bells. Every time my breasts sway, with every step I take, I will jingle sweetly. When I return to my inspection posture Captain Teodric smiles and tightens each screw another half-turn, making me gasp. I am allowed to express my pain and distress; it is the only freedom permitted me in this place. They like to hear me. My cries never earn me any mercy.

Then Teodric wobbles each orb to test the effect. 'Now thank me.'

Obediently I say, 'Thank you, master,' although I hate the bells, even more than I fear the pain: their frivolity mocks me. The Captain must notice the dismay in my voice, because he grabs my jaw in his big hand and yanks my head from side to side, forcing me to look up at him. His fingers bite into my skin; there is no rebellion in my expression now, only aghast submission.

'What are you?' he snarls.

'Whore.'

'What are you?'

'Tits.'

'What are you?'

'Cunt. Just tits and cunt.'

His lip curls in contempt. He releases me. 'Present in the second posture.'

For that I go over to the fountain and bend to set my hands on the marble rim, arching my back so that my bottom is thrust out. The leather skirt hangs from my hips; it does not cover my bare cheeks, it merely frames them. Captain Teodric bends over to inspect the crack of my arse. He spreads my cheeks with his hands, gazing into the cleft of my sex, and sniffs. I've been sugared and pumiced and washed in rose water until I'm smooth all over and as fragrant as possible, but I know he can smell me. The sexual aroma of a woman cannot be hidden. When his rough fingers part my lips I can feel the moisture on the delicate tissues.

'You pass muster.' He sounds bored now. He slams his hand down stingingly hard on my left bum cheek. 'Hurry up. We've been waiting.'

As I stand I know that there will be a red handprint emblazoned on my bottom. It is still burning as I pass into the main chamber of the apartment. There they are, the five others, lounging upon couches about a low table – the Imperial Elite at rest. Three of them are still in their leathers, on duty, while the other two are naked except for their breechclouts. They stop talking as I enter, looking up from their games of backgammon with no acknowledgement but expressions of casual satisfaction. I walk to the middle of the room and then go to my knees; it's what I have to do every time in their presence. I assume the kneeling posture, my wrists crossed at the small of my back, my thighs parted, my breasts thrust out. Captain Teodric takes his place and sits.

For a moment half-a-dozen pairs of eyes are on my breasts, my splayed thighs, my half-hidden sex. Alain scratches lazily at his crotch.

'Good girl,' says Milo absently, and goes back to rolling dice.

Jaffez, conversely, sits up, his attention fully on me. He has a horse tail in his hand, and he drags it across his other palm meaningfully. I feel the colour rise in my cheeks. Jaffez likes to thrash me with that tail until I am red all over and every single one of those hairs stings as it impacts. 'Feeling frisky, Kitten?' he says, grinning playfully. He has beautiful eyes, that man, despite his broken nose and the scar that cuts through his close-cropped hair.

'No, master,' I whisper.

'Well, don't worry. Rurik here has a new way to ginger you up.'

They all snigger at this. Rurik is busy carving something with a small knife: it looks like a slip of wood. He raises his pale eyebrows meaningfully at me, but I don't know what the joke is. Confusion makes my trepidation worse.

There is no such thing as a quiet evening with these warriors. There is no mercy. They are men in the prime of life, raised to be soldiers, itching for action; they are fed well with meat every day, exercised hard and kept in the peak of condition. Each and every one of them is loaded to bursting with spunk and impatient to discharge it. As janissaries they may not marry, and though they may have doxies they are not permitted to bring them within the Court. In here, the innermost apartment before the chambers of the Empress herself, they are not even permitted to entertain themselves with slave girls. I am the only woman allowed to dally here. So I have to serve six stallions, attend to six ravenous appetites, take six cocks in whatever orifice they choose. The appetite of men is a frightening thing. There is never a night when I am not needed by someone, and then as soon as one man stakes his claim the others fall upon me, wanting their turn. I am the hub at the centre of a six-spoked wheel.

'You'll serve us dinner,' says Captain Teodric. 'Get on with it.'

Reprieved, I rise to my work. The air of the room is laden with the pungent scents of hot food and fresh spices, emanating from the dishes on a brass tray over the brazier. The meal has been deposited there by slaves, but as so often it is my task to serve. First of all though I take up a ewer and basin, and pass from man to man so that they might wash their hands. Captain Teodric is always served first. There is no towel; after shaking their fingers they rub them dry on my bare breasts or my braided hair as I kneel before them. My bells get flicked and jiggled, accentuating my humiliation. Darius, who is the bulkiest of the six and must have been born beyond the Southern Desert, runs his dark hands all over my creamy skin, testing my leather bonds to make sure they bite into my flesh in the right places. The harness pattern was his design and he has a special interest in seeing me tied. Sometimes he suspends me on tiptoe from a hook on the wall for hours, gagged and aching. It pleases him to hear my pleading for mercy when he finally releases my mouth, and my sobs invariably provoke him into fucking me.

Jaffez is the last of the group to make his ablutions. As I rise to my feet he grabs me by the waist and shoves the stock of his horse-tail lash up between my thighs. The wooden handle is thicker than most cocks and my vulva is unprepared so far today, so I squeal in shock, nearly slopping the dirty water. The men hoot with derision.

'Ah-ah!' he admonishes. 'Take it, Kitten!'

So I do, biting my lip, shifting my stance so that he can angle the stock and push it inside me, trying to ride out the pain of first penetration. The muscles of his arm clench as he works it inside me. When he withdraws suddenly I gasp, shocked by the loss as much as by the prior invasion. He brandishes the handle for inspection, to appreciative laughter; thick streaks of my cream decorate the dark wood.

'On your knees and clean it.'

I obey, licking and sucking the handle as if it were a cock, as I've been trained. He pushes it all the way to the back of my throat, so there is no chance of me being able to breathe, but I accept it and keep my gaze on his face. I can hold my breath until I go blue without gagging: usage has taught me that.

'Let her go, Jaffez,' says Milo easily.

He releases me and cocks an eyebrow. 'Well? I'm hungry. Don't keep us waiting.'

Trying hard not to betray my relief, I hurry to bring over the warm dishes from the heater. Of course I have to bend over when I place them on the low table in front of the couches, and the men take the opportunity to pinch my buttocks and probe me with sly fingers, trip my ankles and slap my dangling breasts. When I drop a basket of bread rolls they make me kneel and pick up the pieces with my mouth. Milo strokes his fingers right up the inside of my thigh and tenderly pets my sex. Milo, with his hair hanging like a parted curtain over his forehead, thinks I am pretty. He is the least likely of them all to call me a bitch or a slut or a whore, even in the throes of lust; the least likely to mock me; the most likely to stroke me comfortingly when I am exhausted or to tell the others to ease off. But he also likes to put me over his knees and slap my arse crimson, with bare hand or leather belt. Even with unmasked pity in his eyes, he can rarely resist giving my wobbling bottom a thrashing to the point that I am in floods of tears, and only then will he stop and embrace me, rocking me into silence.

They own me. I am theirs. I am an animal on a leash. I am a piece of meat, and there is no right of appeal.

'Are you hungry?' asks Jaffez when they've settled with the bowls of soup that start every meal.

This is usually a trick question, but I answer, 'Yes, master.' It's true: I haven't eaten since dawn.

'Then get yourself a bowl of soup.'

I thank him and obey, dishing up from the tureen. It is a spicy lentil and lamb broth.

'Bring it back here and set it down. At my feet.'

Careful not to spill on the rug, I kneel before him and place the broad bowl between his bare feet; he's one of the off-duty ones. Jaffez leans forwards and spits into my soup.

'Drink it then.'

I don't hesitate; I'm escaping lightly. Jaffez likes to play games. He particularly likes to get me dirty and I've had to accept his piss down my throat before now. I place my hands on the rug and bend forwards.

'Wait.' He puts his foot in the bowl, wriggling his toes as if the broth were a warm bath. The others hoot in amused disgust. 'There.' So I lap my soup from around his foot, and when I've nearly emptied the bowl he lifts his leg, plants his foot against my breast and shoves me back onto my haunches. 'Lick it clean.'

Supporting his ankle with both hands, I clean his foot thoroughly, licking between his toes. 'She tickles!' he complains merrily to the others. Then he adds, 'Now lick it off your tit.'

I look down to see a big soupy footprint on my right breast. I cup the orb with my hand and bow my head; I'm not as supple as a real kitten but my breasts are big enough that I can bring my nipple to my mouth, so I tongue myself as neatly as I can. The bells rattle against my teeth. I receive a derisory applause.

Alain crooks his finger. 'Here, cunt.'

That's what he calls me, never even gracing me with an animal sobriquet. I shiver just from the sound of his voice, and crawl over to him on hands and knees. Alain evokes in me the worst dread of them all; I would not want to be left alone in his presence. He is quieter than most of them in conversation, but that doesn't make him any less of a shaven-headed brute, the blue tattoos up the back of his scalp marking him out as a devotee of some barbarian steppe god. His eyes are sunken and dead. He takes me by the throat and, turning me, pulls me between his knees in exactly the position one would pin a sheep for slaughter, my throat stretched taut. He has used his eating knife to dismember a roast duck while I was otherwise occupied; now he takes the greasy knife and wipes it slowly on my breasts, paying particular attention to my nipples as he cleans the blade. My pulse rockets under his fingers. I hold myself as still as I can but the bells tinkle faintly with the thump of my heart.

'Enough,' growls Captain Teodric as the point of the blade plays with my nipple.

Alain smirks and lets me go. 'Maybe later, cunt.'

He hasn't nicked me this time

'Go wash yourself, you filthy bitch,' Teodric orders. 'Then report to Rurik.'

My eyes blurring, I retreat to a safer distance. The only water to wash in is that which they've already bathed their hands in, but I do my best to scrub off the food grease. The scrap of silk between my thighs becomes soaked and clings to my mound, revealing the split of my sex lips clearly. Then, my skin still glittering with water droplets, I return to kneel at Rurik's feet.

'Other way. Head down.'

I swing round, presenting him with my bottom and lowering

my face to the floor. Rurik's people come from beyond the mountains at the northern edge of the empire; he has a slab-like face with broad cheekbones and pale eyes, and his hair is the colour of wheat that has been left to stand uncut in the field too long. He has a passion for my back entrance and loves to insert things there. His usual amusement is to tie a bunch of silk scarves together then push the knot into my rear aperture so that I have to walk around trailing a multicoloured tail behind me. Not today though. Today he has other plans.

'Know what this is, Kitten?'

I squint over my shoulder. He is holding the yellowish curve of wood he was carving earlier. It's only about the size of a man's finger. It is the peppery, lemony scent in my nose that tells me what it is – not all the spice smells come from the food they're eating, it seems.

'Ginger root, master?' My voice is barely audible over their anticipatory sniggers.

'That's right, Kitten. The hottest in the market. This is going in your arse. Ever had a gingered rump, girl?'

'No, master.' I can only guess what it will feel like.

'Open up.'

I obey, relaxing my iris. My arse is well trained. It has had to take six cocks in turn many a time and it knows how to yield. I know what it is to have six loads of come in my private entrance, squirting out between my cheeks as I crawl away. This ginger finger is moist and slippery and feels cold. It goes in past the ring of muscle easily, the last quarter remaining outside. It's not uncomfortable.

'Kneel up. Face us. Hands behind your head!' barks the Captain.

I hurry into position and feel the first warm glow ripple up the tissues of my violated bottom. There's a big grin on Rurik's face.

As soon as I am in position I am ignored, or at least left alone. They carry on eating and talking among themselves, with only the odd glance thrown in my direction. The topic of conversation is the coming campaign season and whether military success will yield a worthwhile new crop of slaves. There is good-natured disagreement as to which nation's women are the best fucks. And as they talk I feel the cool slickness of the ginger turn to a burning flame inside me, the pungent juices prickling and inflaming my insides. I begin to squirm, secretly at first. I squeeze my arse muscles, but that instantly makes the sensation truly painful and I learn my lesson, unclenching with a gasp.

Rurik chuckles.

As the moments wear on the heat builds unbearably. I wonder if I'm going to burn up. Sweat springs out on my back, trickling down my crack. My breasts quiver. I begin to writhe my hips almost imperceptibly, longing to pull the tormenting plug from my hole. Soon it feels like the whole length of my spine is aflame and tears well up in my half-closed eyes. I start to pant. I long to pee, as if the liquid might put out my inner fire. My labia feel engorged and I can feel moisture oozing from me. The tiny chime of the bells is unceasing as I squirm and shake. At last I can't hold back my anguish and I let out a moan.

'Is it too hot for you, Kitten?' Rurik asks.

'Please, masters ...'

'Have you got an itch you can't scratch?' He comes forwards to pull my silken shred of modesty clean off, and slip his hand between my obediently spread thighs. He fingers my clit, and for a moment it is wonderfully distracting. Then as the itch ignites I realise he has ginger juice still on his hand and now my most sensitive flesh is sparking into torment. I squeal outright. He slithers his fingers into my gash and remarks, 'She's wet as a swamp here.'

He's not wrong. Something – the frustration, the inflammation, some alchemical effect of the ginger itself on female flesh – is making me slathering wet. My sex gapes. He explores me briefly then withdraws.

'Want me to take the ginger out?'

'Oh please, yes! Please, masters,' I moan.

'How about I put some of this nice cool cream up there instead?' Rurik picks up a ceramic pot of golden-yellow syllabub from the table. The thought of its soothing richness in my back passage makes me want to scream with need, but I bite my lip instead and nod frantically. My clit is starting to throb.

'Let's see how much of it is left then,' he says, sitting himself back down and unlacing his leathers. His cock springs out, already stiff enough to summon me with an imperious jerk, but he grips its root between his fingers and sticks the whole thing into the syllabub, scooping out the cream as if with a spoon. It oozes down his length. 'Come on and give me a licking then.'

Darius makes a mock-complaint: 'Hey. I wanted to eat that!'

'You still can, if you like.'

Darius' expression of disgust is theatrical. 'You think I'm eating anything where your cheesy knob has already been?'

'Well, you've had your tongue up her cunt plenty of times. Maybe you like the taste of my knob-cheese, Darius.'

There are general snorts of laughter but the black man and the blond aren't going to start a proper scuffle; they're both too interested in what they're going to be doing to me.

Darius starts to loosen his armour. 'Just don't waste that dessert, Rurik. I want to see it used.'

'Oh, it's not going to waste. Time for the Kitten to get her cream.'

I've crawled to Rurik on hands and knees. I'm yearning to

feel the soothing, rich cream in my abused passage and it's frustrating to have to take it in my mouth instead, but at least it's something – anything will do – to take my mind off the burning between my cheeks. I wrap my lips about the white froth and it melts in my mouth, tasting of honey and saffron, slicking my throat. But underneath the sweetness is meat and salt, and I slide him deep into my throat so that I can lap up the drips and runnels from the underside of his shaft. I feel him thicken, butting against my soft inner flesh. I feel his scrotum tighten under my hand. They are talking over my head, but I can't hear the words because Rurik has his hands over my ears, guiding my head up and down on his cock in the rhythm that pleases him best. I squirm my bottom, whimpering my distress even through my diligent sucking.

Just as I think Rurik is going to add his own cream to my diet, he pulls me abruptly from his cock. Mouth open, lips wet, tongue displayed, I meet his gaze. He rubs his fingertips up his slippery shaft, and I see in his eyes he's saving himself for something more than a blow job. Instead he pushes me into Darius' lap and I go down with a gasp onto my second cock of the day.

There is no cream this time to sweeten the meal. This cock is the colour and hardness of mahogany, broad and impatient. His pubic hair clings in tight curls over his crotch and up the root of his shaft, his scrotal pouch is heavily wrinkled and almost blueish. And he is not the last. I am passed on down the line, one by one, because they are all divesting themselves of their clothes now. I am surrounded by cock and I abase myself willingly, as frantic as the most ardent of worshippers to forget my own misery in the giving of myself to my deity. Among those slab thighs, I bend to make obeisance. Cock is my god. These men with their brawny arms and their smell of sweat and leather, their broken noses and their calloused hands, they are my gods. I know them as a priest knows those he bows and prays to every day. Each cock is different in taste and behaviour and appearance. Some are smooth, some veined and gnarled, some uncut, some shorn of their foreskins. Jaffez has a pronounced list to the right. Teodric's helm looks too massive for the shaft it sits on. Milo seeps with excitement. Rurik's balls clench so hard they seem to disappear into his body. Alain's prick stands up so stiff it almost brushes his belly, but Darius' is too heavy for that, though he gets hard he does not rise. Some of them like to sit back and let me lick, others prefer to thrust into my throat.

I can hear their desultory conversation, like the voices of indifferent gods; they are reminiscing about whores they have fucked and virgins they have despoiled, and comparing me unfavourably to them all.

Somewhere in the middle of this, a hand pulls the ginger plug from me. I moan with gratitude. Then cool and slippery digits probe my burning hole anew, and suddenly the ginger finger is back, but this time bearing a slippery load. They are using it, I realise, to stuff my arse with the honeyed cream. It slips in and out of me over and over. I feel myself filling with sweet dessert, which melts deliciously on my inflamed inner walls and oozes out, greasing my ring.

Then I get to Alain, and Alain has no patience. He picks me up bodily, turns me and slaps my behind down in his lap, spearing my slick anus with his prick in one savage thrust. My sensitised tissues seem to explode. I shriek, twisting in his grip, but he lifts me and slams me down even harder to teach me a lesson. The others curse his lack of manners, nearly choking with laughter. Ignoring them, Alain gets a good grip with both hands and begins to shaft me deep and fast, bouncing me on his thighs. The saffron cream squelches out over his balls.

'Smack her tits!' he grunts.

So I get one man on either side of me and they slap my breasts and my face in turn, stingingly, until Alain lets loose with a snarled blasphemy and blasts his spunk up my back passage. With a spasm of irritation he throws me aside, face down on the couch. I cling to the coverlet with clawing fingers, pressing my face into the cushion.

Almost as fast as he has discarded me, the others move in. Hands descend on my raised, open arse, several of them. Fingers slip into my greased anus from either side, easing me open even further, exploring my depths. I have no idea who is doing what, just that I am being entered fore and aft without distinction.

'I could get my hand up here!'

'Fuck your hand. I'm having my turn.' Rurik shoulders the others aside, kneels up behind me and stuffs his cock up my arsehole. After what I've just been through it's not so hard to take, though it pushes the breath out of me and I grunt spasmodically.

'Hold there, soldier.'

It's Captain Teodric's order. Rurik freezes in position, rammed to the hilt between my buttocks.

'Sir,' he acknowledges through clenched teeth.

In that moment of stillness I become aware that the ginger is still having its effect. My sex dilates and ripples. My clit is engorged. There's a pungent confection of cream and spunk and my own juices oozing down my splayed sex.

'This is not a tavern brawl, soldier! Alain, I'll see you later. Right now ...' I know he's surveying their flushed faces and straining bodies. 'Rurik, get out of there.'

Rurik groans under his breath, but withdraws. I collapse on my belly.

'And get your hand off your cock, soldier!' Teodric snaps. 'Darius, cunt or arse?'

Darius is reclining on one elbow; he'd been watching the procedures rather than taking part. 'Cunt every time, sir.'

'Take her then.'

So he reaches down between my breasts, grabs the harness and hauls me up the length of his big body until I'm lying on top of him. His cock is trapped between us, hard but not impatient. Darius takes the longest of them all to come; he can fuck all night if he chooses to. He laughs at my dazed expression, grips my thighs and then manhandles me into place, slotting me down onto his big prick. He fills me completely and the pressure he exerts, opening me wide, is actually a relief on my inflamed tissues; I can't disguise my gratitude.

'She loves that, the whore,' Jaffez remarks.

'Back you go, Rurik,' says the captain.

My eyes open wide. The men cheer. I hear Rurik's dirty chuckle as he takes his place again, a lot more carefully this time because he has to fit his knees around Darius' thighs. 'Come on, bitch,' he grunts under his breath as he feeds his length into my rear entrance. My muscles put up no resistance, and he slides in smoothly, right up the length of Darius' bone, cock to cock, except for my inner wall between the two engorged members.

'Sweet,' Darius purrs. 'So much tighter now.' He pulls my knees right up so Rurik can get in good and deep without effort.

I realise I've been holding my breath. I let it out in a moan of surrender. My forehead rests on Darius' breastbone.

'Now,' says Captain Teodric, 'think you can fit in there too, Milo?'

Milo is lovingly polishing his wood and the question clearly takes him by surprise. 'What, in her arse?'

'Well I don't think a deviant slut like that is going to be satisfied with just one cock up her butt, do you?'

Three cocks at once?

I open my mouth, but Darius forestalls any sound by shoving his fingers into it, pressing my tongue. 'Shut the fuck up, bitch,' he growls. 'The Captain isn't interested in your opinion.'

That's hardly fair. I hadn't been intending to protest, only to scream with fear. They've never tried this before and I'm far from sure I can take it. My body starts to shake.

'Rurik, sit back and make space. Milo, you up for this?'

'Shit, yes.' He moves in, bending low over my back. There is some tentative jockeying for position, Rurik partially withdrawing to make room for the other man's pelvis, pressing his erect cock down hard manually. I'm not sure what their final stance is because I can't see. It hardly matters. All I know is that Milo spits on his hand to lave his cock-head, because I hear the wet noises, then he presses the slippery ram to my portal right alongside Rurik's prick. Their limbs are a tangled, sweating knot against my rear end. The first forays are tentative and I'm wildly grateful the captain has chosen Milo, who will at least try not to rip me open.

'Open it up, bitch!' Darius snarls through clenched teeth.

It's a lot like the first time I was buggered, it turns out: the pain, the awful feeling of invasion, the fearful desperate clenching of my muscles that is overcome by implacable force, the pop and slide and dilation as the cock has its way. The noises I'm making over Darius' fingers don't sound human, and the soldiers not occupied with their exertions grin and mock.

'Give it to her!' Rurik urges from behind me. 'Get it in there!'

'Fuck. Fuck.' Milo is panting hard. 'I'm in. Fuck.' He is: I can feel my anus stretched wider than it's ever been, like a mouth open in a silent scream.

'Go on then,' answers Teodric dryly. 'Fuck her, lads.'

I've run out of cries. I cling to Darius' broad torso helplessly, unable to believe there's a cock up my sex and two more up my arse – two cocks pressed tight together, skin to skin, in my slippery grip; cream and honey and Alain's jism lubricating their unyielding stiffnesses as they begin to move over each other, inside me. And as they move they press against Darius, who heaves beneath me, grinding my mound.

'Does that feel good, whore?' Teodric asks, lifting my chin. But I have lost the power of speech. My eyes can't even focus on his face. He smiles, satisfied with me at last.

'Nobody's using this end,' points out Jaffez.

'True enough. Hold her up, Darius.'

Darius props me from beneath with one hand and with the other grips my braids and pulls my head back. Now I really am pinned immobile. My mouth sags open.

'Three at the back there,' muses Teodric. 'Don't see why she shouldn't take three cocks up here too. And, Alain, you'd better come or I'm revoking your whoring privileges until the Spring Festival.'

'Yes, sir,' he drawls.

They close in, kneeling up over Darius' head with the terrible uncaring intimacy of fighting men. Jaffez is first in, plunging his cock into my mouth. I'm unable to suck so I just take him, moaning, and he gets off a few strokes before making way for Alain, who yields in turn to the Captain. So they carry on, working and squeezing their own cocks while they are waiting to make use of my open throat, and all the while the other three fuck me arsewise and cuntwise with slow, rolling strokes. My eyes are watering, the tears running down my face. I can barely draw breath. It is all I can do to keep my mouth moist.

I am being squeezed out of existence by all this hard male flesh crushing me. I am full as I have never been full before. My gingered flesh flares to every thrust. In my mind's eye they are not only six individuals but one huge Man that possesses and forces and ravishes my every orifice, their grunting and panting the voice of a single monstrous beast, the scent of their bodies mingling, their cocks one omnipresent cock, inescapable as the oblivion to which it is driving me.

My breath escapes as a long wail.

'Look, she's coming,' says Captain Teodric, far over my head. 'The slut is coming, lads.'

'Oh gods,' groans Jaffez, spurting into my mouth.

His copious gushes nearly drown me, but there is no let-up when he pulls back because Teodric is coming next onto my slack tongue, salty and sour. Someone – I can't tell if it's one or both men, but they are both thrusting frantically – is coming in my back passage and my arse is awash and I think it's both Milo and Rurik together, clawing at me. Even Alain squeezes out three thick white gobbets of spunk onto my lips. And all the time I am still coming, and I do not care if they tear me to pieces with their lust and their need for release, because mine are greater still.

I get fucked a few more times that night, but to be honest I barely register the subsequent occasions, slipping as I am in and out of consciousness. Eventually I pass out face down in Jaffez's lap, with his hand sunk to the wrist inside me. They let me sleep after that, curled on the rug in my usual spot, the Captain's booted foot resting on my head.

Deep in the early hours someone – it's Milo, I recognise the scent of his skin – picks me up and carries me through to my own chambers. I bob back to the surface of awareness in inter-mittent glimpses: darkness then light then darkness again. He lays me between clean sheets, unravels the scarlet harness from about my abused flesh, strokes my face with his fingertips, then leaves me to sleep it off.

I would have him demoted from the Elite, if it were not for the cruel thrashings he subjects my arse to so often.

In the morning my maidservants will come and wake me. They will not remark upon the rope imprints in my flesh or the encrustations upon my skin; my personal attendants are all mute now, by birth or surgery. I cannot bear the twittering of female chatter, and the executions necessary to quell gossip became tedious. They will lead me through to the bath of warm water they have prepared and I will soak away the aches, bruises and scents of the previous night. Then I shall be dried with towels of softest lambs' fleece, and perfumed and clothed in cloth of gold and finally masked. I shall ascend my palanquin and be carried through to my throne room, flanked by my faithful and devoted janissaries. Zoë Eiparthanos, Ivory Empress, ruler of half the world.

Tomorrow I will once again have the lives of millions in my hands. I will have executions to order, punishments to inflict, military strikes to plan. I must receive the embassies of distant kingdoms, discern the twists of treachery, judge the innocent from the guilty, issue orders for new towns to be founded and temples to be built. I must tax the loyal and quell the disloyal. I must save and I must lay waste. I must decide every moment which of a thousand scheming ambitious men to trust with the business of empire, and while my trust means wealth, my slightest doubt means death. So they lie to me. They lie and lie and lie, and still I must judge and decide.

How can anyone bear such responsibility? How can anyone wield such power without going mad? It is like a cloak of fire that, wrapped about the shoulders, will burn the wearer to ashes.

The answer is that such great power must be burned off before one bursts into flames. My Imperial Elite see to that. Nightly they drag my incandescent form to earth and pin me there. They reduce me to mere matter in the crucible of their lust. They remind me what it is to feel helplessness and fear and pain and relief as all my subjects know them; they remind me that I am mortal. Neither god nor demon. Human.

Most loyal, most necessary of men: my janissaries.

Darkling I Listen

Darkling I listen; and, for many a time
I have been half in love with easeful Death
John Keats, 'Ode to a Nightingale'

The young woman sat before the white marble tomb of the Elerin family, and as she spoke to the ghoul she drew spirals in the sand with a twig. Exploring ants clambered in the furrows left by the stick and she watched them incuriously. A mane of dark hair almost hid her face. She wore an unbleached shroud that sagged from one shoulder, exposing the smooth brown skin beneath and part of the curve of one breast. In contrast the ghoul squatting before her was naked, its livid hairlessness mottled like a bruised toadstool, and being a ghoul it shifted uncomfortably in the light although the sun was setting and the clouds stained pink, blinking rapidly over sensitive pupils that refused to contract. It was almost blind in daylight, even crouched here in the tomb's shadow; only its interest in the girl's tale staved off its nervousness.

'Once upon a time,' she said, wriggling her bare toes in the dust, 'there was a maiden who lived with her father in a wagon. The wagon was pulled by two mules. Her father was a great traveller and had been all over the world. The girl was only fourteen, so she had not been so far, but she lived in the wagon and was happy, even though they were a long way from their own home.'

It was a young ghoul, much smaller than the woman, and had no memory of its humanity in the days before it was stolen from its mother; nonetheless, it had a liking for stories and games that marked it out from its larger brethren whose pastimes were of a more peculiar nature. Ghouls, as is well known, do not breed amongst their own kind – though they can quicken a human womb, living or dead – and they have a habit of acquiring other people's children.

'She had a talking bird in a cage that hung from the front of the wagon, and a small yellow dog that ran along beside the wheels when they were on the road, and with the company of these and her father she didn't miss her mother, who had died a long time ago. She didn't remember her mother at all. The wagon was painted dark blue, with stars in yellow on the boards and the awning.

'The maiden's father was an astrologer and a worker of small magics. He could make fire turn all sorts of colours, and pull the little yellow dog out of an empty bag, and persuade the mules to speak in funny voices. But mostly he read the stars, and told people's futures from their birth hours. That was how he made his living and looked after his daughter. I don't think he was very good, because otherwise he would not have come to Krisilith. Or maybe he would not look at his own star chart. I don't know for sure.'

She stubbed out the small life of one of the ants and dragged her twig into a new series of loops.

'They rode into Krisilith along the coast road, coming down from the cape of Het where the Baron himself had asked the astrologer to read his stars. The maiden was excited – she liked travelling to new places. She asked her father about the city, because he was a scholar and knew everything, even foreign lands. He said that Krisilith was famous for three things: firstly because it was the biggest seaport on that coast, secondly for the sweet sticky breads that they made there, and thirdly because there were really two cities in Krisilith, one for the living and one for the dead. He said that the living city was built all around the skirts of a hill, and on the hill were stone houses for the dead people, and a palace for the dead barons, and empty marketplaces and court-houses and chapels and public baths and even a library in which they kept copies of the writings of poets and histo-rians. Everything empty and silent. The houses had beds and tables and chairs in for the dead people to use. And the living people would come in the daytime to pay social calls and leave food and drink for their relatives, but they would never go there at night, and though they treated their ancestors to the best they had, they never gave them any shoes, just in case the dead people should decide to pay a visit to the living for a change.'

The ghoul made a noise that sounded a great deal like a snigger.

'That all sounded very strange to the maiden, who tried to imagine the dead people coming out of their houses at night and going about their normal business under the moonlight just like other people.' She tilted her face up into the last warm fingers of light. Her bronze-coloured eyes were rimmed by dark shadows, the face that caught that sun a little too thin for her age and the line of her mouth a little too hard, an observer might have decided. 'Among the maiden's people, in the dry mountains far away, the way with the dead was to bury them in a sandy place and pile rocks upon the grave, to give them a narrow bed alone and not a city. But this was another country and another people, and if they had strange ways what of it? It was not so odd, she thought, as the raft villages in the swamps of Iol, or the rock mazes of NaBrith in which the priests danced and chanted.

'So they rode into Krisilith in their wagon, and the maiden looked all around her with fascinated eyes. She saw the tall red-stone houses and the white awnings stretched between the roofs to shade the narrow streets from the sun. The people of the city hurrying up and down the choked streets and pressing around the wagon were sandy coloured with big hands, and they wore stiff dark clothes that looked too tight and hot for them; they stared a great deal at the wagon and the man and the maid who must have looked very strange and foreign to them. Some followed the wagon to the marketplace and asked where they had come from and what was their news. The astrologer was pleased to have made such an entrance, and he stood on the box of the wagon and told all who would listen that he was a reader of men's fates and that he had been recently patronised by the Baron of Het. Then he paid for a room in a fine inn and locked himself away with his daughter to await the first summons.'

The sun slipped behind a ribbon of cloud low on the horizon as the young woman spoke these words and at once the air darkened. The ghoul relaxed visibly and glanced around it, before reaching under the doorstep on which it sat and feeling around in the space beneath. The girl paid no attention, even when the ghoul retrieved a withered human hand and began to gnaw pensively upon it, chewing off the skin and crunching the small bones between its teeth.

'That was the way the astrologer worked,' she continued. 'When word got around, then the wives of rich men would send to him, wanting to know if their husbands would prosper, or whether they would find love. Then when the women were all talking of his fame and his fine and accurate predictions, then the merchantmen and the nobles would stoop to consulting him. This was what he expected. But this time in

Krisilith the well-dressed servants were slow to appear. And when he asked the innkeeper some questions in the privacy of his room, it became known to him that the chief priest of the city had spoken out against astrologers and alchemists, accusing them of witchcraft and poisoning, and crying for such blasphemous enquiries to be silenced.

'"Perhaps this is not a good place for us to stay," sighed the man to his daughter as they ate their dinner together, but hardly had they dropped the bones to the yellow dog than a soldier entered at the door and presented a summons to him. The astrologer was to go at once to the castle and there read the stars for the old Baron of Krisilith, who had taken to his sickbed. The maiden's father swept his charts and papers into a bag and hurried off at once with the soldier, leaving the girl to wait. She did not dare to leave the inn alone, so she sat on the balcony and watched the lamps of the city glimmering in the dark lanes.

'Her father did not return until after the midnight bell had been tolled, when she had fallen asleep in her seat with the dog curled up around her feet. When he came in he was pale and worried; she asked what was wrong and he said, "We must leave as soon as the city gates are opened in the morning. We must get out of the barony as soon as we can. The Baron is dying, and will not see many more days; more than that, I see the signs of poison in him, not of sickness. I did not dare tell him the full truth of my reading, but the courtiers there took from me the chart I had scribed, and have guessed the truth … If they did not know it already. I am afraid that whether I am right or wrong, I will be blamed for the outcome." So the two packed their few belongings, and before dawn the maiden crept downstairs to harness the mules.'

The young woman's dark hand clenched around the stick

and the muscles in her forearm knotted visibly. Her hand was slender and scarred, the nails rather tattered. The nails of the ghoul, of course, were hooked like a cat's claws.

'But while she was in the stable,' she continued in a low voice, 'she heard the sound of many people in loud boots, and when she looked out through a crack in the plank door she saw soldiers pushing into the inn, all carrying weapons. In a few minutes they were back down, shoving the girl's father in front of them. He had blood on his face. They had the little yellow dog on a piece of rope too, and it was barking and trying to run round in circles. The whole group hurried out of the inn, shouting and pushing aside the innkeeper and his servants who had rushed out to see what was happening. The maid did not know what to do, so she ran and hid in the hayloft over the stables, where she could see the mules when she looked down. She stayed there all day, frightened to come out, hoping that her father would come back, crying to herself in the dusty hay. Nobody found her. Then late in the afternoon the soldiers came back, and they pulled the wagon out into the yard, and then they led the mules out and hitched them up to it. The girl was terrified that she would never see her father or her home again if she let them out of her sight so, greatly daring, she put a piece of sacking around her dark head and she sneaked down out of the hayloft when they had left the yard and followed them through the city.

'It was easy to follow them. A big crowd was moving with the soldiers, whistling and shouting, and the mules moved slowly. They processed through the narrow cobbled streets to the marketplace where her father had first announced himself to the populace, and there he was again, waiting, but this time with a retinue of soldiers and a line of priests, and in the centre of it all a heap of kindling as big as a cart.

The Baron was dead, you see, just like her father had feared.'

The girl paused in her tale. The yellow orb of the sun had disappeared now except for the brightness it left on the horizon, and the sky was a pale eggshell blue, streaked with pink clouds. She let the stick fall into the dust, and slipped her arms about her knees instead. Her head drooped.

'The maiden had to watch from between the shoulders of everyone else in the crowd, as the priests made their formal condemnation of her father for sorcery and the late Baron's murder. The crowd spat on him and threw stones, until the soldiers got nervous and stopped that. He looked very small, and old, and he kept shaking his head. They didn't let him say anything. They had her dog there, and when the crowd started booing and getting really loud they cut its throat and dropped it on the kindling, which they lit. And a big man with a butcher's axe stepped out and hit both the mules between the eyes with the spiked end, and they dropped in their traces. And they cut the mules loose and tore the wagon to pieces and heaped the flames with all those bits of wood. The fire rushed up high. She thought she could hear the bird shrieking as it burned. Then . . . ah,' she faltered, her voice breaking up into a croak, 'they took the maid's father and tied him to a cartwheel and broke his arms and legs with a big hammer, and then they threw him onto the fire too. The maiden did not watch him burn, because she was crying.'

The ghoul paused in its gnawing and regarded her solemnly.

'They heard her.' The girl cleared her throat with a growl. 'They heard her crying, and someone looked at her and started shouting, "Look, here is another one!" And suddenly they were all trying to grab her and she had to run through the crowd. Hands caught at her but she bit her way free and tore loose from her shawl and dodged from them, and because the crowd was so noisy most people did not know what it was that they were supposed to do when they saw her, so that she got to the edge of the marketplace and ran down a street. She could hear feet pounding behind her. She saw a big wall in front of her with a gate open in it, and people coming out of that gate. She thought it must be the city wall, it was so tall and so long, so she dashed through into the open space beyond. But there were houses there too, though much smaller and further apart than before. She dodged down the wide lanes between the white houses, turning left and right, and finally hid in a porch because she was too breathless to run further. She heard the noise of the people following her, but they were grumbling and uncertain. She crouched down low behind a great urn full of sand and rosemary as they came near, and she saw their feet pass close to her head, leather boots with bright nail heads, and heard them say – though she could hardly understand their accents – "It's nearly sunset; leave her for the dead." Then they went away, leaving only their footprints on the sandy path.'

The ghoul resumed its repast, but its eyes were fixed upon the storyteller and its pointed, slightly mobile ears turned in her direction. She paused to run her hand slowly through her hair and look about her.

'When the maiden came out of hiding, she saw the mistake she had made. She was not outside Krisilith. She was standing at the base of a rocky hill, and all over the hillside wound the neat lanes of small white buildings and little sandy paths, while below her, circling the base of the slope, was a wall behind which crouched the darker houses of the city. There was no other person in sight. These buildings here were low and clean, with spaces in between where there were almond trees and cork oaks and tamarisks growing among long pale grasses. It was very dry and very silent. When she looked back cautiously towards the wall, she saw that the distant gate was now closed. She realised that she must be in the inner city of Krisilith, the town of the dead. She was a little afraid, but not so much afraid as she was of the living city. She began to walk about, wondering if there was some way beyond the buildings to the open country, but mostly with no idea in her head except pain and thirst. She was hungry and exhausted, and her father was dead. She had no home and no family. She was starting to feel cold now that the sweat of her running had dried and the sunset breeze was picking up.

'She walked past the basin of a fountain in which there was no water, and crossed in front of a columned building on which pigeons were starting to roost. It was growing dark now. The birds were the only living things she had seen in the city of the dead, until she passed a square tomb with blind stone windows, just like any of the others, and she heard the sound of rock scraping on rock. She turned in time to see the door of the tomb swing open and a face look out at her.

'It wasn't a human face. There were too many big teeth in it that had pushed the mouth forwards into a muzzle. The creature looked at her, stepped forwards into the dusk and showed her all those teeth in a big hungry grin. There were other creatures like it behind the first. When she saw the whole animal, the maiden thought at first it was a big hairless baboon, and then she realised it was a *ghûl*, such as she had heard of in her father's stories. They live in her home country too.'

The ghoul meeped enthusiastically. A shadow of a smile crossed the girl's face for a moment.

'The maiden ran again – though she was tired, though she really did not think her shaking legs could drive her onwards more than a few paces. The path led her uphill, and with the creatures only yards behind her she floundered up the rise. On the crest was the tall figure of a man in grey robes, almost blending into the dusk. She ran towards him, and he did not move, and as she reached him she flung herself forwards to snatch at the hem of his robe and call, "Save me, kind sir!"'

The ghoul gave a kind of shudder and dropped the remnants of the chewed hand.

'She thought,' said the young woman slowly, choosing her words with care, 'that if he stood there unafraid of the *ghûls* then he must be a sorcerer. Her hands grabbed the robe, which was very dusty, and for a moment it felt like there was nothing underneath it, just empty cloth, and then the man jerked round to look at her and threw his hand out at the creatures behind and said, "Stop." And the *ghûls* stopped as if they had run into a wall, crouched to the ground in front of him and fawned like dogs. The maid didn't look up, she didn't dare move, she thought she was going to be sick. And she was thinking, Even if he is a necromancer, what is he likely to do to me that the *ghûls* will not surely do?'

The ghoul before her shook its head nervously.

'The man said to the maiden, "You can see me?" – which seemed to her to make no sense at all. She repeated, "Kind sir, save me, please! Send them away!"

'The man asked her name then. He had a soft voice and an accent that worried her somehow. "Zulkais en Taherin," she told him, and to this he replied, "Ah, you are the daughter of Taherin Ahmin Multire, the astrologer, who died today on the fire." This was a surprise to her and she asked miserably, "You know what happened to him?", to which he said, "I was there." And at that point she realised that in her distress she had implored him entirely in her own language, and what was troubling her about his tones was that he had replied in the same tongue.

'She had to look up at him then, and did so fearfully. At first it struck her that he had no eyes, but she blinked and saw that she was mistaken, though they were rather dark. He did not look like one of her people, nor like the inhabitants of Krisilith. He was, she thought, very sallow, the hue of old bone, and had long hair the colour of charred wood, white and black. She saw these things despite the dusk.'

At this point the ghoul broke into a rapid glibbering. The young woman listened, inclined her head gravely and raised one bare shoulder in a shrug. The dying light around them was staining earth and sky blue. She continued with the same caution.

'The man was watching the maid curiously. "I am surprised that you saw me," he said after a little time. "It is unusual. I have met only one other recently: an old man who lived alone and prayed a great deal, and was accounted quite mad by his relatives." And the maiden, who had swiftly learnt that it was better to look straight at him or not at all, because if she turned her head away – to look at the grovelling *ghûls*, for example – his appearance would shift at the edge of her vision in a manner that was not pleasant, well, she asked humbly, "Are you dead, sir?" because it seemed perfectly likely that he was one of the inhabitants of the tombs around them. But she saw him smile, or thought he did so, and he replied, "No."

'Then he held out his hand to her, and she took it after a moment's hesitation. The sensation was … disquieting, but only for a moment. She tried to stand, but her legs gave way and he had to pick her up and carry her. He took her to one of the tombs, leaving the *ghûls* waiting in the dust, and when he laid his hand upon the door it swung open before him. They entered the small building, all the lamps in the wall niches flaring into life as they crossed the threshold, and the girl saw that they were in a room with a table laid for a feast, with chairs and fine linen. The man let her sink into one of the chairs and seated himself opposite. The funeral must have been that very day, for the food on the table was untainted, the flowers still fresh, and there was no stink discernible from the corpse that reclined on the bed, visible through the doorway to the inner room. Nevertheless the girl shivered in that cold presence, and at a glance from her host the inner door swung shut.

'"Eat," the sorcerer suggested, and watched as the maiden fell to, slowly at first, then with desperation. He waited while she devoured pomegranates and spiced lamb, sheep's cheese and figs and sweet white bread, and washed them down with a bright red wine. The maiden's head was spinning by the time she had finished. Her companion at the table said nothing, neither did he eat, but only watched her gravely. When her hands fell still at last he said to her, "You may stay here in the city, Zulkais. It is a refuge from your enemies at night, though you must be wary during the day. I will give my hounds instruction that they are to care for you. But you should eat from these votary gifts, and not from the meat they may offer to share with you. I will return from time to time to see how you are." With those last words he rose and left the room, and the maiden's head slipped onto the table and she slept until dawn.'

The young woman stopped talking. Twilight was creeping upon them. The trees sighed in the light wind. 'That is the first part my story,' she said. 'The maiden lived in the necropolis for some years, just as he had suggested. She learnt to wake by night and sleep lightly in empty tombs by day. She stole her clothes from the dead people and ate the meals left for them by their living families, and when those offerings were scarce she pulled fruit from the trees and trapped small birds. She learnt the speech of the *ghûls* and their dances in the moonlight and their strange lore, though she never shared their meals and she never followed them through the secret doors that each tomb has. She kept away from the living, always beyond their reach and out of their sight. She nearly forgot the speech of humans, and she grew odd and wild and unsightly, so that anyone who met her by chance would take one look and back away. Sometimes her host would call by on his travels. She grew to like that.

'Then one summer's evening she had bathed in the spring by the eastern foot of the hill, where the water of the dead runs through the culvert under the wall into the city of the living, and she was sitting upon the pool's edge in the last light, combing out her wet hair. She had wrapped a pall-cloth from a bier about her damp body. It was an evening very like this. And she looked around at a small noise to see that her host had arrived unannounced and was sitting just behind her in his robe of grey. He did that, you see. She would never know when he was coming, or see him arrive. He would simply be there. Then her host, whose name she knew by now was Mor –'

The ghoul cut her off with a hiss, revealing teeth designed to break open thigh bones.

The woman looked at it without fear. 'Whose name is not spoken except during holy rites,' she amended.

The ghoul glibbered.

'The sorcerer? I will call him the sorcerer if you prefer. The sorcerer gave the maiden a comb made of ivory and gold that day. He often brought her presents, strange things that she kept simply out of delight: a lyre made of a tortoise shell; a pair of silver trefoil brooches; a mask of beaten gold; a necklace of jade so heavy that it crushed her breasts; a cloak of feathers as brightly coloured and iridescent as the wings of butterflies. She had no use for of any them, except for one that was clearly the tip of an ivory tusk, curiously carved, for which instinct and need had tutored her inexperienced hands, and which she had grown greatly fond of. But the comb was of use to her that moment, better than her fingers. She began to work it through the tangles of her long hair.

'"Let me comb your hair for you," said the sorcerer. It was something he had never suggested before.

'So, sitting between his knees with her back to him and holding the pall-cloth closed over her breast, she let him work the fragile ivory teeth through her locks. His hands were unhurried and careful. She liked the feel of them on her hair, the soft tugs of her scalp, the shivers that worked down her spine as an accidental brush of a finger tickled the nape of her neck. She could see his pale foot, as bare as the feet of the dead, which emerged from under the hem of his robe and rested on the step next to her. She could feel the solidity of his thigh and knee as she leant against him. They did not talk. He never spoke very much around her, though he seemed to seek her company. His quiet hands, his dark eyes, the hint of a hooded smile now and then, were all she had from him to think on through her days alone.

'She watched him twine her dark locks about his pale fingers, as if appreciating the contrast in colour. When he began to stroke her neck she shivered with pleasure and made no protest. After a moment's hesitation he moved again, his fingertips caressing her skin, tracing the lines of her vertebrae, the curve of her shoulder, the hidden paths of her veins. The pleasure of the sensation was pure and elemental. She wanted to arch like a cat and purr, but she forced herself not to wriggle out of terror that he would stop. She was not used to being touched. No human had hugged her or patted her hair or held her hand in years, and her reaction to this now was almost too intense to bear. Her lips parted and her breath came quicker between them. Her eyelids fluttered, suddenly heavy, her eyes unable to focus.

'"Do you like this?" he whispered, his lips close to her ear. The question was too ingenuous; it did not do justice to the riot of sensation his fingers were evoking, so she only murmured agreement. In response his fingers slipped around to the front of her throat and stroked her down to her collarbones and up to her chin, which she raised for him. Her pulse was beating harder, faster, and she knew he could feel it. "Yes. You like it," he said, and "Yes," she replied.

'"Your skin is so warm." His voice was low. "Life burns under it, like sunlight." His fingers descended to her breast-bone and at his touch there she spasmed with shock, unable to help herself, and he cupped his other hand about the swell of her shoulder to still her. Then gently he drew the cloth from her grasp and let it drop, baring her breasts. She made a little noise then in her throat, her hands curved uselessly in mid-air, neither defending her modesty nor knowing where to go. Making up for the loss of the garment, a blush warmed her from top to toe. Long pale fingers swept down, tracing the curve and swell of her flesh, circling a nipple which tingled to aching. "You have grown and changed, yet you are still Zulkais, my necropolis child. I hardly know what to do with you."

'"Do this!" she told him, and heard him smile. "And this?" he asked. His cool fingers found their target and closed upon the little bud of flesh, teasing with little circular caresses. Her nipple stirred to his touch, stiffening at once, her areola dimpling. She felt suddenly as if her skin, too alive with sensation, did not belong to her at all, that it was as strange as a new garment. She leant back into him, moaning a little, as he tugged at her. "So soft," he murmured: "So tender. You are too young, Zulkais." The maiden protested at that. He sighed then and his fingers played on her one after another like a harpist striking rippling chords. "Not too young for love. But too young to love me."

'She pressed her face against his arm, the grey robe rough against her cheek, and begged, "Don't stop." He slid his other hand down her spine and began to rub her back, low down, his fingers pressing into the muscle. She felt as if her whole body might open to let him in, as if her bones were turning to water. "Do you know what you want?" he asked, and though she did because she had watched birds and animals and the *ghûls* and remembered enough of life outside the walls of her sanctuary, she could not bring herself to answer except by moving to his touch. She knew she wanted this to go on. She did not know how she could have lived so long without this exquisite taunting pleasure.

'His second question was, "Do you know what you're doing?" and his voice by that time betrayed a huskiness, a strain. "You'll show me," she moaned, capturing his hand and moving it across to the other breast. "Show me how."

'He cupped that breast, hefting it to a smooth bulge, the nipple poking out dark between his fingers. His other hand, kneading her spine, had turned her lower body to molten turmoil and she could feel it oozing out of her, hot and wet. "Pleasure is hardly my domain," he said. "But release, certainly."

'She could stand it no longer; she pushed back against him, wriggling up from between his thighs into his lap, driven by the instinct to press herself to him. Taller and bulkier, he took her weight as if it were nothing. He wrapped his arms about her, one hand on her body stroking her from breast to thigh, one tipping back her head so he could kiss her throat, pinning her against his torso. His mouth was no warmer than his fingertips and she shivered delightfully, urging him with little whimpers of need. His hand slid over her damp pubic curls and down between her thighs. He gripped tight, his fingers mired in the slipperiness of her split sex, pressing at the portal of her maiden hole. And she felt it, under that strong grasp: ripples of pleasure running through her whole body, wave after tiny wave. It wasn't a full climax – it was too faint, more like a shadow that runs on the ground ahead of the solid body that casts it. But it steadied her and she grew still, gasping, in his arms.

'"Zulkais, do you know who I am?" he asked, and that question, the third in a row, fell with audible weight. She sought to focus her mind and answered him, "You are the god of the *ghûls*." "And that does not trouble you," he wondered, but she answered with a trembling voice: "Why should it?"

'He stood then, holding her as she slipped from his lap, and turned her to face him. She tried to press against his robed body, but he held her a little from him and her belly clenched. He stooped and picked up her pall-cloth, knotting it at her shoulder, then kissed her mouth as softly as the fall of petals, his hand cupping her cheek. She stared up at his grave face as he told her, "I need to take you from this place before this goes further. There are things you should know."

'She shivered at that. The afterwash of his touch was fading into an ache of tormented loss. "I don't want to leave," she protested. So he promised that it would be for a little while only, and though she said how frightened she was of Out There, he would not change his mind, telling her, "I'll be with you. No one will see either of us."

'So he took her away. He wrapped her in his arm and stepped with her between the leaves of the world with less fuss or effort than the release of a last pent breath.'

The young woman fell silent for a moment. The ghoul's unblinking eyes reflected the twilight like dim moons. If its face had been human, an observer might have ascribed to it an expression of fascinated horror.

'He took her to many places and showed her many things. The house of a tailor, where a young mother dozed over a crib and a cat lay purring where it had no right to be. A gallows tree by a harbour. A pyre lit for a king who did not lie there alone. The back alley behind a tavern, where a man lay in a puddle darker than the rain that fell upon his upturned face. A battlefield after nightfall, where stooped figures moved about the fallen with lanterns in one hand and knives in the other. A ship locked tight in sea ice, its rigging curtained in frost. "I am here," he said. "In this place with you, and in that. In every tomb and in every house I am there. Do you understand?" And she nodded, wide-eyed.

'Now, for the first time, she doubted him. "Am I seeing you as you really are?" she asked. He answered her: "You are seeing me as I am to you. A man may be an indulgent father, a zealous lover, a loyal friend and a cruel master all at the same time. Which is real?"

'She looked long and hard into his eyes then, but he did not change, did not become the thing she had once been dismayed to see from the corner of her vision. He brushed back a strand of hair from her face, and spoke softly, as if his words were too painful to say louder: "Know this. You will not get from me the things you might get from a mortal man who loved you. Neither children nor grandchildren, neither growing old together nor my growing to need you, neither honour nor a place in the wider world. From me you will only get sunset moments."

'Then he took her to one last place. It was a room the maiden did not recognise, filled with things that glowed and flashed and beeped that she could not name, with a bed of a kind she had never seen before, and in the bed a woman she did not know. There were tubes puncturing her arms, and she seemed to be asleep. Her dark hair was cut short and though she was not fat there was something doughy and unformed about her face and a grey cast to her skin. The maid shrank back against the sorcerer, asking, "Who is this? I don't know her."

'"Years ago," he said quietly, "when she was fourteen, she and her father entered the wrong neighbourhood and were set upon by thieves. She was beaten unconscious. Her father was set alight in his own automobile and died. She has been in a coma since that day and will never wake up. She might die in fifty years' time or tomorrow. In the meantime a part of her has taken flight down the seven hundred and seventy steps below the mansions of her dreams, to another place."

'The maiden's heart felt like a stone sitting under her ribs. She didn't understand all the words he'd used, but she understood their import. "I don't recognise her face," she whispered, and he replied, "She grows old faster than you do. She is now thirty-one. What do you want me to do, Zulkais? The choice is yours."

'"I want to go home, to Krisilith," said she.

'So in the blink of an eye he took her back to the city of the dead, and when they arrived on the balcony of the palace of the dead barons it was still sunset just as it was when they had left, though it might have been another day entirely, for very little changed in that place. And it seemed to the maiden that as she stood upon the high building she might also still be sitting by the spring combing out her hair, and she might also be lying alone in a room, asleep for ever. Her legs were suddenly wobbly with shock. The sorcerer set her down upon a couch made for the dead barons to hold public audience upon. For a moment he knelt at her feet, looking up into her face, his hands touching her ankles.

'"Why did you have to show me those things?" she asked, unable to speak in more than a whisper. "I would have been happy not knowing." To which he answered, "Yes. But to leave you ignorant would have been to ... take advantage. I want to be fair to you."

'She opened her eyes wide at that. "Fair? You?" she said, which made him bite his lip. "You are right," he acknowledged. "I am neither fair nor just. Only, sometimes, I am merciful."

'"Not this day," she told him, and he looked thoughtful, answering, "Yes. Already you have changed me a little, Zulkais. What are you going to do next?"

'"Me?" she asked.

'"You, Zulkais. I will not make the choice for you. You are free."

'She closed her eyes. When she opened them again a heart-beat later he was no longer kneeling in front of her but standing at the stone balustrade with his back to the view over the necropolis and the wall and the city of the living. She shivered because she could still feel the lingering touch of his fingertips on her ankles. Though no bigger than any other man he seemed to fill her field of view, fill the landscape beyond, fill all the world. And he watched her, his face sombre and motionless and only his hair shifting a little in the breeze, like a drift of ashes from a cremation platform. The maiden, caught in his implacable gaze, heard again the questions he had asked:

Do you know who I am? Do you know what you are doing? Do you know what you want?

'And in the silence she heard the answers inside her. Her heart was beating fast, not just with fear but with vertigo. She had looked into an abyss.

'Then she rose up and went over to the sorcerer, and put her hands upon his chest. She heard the intake of his breath, but he did not move. He might as well have been a memorial statue. She had to stretch up to bring her lips to his, hesitantly, with many false starts, her heart in her throat, her eyes brimming with tears. She kissed him.

'Like a statue coming to life he folded his arms about her and pulled her to him. His kisses were strong and hungry and felt quite human; in moments he had taught her how to yield to them. She felt her whole body melt against his, changing its shape and its nature, her stomach to his stomach, her thighs parted by one of his, her breasts crushed to his chest. It came to her that the one thing she'd never thought to question was how much he wanted her. Now that question was answered forcefully, by the fierce grasp of his hands on her hips and by the need in his kisses. He ate the breath from her throat and she had to pull away from him in the end, gasping. He laughed softly, and that sight was so novel to her that it was almost more frightening than anything that had gone before it. "Do you know what you want?" he asked again.

'"This," she answered, running her hands down his torso, forcing them between her body and his until her fingers found a hardness they'd never known before, a jutting thing that seemed to her improbably angled. "Oh?" he asked. He might have been teasing; she could not tell. She lost her nerve and retreated to his chest again, drawing open the overlaid panels of his robe to reveal the bare chest beneath. He shrugged the garment off his shoulders, letting it hang from his belted waist, revealing a torso the colour and sculpted smoothness of bone. Entranced, she ran her palms over his skin. Her hands looked very dark against him. "I want this."

'"As I want you." His hand went to the knot at her shoulder and the pall-cloth fell away, revealing her to his gaze and his touch, her bronze gilded by the sunset glow. Some part of her mind noted than neither his pale skin nor the white streaks of his hair were even tinted by the ruddy light. "Every part of you." So saying he picked her up and carried her bodily over to the couch, moving over her as he laid her back upon the dusty cushions. His mouth grazed her lips, her throat, her breasts. He licked her nipples until they stood up all shiny. Oh, she liked that, she found; it woke in her a fierce hunger that made her grip him hard. Then he crouched lower, kissing her belly and navel, his hair falling over her like a caress, his hands pinning her down. His mouth made her squirm and she laughed out loud. "Ticklish?" he asked her and when she whimpered, "Yes! No!" he drew her thighs apart and bent his head between them, wondering, "And here?"

'His mouth found her and, oh, it was bliss. Bliss better than anything else – sweeter than the taste of the year's first ripe persimmon. She writhed beneath him, feeling his tongue sliding about upon her pearl, the hardness of his jaw pushing into her softness, his wetness mixing with hers. First she wanted to push him off and then pull him into her, and then she felt as if she were opening up like a chasm in the earth into which they must both fall. Then she thought she would burst in his face and spurt down his throat, and then she knew he would tear her apart – and then he was doing it, or she was doing it, and the movement of his mouth was working right through her body and her breasts were shaking as she arched her back and clawed the cushions beneath her, and she cried out as Death took her plunging through the void.

'But still she lived. She lay shaken as he knelt up over her. When he kissed her she could taste herself on his lips and tongue. He whispered her name, smiling darkly. He touched her with his fingertips, stirring the gloss on her skin, stroking the flat belly that quivered with her every heartbeat. "Now," he said softly, drawing her hand up into the folds of his robe, parting the cloth for her so that she could wrap her fingers round the erection she found there. "Do you know what this is?" When she nodded he kissed her again. "Do you know what I'm going to do with it?"

'"You are going to put it inside me," she said, quivering. Her hand was measuring his cock from root to tip, shocked by its cool hardness. She found a distinct head that she had somehow not been expecting, a sheen of slickness, a muscular kick against her palm. His lips brushed over hers. "And you want me to do that?" he asked.

'"Yes," she told him, "I want it." And his eyes flashed his pride at her. But it was his fingers that went to her split first, finding her moisture, exploring the contours and depths and the sensitivity of her. She felt her stomach flutter again as he touched her in secret places, making her moan and surge. Then he took her spilt butter and anointed his cock while she watched in fascination.

'"Come here," he murmured, sitting back and pulling her upright. He lifted her astride his lap as he turned to sit upon the edge of the couch and, holding her about the waist, her breasts pressed to his bare chest, he gripped himself tight and let his cock kiss her cleft, sliding up and down in an abundant wetness. Even when he first essayed a push it did not hurt because her body was used to another ivory tusk. Only, though it did not hurt, still it frightened her a great deal as he eased her down upon his length; to have a living man inside her was hard to believe, to have *this man* – or this thing that looked like a man – so close, so intimately encompassed, was almost unendurable. She made a moan of terror, realising how much trust she had to find. And then he was in all the way, filling her up. "My brave girl," he breathed. Then he kissed her, settling her weight half on his thighs, half on his cupped hands. "My Zulkais."

'She clung to his shoulders, wide-eyed and flushed. "Now touch yourself," he whispered. "I want to see you touch yourself." Carefully she slipped one hand between their bodies and fingered her clit. Her face was level with his, their lips brushing. When he spoke she could feel his cool breath: "Does it feel good?"

'She nodded, unable to speak coherently. Squeezing her bottom in his hands, lifting her weight, he worked her up and down on his shaft, shifting his hips and thighs to open her still further. "I want you to come on me," he told her, but after that they spoke no more, too busy keeping their rhythm steady and their panting under control, too busy watching the sensations and emotions blossoming in each other's face, too busy snatching breathless sticky kisses – until the maiden felt the rush of heat flooding her and knew she was coming with a man's hard cock thrust to the hilt inside her tight sex. She shook her head wildly and scrunched her face and squealed, unable to help herself. It was not a dignified moment. She was sure he would be laughing at her, but when she met his gaze again she found his dark eyes serious and tender. "Yes, that's it," he whispered, kissing the sweat from her temples. "It's over. You've done it."

'Of course it wasn't over. Not then, and not for a long time because he next rolled her upon the cushions and delved her slow and carefully, then long and hard, and the pleasure was not so sweet as that she'd felt under his mouth or her familiar fingers, but much deeper. Her body was supremely ready for this, readier than she could be herself, and she was grateful that it knew the way as he pushed her to the edge of endurance then over the edge into rapture, all over again. He made her scream and claw at him and beg before she was done, before he let his own need lay him waste. Then he lay with her until they had both recovered enough to begin all over again.

'The light never changed. He held it there, at that golden sunset moment before the onrushing dark. He held her at the edge of oblivion then let her fall asleep sprawled on top of him, and his hands were tracing the lines of her back as she slipped into unconsciousness.

'And that is all the story ... That's the end. Everything else is only sunset moments. I don't know what will happen to ...' The young woman's voice died away. The shadowed form of the ghoul sat in contemplation. What it had made of the tale was impossible to discern.

Then both heard a chittering call and stood to look down the hill, towards a grove of lemon trees that clustered round a cracked and dusty well. Indistinct in the deepening dusk, to the woman's eyes – clear to those of her companion – a group of capering, naked ghouls emerged from under the canopy. In their midst walked a tall figure, straight where they were crooked, calm where they danced and jostled, clad in a grey that seemed to blend into the colours of the gloaming hill. It can be assumed that what the ghoul saw differed from that which the girl perceived, but both pulled in an anxious breath at the sight. The young woman's heart, at least, knocked painfully in her chest. The grey figure lifted its head as if gazing towards them.

They started downhill quickly, the ghoul loping sideways, the girl treading carefully on the unmade path. Her wounded, feral eyes had softened and her face had taken on a new cast, one more suited to someone of her age, her eyes bright and eager. But there was no one close enough to her to see this through the evening shadow, except for the ghoul, and ghouls have no interest in human emotion.

Visit the Black Lace website at
www.black-lace-books.com

FIND OUT THE LATEST INFORMATION AND TAKE ADVANTAGE OF OUR
FANTASTIC FREE BOOK OFFER! ALSO VISIT THE SITE FOR . . .

- All Black Lace titles currently available
  and how to order online
- Great new offers
- Writers' guidelines
- Author interviews
- An erotica newsletter
- Features
- Cool links

BLACK LACE — THE LEADING IMPRINT OF
WOMEN'S SEXY FICTION

TAKING YOUR EROTIC READING PLEASURE
TO NEW HORIZONS

LOOK OUT FOR THE ALL-NEW BLACK LACE BOOKS – AVAILABLE NOW!

All books priced £7.99 in the UK. Please note publication dates apply to the UK only. For other territories, please contact your retailer.

To be published in February 2009

SEDUCTION
Various
ISBN 978 0 352 34510 3

From the enthralling gaze to the masterful kiss, the arts of the seducer are legendary and this anthology will draw you into a sinfully sensual world where the urge to seduce or be seduced is irresistible. Written by some of today's most talented and imaginative authors of female erotica, each story explores the timeless fantasy of giving in to temptation. Elegant, feminine and alluring, this collection will leave you longing to surrender over and over again.

To be published in March 2009

THE CHOICE
Monica Belle
ISBN 978 0 352 34512 7

Poppy Miller is an exceptionally bright and ambitious student at a top British university. Determined to make her mark in politics, she has her mind set on finding a husband with similar aspirations to herself. Stephen Mitchell, a second-year law student seems to fit the profile and the young pair plan a future together. But then Dr James McLean, a rakish don, appears on the scene. Poppy can't help feeling drawn to the older man, and the campus stories about his colourful past and masterful character only increase her fascination. She knows that a liaison with the darkly seductive McLean will change the course of her life, but perhaps deep down that is what she wants after all? Poppy has to make a choice: should she go with her head or with her heart?

To be published in April 2009

THE APPRENTICE
Carrie Williams
ISBN 978 0 352 34514 1

In desperate financial straits, aspiring writer Genevieve Carter takes a job as a
personal assistant, only to discover that the middle-aged woman she will be
working for is none other than her literary heroine, Anne Tournier. However, her
new employer expects rather more from her assistant than was implied in the
advert and Genevieve gradually becomes enmeshed in a web of sexual intrigue and
experimentation with younger and older men and women. Then, by accident, she
learns that she has been cast as the heroine of an erotic novel that Anne is writing.
Determined to get her own story out first, Genevieve starts a blog where she relates
her sexual liaisons to a growing and appreciative readership. Lured by the prospect
of a lucrative publishing deal, a competition ensues between mistress and apprentice, one which will push Genevieve to her artistic and erotic limits.

ALSO LOOK OUT FOR

THE NEW BLACK LACE BOOK OF WOMEN'S SEXUAL FANTASIES
Edited and compiled by Mitzi Szereto
ISBN 978 0 352 34172 3

The second anthology of detailed sexual fantasies contributed by women from all over the world. The book is a result of a year's research by an expert on erotic writing and gives a fascinating insight into the rich diversity of the female sexual imagination.

Black Lace Booklist

Information is correct at time of printing. To avoid disappointment, check availability before ordering. Go to www.black-lace-books.com.
All books are priced £7.99 unless another price is given.

BLACK LACE BOOKS WITH A CONTEMPORARY SETTING

BLACK LACE BOOKS WITH AN HISTORICAL SETTING

- ❑ DIVINE TORMENT Janine Ashbless — ISBN 978 0 352 33719 1
- ❑ FRENCH MANNERS Olivia Christie — ISBN 978 0 352 33214 1
- ❑ LORD WRAXALL'S FANCY Anna Lieff Saxby — ISBN 978 0 352 33080 2
- ❑ NICOLE'S REVENGE Lisette Allen — ISBN 978 0 352 32984 4
- ❑ THE SENSES BEJEWELLED Cleo Cordell — ISBN 978 0 352 32904 2 — £6.99
- ❑ THE SOCIETY OF SIN Sian Lacey Taylder — ISBN 978 0 352 34080 1
- ❑ TEMPLAR PRIZE Deanna Ashford — ISBN 978 0 352 34137 2
- ❑ UNDRESSING THE DEVIL Angel Strand — ISBN 978 0 352 33938 6

BLACK LACE BOOKS WITH A PARANORMAL THEME

- ❑ BRIGHT FIRE Maya Hess — ISBN 978 0 352 34104 4
- ❑ BURNING BRIGHT Janine Ashbless — ISBN 978 0 352 34085 6
- ❑ CRUEL ENCHANTMENT Janine Ashbless — ISBN 978 0 352 33483 1
- ❑ ENCHANTED Various — ISBN 978 0 352 34195 2
- ❑ FLOOD Anna Clare — ISBN 978 0 352 34094 8
- ❑ GOTHIC BLUE Portia Da Costa — ISBN 978 0 352 33075 8
- ❑ PHANTASMAGORIA Madelynne Ellis — ISBN 978 0 352 34168 6
- ❑ THE PRIDE Edie Bingham — ISBN 978 0 352 33997 3
- ❑ THE SILVER CAGE Mathilde Madden — ISBN 978 0 352 34164 8
- ❑ THE SILVER COLLAR Mathilde Madden — ISBN 978 0 352 34141 9
- ❑ THE SILVER CROWN Mathilde Madden — ISBN 978 0 352 34157 0
- ❑ SOUTHERN SPIRITS Edie Bingham — ISBN 978 0 352 34180 8
- ❑ THE TEN VISIONS Olivia Knight — ISBN 978 0 352 34119 8
- ❑ WILD KINGDOM Deana Ashford — ISBN 978 0 352 34152 5
- ❑ WILDWOOD Janine Ashbless — ISBN 978 0 352 34194 5

BLACK LACE ANTHOLOGIES

- ❑ BLACK LACE QUICKIES 1 Various — ISBN 978 0 352 34126 6 — £2.99
- ❑ BLACK LACE QUICKIES 2 Various — ISBN 978 0 352 34127 3 — £2.99
- ❑ BLACK LACE QUICKIES 3 Various — ISBN 978 0 352 34128 0 — £2.99
- ❑ BLACK LACE QUICKIES 4 Various — ISBN 978 0 352 34129 7 — £2.99
- ❑ BLACK LACE QUICKIES 5 Various — ISBN 978 0 352 34130 3 — £2.99
- ❑ BLACK LACE QUICKIES 6 Various — ISBN 978 0 352 34133 4 — £2.99
- ❑ BLACK LACE QUICKIES 7 Various — ISBN 978 0 352 34146 4 — £2.99
- ❑ BLACK LACE QUICKIES 8 Various — ISBN 978 0 352 34147 1 — £2.99
- ❑ BLACK LACE QUICKIES 9 Various — ISBN 978 0 352 34155 6 — £2.99

To find out the latest information about Black Lace titles, check out the website: www.black-lace-books.com or send for a booklist with complete synopses by writing to:

Black Lace Booklist, Virgin Books Ltd
Virgin Books
Random House
20 Vauxhall Bridge Road
London SW1V 2SA

Please include an SAE of decent size. Please note only British stamps are valid.

Our privacy policy
We will not disclose information you supply us to any other parties. We will not disclose any information which identifies you personally to any person without your express consent.

From time to time we may send out information about Black Lace books and special offers. Please tick here if you do not wish to receive Black Lace information.   ❏

Please send me the books I have ticked above.

Name ....

Address ....

....

....

....

Post Code ....

Send to: Virgin Books Cash Sales, Random House,
20 Vauxhall Bridge Road, London SW1V 2SA.

US customers: for prices and details of how to order
books for delivery by mail, call 888-330-8477.

Please enclose a cheque or postal order, made payable
to Virgin Books Ltd, to the value of the books you have
ordered plus postage and packing costs as follows:

UK and BFPO – £1.00 for the first book, 50p for each
subsequent book.

Overseas (including Republic of Ireland) – £2.00 for
the first book, £1.00 for each subsequent book.

If you would prefer to pay by VISA, ACCESS/MASTERCARD,
DINERS CLUB, AMEX or MAESTRO, please write your card
number and expiry date here: ....

....

Signature ....

Please allow up to 28 days for delivery.